SHE HAD IT COMING

Carys Jones is a thriller writer based in Shropshire where she lives with her husband, daughter and dog. When she's not writing she can often be found indulging two of her greatest passions: either walking round the local woodland or catching up on all things Disney-related. Her favourite authors are Megan Abbott, Amy Engel and Taylor Jenkins Reid.

Carys is represented by Emily Glenister of DHH Literary Agency. *The List* and *We Are All Liars* are published by Orion books.

www.carys-jones.com

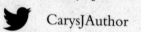 CarysJAuthor

SHE HAD IT COMING

Carys Jones

ORION

First published in Great Britain in 2023 by Orion Fiction
an imprint of The Orion Publishing Group Ltd
Carmelite House, 50 Victoria Embankment
London EC4Y 0DZ

An Hachette UK Company

1 3 5 7 9 10 8 6 4 2

A CIP catalogue record for this book is
available from the British Library.

ISBN (Paperback) 978 1 3987 1201 0
ISBN (eBook) 978 1 3987 1202 7

Typeset by Born Group

Printed and bound in Great Britain by Clays Ltd, Elcograf S.p.A.

MIX
Paper from
responsible sources
FSC® C104740
FSC
www.fsc.org

www.orionbooks.co.uk

To my mum. Because no matter what, you've always got my back, even when I was a little sh★t as a teenager

PipAh,

Was it me or did we sit through the LONGEST Maths lesson ever today? Like seriously, algebra is just ridiculous. We will legit never need it. Like, ever. Basic math, sure. But letters and all that crap? No. No way.

Did you see how serious Hannah was taking it all? Can't you just imagine her going home and printing out all the revision notes, pouring over them until she falls asleep? It is actually pathetic. To need to try that hard at anything. She's going to spend her whole life trying too hard and always coming in second. Sucks to be her!

I'm thinking we should hang by the park Friday night. Yes? I heard about a party over at Tristan Jenkins' house but I KNOW you won't go. That you can't stay out past ten blah blah blah, you're no fun. But you're my bestie so I love you and it's OK.

Seriously though – start wearing that Wonderbra I stole for you from Debenhams. PipAh, you NEED it. Like really, really need it. Your tits are taking forever to come in and trust me, guys will defo give you more attention with that bra on. Right now you look like a boy. No offence.

Write me back! And send me some of the answers from Maths as I really wasn't listening.

Love you,

H

xoxo

I

November 2003

It was cold. And damp. Those were the only two things which occupied Pippa's mind as she jogged on the spot, bare legs already flecked with mud, dark hair pulled back in a ponytail. She longed to be back in the warmth of the minibus with her headphones on and her Walkman playing. Instead she was standing beneath a slate sky, teeth chattering.

'I'm fucking freezing,' Heather Oxon hissed beside her, the words carried away on a foggy breath.

'Me too,' Pippa agreed tightly. Her Nike trainers were already soiled beyond recognition and the run hadn't even started yet.

They were all gathered on the edge of a field, the estate of Sefton Park sprawling beyond them. A dozen sixteen-year-old girls wearing matching cream shorts and burgundy polo shirts. They all had their hair neatly tied back, subdued and sleek, it was only Heather's whose glowed even in the absence of sunlight.

'Highlights,' she'd bragged two weeks previously when she had them done. 'I went to that new salon in town.'

Hair colouring of any kind was banned at Waterbridge Preparatory School. Along with nail varnish. Lip gloss. Piercings. Not that those rules ever seemed to apply to Heather.

She flashed Pippa a smug smile as they kept jogging on the spot, waiting to be released like a pack of dogs before a hunt. Her lips were pink and glittery. 'We'll be away from old Charnley soon,' she said, rolling her eyes at the heavyset PE teacher watching over them, legs like tree trunks planted deep in the mud. A thick coat covering her top half. Miss Charnley wasn't shivering like her students; she watched them with pale blue eyes, gaze sharp.

'Girls.' Her voice was a bark over their heads. 'Do remember that we are guests here at Sefton today, that it is a privilege to conduct our cross-country run within their grounds. Remember that *at all times* you are representing the school.'

'As if we could ever forget,' Heather whispered, colour gently blooming in her pale cheeks as she jogged up and down.

'Three miles,' Charnley declared, raising a whistle up to her lips. 'Do your best.'

'And make sure you follow the route – it has been marked with flags across the estate,' Miss Rogers, the younger teacher, also Pippa's form tutor, nervously added, peering at the girls from behind her glasses.

'Ready . . .' The whistle was clenched in Charnley's cream teeth, hampering her words.

'Set.'

The jogging stopped. The girls became coils, tightening, preparing to be unleashed. Pippa swallowed, focusing on the mud at her feet, straining her shoulders against the strings of her flimsy backpack which hung down her back, proudly displaying the school's logo – two ravens in flight above a coat of arms. Pippa still wasn't sure what it was actually meant to symbolise. Every girl wore the same bag. And within every bag was the same water bottle, equally branded.

Heather coughed loudly, a tactic Pippa recognised. It was pointless to deploy it here. They were just with the girls from their class, this was merely a practice run. It wasn't even that Heather was competitive – she didn't care about winning. For her the real sport was making others lose.

'Go!'

The blast from the whistle was shrill, juxtaposed against the calm of the Sefton estate. Barely a second afterwards, a dozen pairs of feet scrambled forward, flicking up mud, expensive trainers sinking into the wet earth.

For ten minutes they ran. Arms pumping by her side, Pippa kept up with the pack, felt the cold slap of mud against her legs. She knew the estate of old. All the girls did. They'd all come here since they were young for picnics, walks, seasonal events. Pippa first met Father Christmas in the main house, the mansion. Though she couldn't see it now. Their route was taking them along the edges of the estate, over the river and past the deer park.

The cold began to lose its bite the more she ran. She let her mind start to wander to what she'd do that night when she was back home. First she'd take a long, hot bath. And then after dinner she'd curl up on her bed and watch some more episodes of *Smallville*. She'd be alone in her little universe, just her and the fairy lights over her bed, the portable TV and the DVD player in the far corner. Her room was a safe place. Her room was— 'Hey.' Breath warm against her ear, nails sharp against her upper arm as they began digging in.

Pippa slowed, several girls passing her.

'We're not actually doing this stupid run.' Heather was still holding her arm, nails painted ivory. Like bone. 'Come on.' Her blue eyes were bright against the gloom of the November afternoon.

Beside her Pippa shrank, feeling that with her brown hair and chestnut eyes she blended in with the mud, the fallen leaves which littered the ground. Heather was summer, all shine. Pippa exuded the gloom of the season. Her shoulders hunched, her feet sinking deeper into the mud. 'You sure you really want to sneak off and risk pissing off Charnley?' She countered lamely, already knowing her words were in vain. Heather never completed a cross-country run. Or a test. Or even sat through an entire assembly. It was as if the rules of the school, even the entire world, didn't apply to her. Something which Pippa was both mesmerised and repulsed by. Because rules mattered. Hard work mattered. But not to someone glossy like Heather, born with beauty into wealth. Pippa watched the profile of her friend, the question hanging between them. Pippa was playing the part she always did, being devil's advocate. Heather's pretty features crinkled with annoyance.

'Fine. We'll do a shortcut.' Releasing her, Heather walked on, her stride slowing to a saunter as she veered left, away from the fluttering red flags of their assigned route, towards the river. Pippa knew the route she was taking, was just as familiar with the estate. They would walk along the river, follow its curve until the bridge and then pick up the trail again, jog their way to the finish line.

Pippa glanced back and saw only mist and wet grass. They were beyond the gaze of Charnley and Rogers. 'The others will tell,' she warned. Knowing they wouldn't. No one spoke out against an Oxon.

'Let them,' Heather laughed, the sound soft like silver bells. She pulled off her bag and reached into it, pulling out a pack of cigarettes and a red plastic lighter.

'No.' Pippa immediately shook her head. She knew that her parents would implode if she got caught smoking. Never mind what the school would do. But if Heather cared about such consequences she didn't show it, raising

5

the cigarette to her lips and flicking on her lighter, shielding it with one hand from the wind that swept across the estate.

'You're so fucking square,' she complained on her first exhale, smoke dancing around her.

Pippa had no rebuttal. They walked along the river, towards the main house, the mud beneath their feet easing as they reached a more solid path. Out of the corner of her eye she watched Heather and wondered, as she so often did, why they were even friends.

'We need to go to the party Friday night,' Heather declared grandly, 'the one at Tristan Jenkins' house.'

Pippa hated Tristan Jenkins. Heather knew this. He went to the boy's school on the other side of town and had frosted tips and an attitude. He acted as though everyone was beneath him.

'I don't know.' Pippa prepared to list a reason of excuses for why she couldn't attend.

'If you think he won't want you there, don't worry. If you're with me you'll be fine.'

Pippa's pace slowed.

Heather looked back at her, smile bright and wide. 'I'm like your passport to boys. If it wasn't for me none of them would even know you were alive.'

Pippa needed to look somewhere, anywhere. To stare at Heather's satisfied smile would be like staring directly at the sun. Her gaze landed on the river, dirty water rushing along in a gathering current. Ducks bobbed along the surface.

'Hey, don't be sensitive,' Heather chided her. 'I'm just being honest with you. That's what friends are.'

Grinding her teeth together, Pippa recalled all the times Heather had been honest with her in the past week.

Your thighs are getting too big.

6

Your breath is rank today.

Did you mean to wear those shoes?

Pippa sounds like a dog's name, don't you think?

It must be nice being so plain, you're easier to forget.

And worst of all, what she had said the previous Friday as they swayed side by side on the swings at the local playground, the sky dark and pricked with stars above them, Heather drunk on the vodka she'd stolen from her parents' liquor cabinet.

Your parents don't love each other.

The declaration had slapped Pippa into sobriety. Her parents *did* love each other. They'd been married for twenty years to prove it. Her home was a stable one, a secure one.

'Oh my God, why are you being such a moody bitch today?' Heather yanked on Pippa's arm, drawing her gaze away from the river. 'If I'd known you'd be like this I'd have asked Claire to ditch with me.'

Claire Howden, who Heather had humiliated the previous Tuesday after asking her in front of the whole Algebra class whether she'd finally got her period yet. Claire, who had found Pippa after the class had ended, and whispered, 'Someone needs to bring her down a peg or two.'

Claire was short, only reaching Pippa's shoulder. And she was kind. Possibly one of the kindest girls in their year. Heather had only lashed out at her because Claire had received a better score in their algebra test. And scores mattered. Heather needed to gather good scores like a magpie hoarding treasure because they were the currency to a good university, a good life. But rather than work hard and study, she mastered manipulation, how to trip up the competition.

'And I got my period last year,' Claire had added, green eyes glistening with tears.

'Hey, it's fine.' Pippa had given her a reassuring hug. 'You know how Heather can be.'

'I don't know how you can stand to be friends with her.' It was a comment Pippa had heard many times before. But she and Heather had a shared history, years behind them. Pippa knew all the boys Heather had kissed, had held her as she wept over some of them. And Heather knew that Pippa wasn't yet ready to date, that schoolwork came first.

'One day you'll understand,' Heather would sometimes gasp between heartbroken sobs, 'when you finally find someone who wants to kiss you.'

Whenever she said it, Pippa had to bite her tongue from informing her friend it was a two-way street, that she'd need to want to kiss them too, but she'd yet to find a boy she actually liked. She was too busy studying, focusing on the future. Boys were a distraction she didn't want. Heather had already demonstrated the endless drama they caused.

'Hey!' Fingers clicked before Pippa's eyes, nails polished and long. 'Can you actually fucking listen to me for once?' Heather demanded hotly.

'Right.' Pippa bowed her head. 'Sorry.'

'What are you even daydreaming about?'

'Nothing.'

Someone needs to bring her down a peg or two.

'Actually, can we stop a sec?' Pippa reached for her bag, cautiously threw a glance over her shoulder.

'What is it now?' Heather dropped the last of her cigarette to the ground, stubbed it out with the muddy toe of her trainer.

'I need a drink.' Pippa grabbed at her water bottle, fumbled with the lid. It was so quiet within the grounds, the noise and bustle of the cross-country run now far away from them, on the other side of the estate.

8

'Fine.' Heather shook off her bag and mirrored Pippa's movements. 'I suppose we do need to kill a bit of time.'

'Exactly,' Pippa agreed, drinking deeply, the cold water soothing against the back of her throat. She watched Heather's throat as she swallowed from her own bottle. Thinking of that night in the park. Of the squeak of the swings. The sting of the vodka.

Your parents don't love each other.

It was one thing to trample on Pippa day in and day out. It was another to come for her parents, her home.

2

Sunset Blush.

Caramel Delight.

The two colour swatches were side by side on the island in the kitchen. Above them, Abbie Parks cradled a fresh mug of coffee in her long fingers, elbows propped against the granite. It was eleven in the morning. She knew this without turning her head to check the clock on the wall to her right. The routine of her days was so deeply ingrained within her it had become part of her DNA.

'Redecorate the kitchen,' John had suggested only a week ago before picking up his briefcase and leaving for work.

Abbie freed a hand from her mug, let her fingers stroke against her cheek. It had been so long since her husband had left the whisper of a kiss there. He used to hover in the doorway, dark eyes gazing at her hungrily.

'Duty calls,' he'd moan, leaving a lingering kiss on her lips. His hair was jet black then. Now it was peppered with grey.

'Pick a paint . . . pick a paint . . .' Abbie shuffled the two samples, studied them from different angles. The walls of the kitchen were currently eggshell blue, a project from the previous summer.

If she chose a paint, she could get in the Range Rover and drive over to B&Q, pick up a few tins of it. Then, since she was already up town, she could stop by the shopping centre, grab a coffee, maybe even shop for a new dress. Carol's book club was next week and she had nothing to wear.

Her white-tipped nails tapped against the island top, louder than both the ticking clock and the weary exhale of her breath.

Pick. A. Paint.

A soft pink or a sickly cream. Those were her choices. She looked up at the walls, wondering which John would prefer, if he'd even notice. He used to see everything, every small change within the home, be it a new towel in the downstairs bathroom, or a cushion moved a few inches to the left on the sofa. His mind was as sharp as the tools he cut people open with, and his keen eye was always dissecting their home. But in the past few months he'd failed to comment on Abbie changing the front door mat, the toothbrush holder in the main bathroom and the sheets on their bed, from blue to dove grey.

'He's just so busy these days,' she'd lamented to Carol over Earl Grey and macarons at their last book club. 'I feel like he lives at the hospital.'

Surgeon's widow. She'd heard the phrase bandied about the hospital in the past, when she was still a nurse, but never thought it would one day apply to her. But now her husband was always at St. Jude's either stitching someone up or cutting them open. When she met him he was still in training, yet to decide upon a speciality. And she was right there with him, handing him the scalpel, the forceps. Holding the clamp. Abbie used to spend her evenings scrubbing blood stains out of her nurse's uniform. Now the stains were Merlot on cream carpet.

'Come on.' Abbie drained her coffee and looked to the clock. Not even 11.05. Wearily she rubbed at her brown eyes, tucked a loose strand of chestnut hair behind her ear. If Pippa were home she'd help her decide. And she'd do it quickly, decisively, with the cutting brutality teenagers possessed. Brushing the samples to one side, Abbie decided to let her daughter choose. Then together they could go and buy paint on Saturday, make a trip of it.

Biting on her lip, leaving lipstick smeared on her teeth, Abbie approached the calendar pinned to the double-doored fridge with magnets of past holidays to the Grand Canyon and Aspen. She checked the entry for Saturday.

Pippa – Piano 10am, Cross-country meet 2pm
John – On call

Abbie winced. Cross-country meets were the worst – always in some far-flung part of the county where she'd have to stand around in the cold and sip tea from a flask while Pippa got covered in mud, which inevitably ended up staining the leather in the back of the car. The schedule allowed no time for shopping. And no support from John.

Her footsteps rang through the empty house as she walked from the kitchen, to the hallway, to the large living room where her phone was resting on a side table. Grabbing it she began tapping out a message, infuriated by the small keys and how difficult they were to work with her nails. Pippa's fingers darted around the keys of her own model of the same phone with such speed it made Abbie dizzy.

'With that sort of dexterity, you should really think about following me into gastroenterology,' John had noted recently, peering at her from behind his copy of *The Times*.

But that wouldn't happen. Abbie knew that before her daughter probably did. Saw how her little girl's attention would drift, how she had to fight to focus. Pippa was a dreamer. And Abbie told her husband as much.

'Dreams don't pay the bills,' he replied stiffly.

But surgeries did.

Abbie manoeuvred the phone in her hand; it felt too heavy in her palm. She'd yet to get accustomed to its weight but John had insisted that they all have phones, citing that it was 'the way forward'. Whatever that meant. Carefully Abbie tapped on letters and the space bar and carefully wrote out a message for her husband:

John, is the calendar in the kitchen wrong as it says you are working this weekend but you were on call last weekend. Isn't it supposed to be once a month? I'm confused. X

Message sent, Abbie drifted into the dining room, noticing that her peonies, gathered in the centre in a slim glass vase, were beginning to wilt. She backtracked to the lounge and her phone and wrote out another message.

And, also John, we need fresh peonies. X

When she returned to the kitchen Abbie glanced briefly at the clock. Half eleven. She still had a few hours to herself before she had to do the school run and collect Pippa.

Through the large windows above the sink she saw the long lawn wet with rain.

'Great,' she muttered tightly, folding her arms to her chest, the cashmere soft on her skin. Pippa would surely be slathered in mud when she collected her. If only she could have selected an indoor sport for her final year at school. 'Something more civilised,' Abbie had urged, 'like ballet or netball.'

'Cross-country running builds character,' John had deemed. 'Determination. Endurance. Skills she will need. Besides, doesn't Heather do it? If Heather does it, you know Pippa will,' he added dryly.

Even the memory of the name made Abbie's mouth turn down in a sour gesture. Heather Oxon, as golden as her mother. Her mother who still worked, despite the money flowing down from her geriatric parents, was a GP at their local practice. Teeth clenched together, Abbie turned on the tap, let it run to scalding, and then pushed her hands under it, washed them until they turned pink, as outside the rain picked up and lashed angrily at the glass.

As she stalked her way through the kitchen, hands stinging, she passed the island and the two swatches peered up at her.

Sunset Blush.

Caramel Delight.

Today she had one decision to make. Such a simple one. She didn't need to measure IV fluids, fit a venflom, calm a stressed patient. All she needed to do was pick a colour. One fucking colour. With a swipe of her hand she swept up the swatches and marched to the bin, opened it with a tap of her foot and dropped them inside. Then she made for the lounge, making a beeline for her brick of a phone. Picking it up she poked at a button, the green and black screen glowing. She had no new messages. No alerts.

It made sense since John was in theatre all day and he was the only person who ever messaged her on it. But considering his insistence on her getting one, he failed to ever reply to her on there. And he was always firing off messages to his colleagues, even at the dinner table at night, his slim fingers working the device as fast and frantic as Pippa's did. Abbie studied her own phone for a beat longer, considering shoving it in the bin along with the swatches. But then what if Pippa needed her? It was a comfort to know they had this lifeline, this connection. That buried at the bottom of Pippa's backpack was her own phone; that one phone call was all it would take to bring Abbie running. And she'd be there in a heartbeat. If her daughter needed her, she'd drop absolutely everything.

3

Face burning, legs streaked with mud, Pippa ran. She rounded a corner and was on the straight that signalled the end of the run. The end of her shortcut. Ponytail swinging behind her, she kept up her frantic pace, needing to flush her cheeks, soil her shoes. To present as though she'd run three miles.

Up ahead, where the path widened she could see several girls who had already finished, doubled over, hands clasped to their knees as they caught their breath. Pippa kept running. Listened to the slap of her feet on the wet ground. Her own harried gasps. The pulse of her heart echoing in her ears. She didn't look back.

Miss Charnley presided over the invisible finish line, checking names off the list attached to a clipboard in her wrinkled hands. Pippa slowed only once she had passed her, not caring about the digits being written down.

'Good time,' Miss Charnley briskly commended her, gaze almost instantly shifting back to the path Pippa had just run down and the next girl along.

Hannah Edwards – the first of the girls to recover and straighten up, so presumably the winner – watched Pippa, eyes narrowed. She walked towards her, one hand wedged against her hip, the other swinging at her side. Her white blonde hair had fallen free from her ponytail, too short to be held captive for an entire run. 'Where'd you creep up from?' she asked, openly suspicious. Her cheeks were cracked like flaking porcelain where she'd piled too much concealer over angry acne.

As the fire in her chest eased, Pippa reached for her back-pack and the drink inside, briefly flicking her gaze up towards Hannah and offering her a nonchalant shrug. 'I decided to start slow and sprint more at the end.' She gulped her water down too greedily, letting it dribble down her chin.

'Not a wise approach.' Hannah's tone was stern. Now both hands were on her hips and she was looking towards the stragglers crossing the finish line. 'You ditched Heather then?'

'Yeah.' Pippa dragged the back of her hand across her mouth, put her drink away. 'You know what she's like, would rather talk than run. But I need the time.'

This Hannah understood. She nodded sagely, continuing to study the final finishers with the haughty stare that came from being the most athletic in her class. 'Not like Heather needs a decent time.' There was a bitterness to her words which Pippa could almost taste, as Hannah's nose crinkled and she turned away from Charnley and the end of the run. 'Some of us have to actually work for things.'

It was as cold within the minibus as it was outside. Even bundled inside her hooded sweatshirt, school emblem bright across her chest, Pippa shivered. Beside her the window fogged with condensation and the engine hummed so loudly it made the metal vehicle shudder as it idled on the spot.

'Can we fucking go already?' Olivia Smith groaned in the seat behind. 'We've been waiting here like twenty minutes.'

Across the short aisle Hannah clicked her long fingers, signalling for silence. There was a collective hush among the girls. No one rustled in their bag, or tapped on the hard buttons of their phone. 'Someone is missing,' she declared with authority. Pippa felt all eyes pass over her, to the vacant seat at the back of the minibus.

The minibus door opened with a sputter and then slammed closed. Pink-hued and panicked, Miss Rogers stood behind the driver, addressing her class. 'Has anyone seen Heather?'

No one spoke.

'She's not finished the race,' the young teacher continued. 'Has anyone seen her?'

Pippa raised her hand, hating the heat she could instantly feel from everyone staring. 'She and I were running together,' she said, wilting with shame, 'but she wanted to do this shortcut and we . . . fell out about it. So I took off and doubled back to catch up with everyone else.'

'What shortcut?' Miss Rogers' voice was harder than usual. Normally she was chirpy with the girls, eager to blur the lines between friendship and authority. Now it was very clear which side of the line she was standing on.

'Along the river.'

Miss Rogers darted out of the bus. Questions were tossed between the girls like tennis balls, back and forth.

'Where do you think she is?'

'I bet she took off.'

'Gone somewhere to smoke I bet.'

'Do you reckon she went home?'

'Doesn't her boyfriend live near Sefton Park?'

This last question irked Pippa. There was no boyfriend in Heather's life, surely everyone knew that. There were boys, sure, but none of them held the honour of being singularly attached to her.

The door to the bus squeaked open once more. Rain peppered the glass beside Pippa, the world outside turning from silver to grey as the clouds thickened.

'Right, everyone off.' Miss Charnley gave the order and then blew her whistle. The sound bounced around the bus, shrill and deafening. 'Now!'

In a shivering, damp line the girls gathered by the minibus. Another headcount. Still it came up short. Still Heather had not materialised.

'Pippa,' said Miss Charnley, pointing a gnarled finger in her direction, 'show us this shortcut you took. Half of you will come with me and we'll look for Heather along the river. The other half will go with Miss Rogers and repeat the run.'

Groans of displeasure rippled through the air.

The blow of the whistle instantly silenced them. 'Enough,' the old woman snapped. 'Stop complaining about the cold. And the wet. Heather may well have injured herself and currently be in a lot of pain. We need to find her. No one can run unassisted on a sprained ankle. Now show some solidarity, girls. Come on!'

Pippa stepped forward to follow Miss Charnley and her assigned group when Hannah grabbed her shoulder, drew her back.

'We all know she's just sodded off somewhere,' she declared through gritted teeth.

'She's going to love knowing how we all had to search for her in the bloody rain,' Olivia added, her pretty face pinched with anger.

They could all picture it – Heather snuggled up safe and warm, probably by a crackling fire beneath a soft blanket, manicured hands clutching a steaming mug of hot chocolate, golden head turned to the window, watching the rain, watching the day darken. Laughing at her peers.

'Show me where you went,' Miss Charnley instructed as they returned to the start of the run. Already Pippa's hoodie was soaked, rain running down her cheeks, dripping off the end of her nose. 'You'll be reprimanded for taking the shortcut later,' she coldly assured her.

Pippa could feel herself sinking deeper into the mud. She could already imagine her father's face when she had to tell him why she had detention. How his expression would sag with disappointment before he drifted off into another room. She wrapped her wet arms against her chest. Her mum wouldn't care. She didn't sweat the small stuff, she understood what really mattered. Pippa knew as soon as she was home her mum would run her a bath, cook her favourite dinner, listen with concern as she described the hunt for Heather in the rain. Feeling warmed by this future, she pointed up ahead to where the path diverged, turning away from the bridge and following the river.

'I told Rogers we should monitor you girls during the run,' Miss Charnley lamented, shaking her head from beneath the protection of the hood of her waterproof coat. 'But no, she insisted you girls were to be trusted.' She began to trudge towards the river, her small entourage following. 'I told her,' she threw the remark over her shoulder, her words almost silenced by the hiss of the rain, 'never trust a teenage girl.'

4

Raindrops splattered against the roof of the large conservatory. Abbie felt comforted by the sound. The familiar folds of her day were now wrapped around her as she settled beside the small log burner pressed against the brick wall of the house, her legs curled beneath her, a wool blanket draped over her knees. The wicker of the chair creaked each time she moved. Abbie was reading. Absorbed in the words on the page, everything else – the house, the rain, the slate grey afternoon – all slipped away from her.

The fire crackled.

Abbie read on. She was playing catch-up, she knew that. Carol had already finished the book ahead of their club the following Thursday.

'It's a good one,' she'd enthused at the school gates that morning. 'You're going to love it.' Her mouth had widened into a Cheshire-cat grin as she peered out from beneath her vast umbrella. 'I went for something more exciting this month.'

Abbie had looked at her expectantly from beneath the protection of her own umbrella, adorned with daisies which made a perfect chain around the rim.

'It's a thriller.' Carol's eyes had glowed in the dim morning light and Abbie felt a tremor of titillation dance down her spine. So often they were reading literary works, books that were so slow-paced they seemed to Abbie at times to barely move. And she didn't like how the slowness on the page reflected the decay of her own life, her own time. Everything so lethargic, so routine. Devoid of the flare of excitement she so desperately needed. 'There's a murder in it,' Carol added.

Right then, Abbie felt fully invested and determined to make extra effort to actually read the book for this month's club instead of just skimming the final chapter the day before the meeting and trying to piece everything together.

'It sounds exciting,' she told her friend earnestly.

'I think we could all do with a bit of perking up.' Carol's usual smile faltered. But like a record skipping, it quickly returned, the fault forgotten. 'So make sure you actually read this one.'

Abbie was grateful for the dull morning concealing the blush which had spread across her cheeks. She'd hoped her inability to finish earlier books had gone unnoticed. Clearly she was wrong. She should have known. The mothers of Waterbridge didn't miss a trick.

'They're doing the run today,' she offered, keen to change the subject. Carol was nodding as they turned from the gates, walked back towards their heavy-duty 4x4s, wasted on the polished streets of their suburban life.

'Oh yes, over at Sefton Park.'

Abbie chanced one last glance over her shoulder, at the high iron gates which marked the entrance to the school. Pippa had stopped resisting her mother's desire to walk her in every morning long ago, probably sensing that she needed that brief moment of socialisation with the other mums. A shudder of shame passed over Abbie. Pippa was too wise for her sixteen years, too attuned to things like her mother's desperation for contact. For friendship.

She's just mature for her age. Abbie told herself this often and knew it to be true. Pippa wasn't swept up in boys, pop bands and make-up. She was thoughtful, introverted. Traits she must have picked up from her father.

At sixteen Abbie had been nothing like her daughter. She had been wild and rebellious, with bleached hair and a taste for late nights. Her mother had despaired, lamenting that Abbie was too like the father she had never known, had grown up without. 'He was always only ever looking out for himself,' the tired woman would seethe. So Abbie had done what she could to prove her mother wrong, which meant nursing, an industry focused on caring for others. That'd show the old bitch. Abbie wasn't like her father. She cared about people. She'd care about her own family when she made one. She was a *good person*.

'Won't be nice in this rain.' Carol had one hand on her car door, about to pull it open.

Abbie blinked at her, felt her train of thought derail and crash noisily in her head.

'The run,' Carol added gently.

'Oh, of course.' Abbie blushed again. 'No, no. I can't think the girls will enjoy it in this weather. Though I'm sure Hannah will set an amazing time.'

'She loves to come first,' Carol beamed proudly, closing her umbrella and shaking off the rain. Abbie waved at her friend as she settled behind her steering wheel and then moved over to her own car. The rain was picking up, bouncing on the tarmac around her. Pippa would surely get drenched out at Sefton Park. Abbie made a mental note to turn the immersion heater on when she got home.

A crackle of heat in the wood burner. Abbie turned the page in her book. She wasn't yet at the murder but was keen to arrive there before she had to go and collect Pippa from school. What time was it? She glanced up, peering towards the fire and the wall clock above it.

It read three o'clock.

Shit.

Now she risked being late. Which really wouldn't do. Abbie swept the blanket from her knees, quickly folded it and returned it to the ottoman. Through the windows of the conservatory she saw her rain-slicked garden, lawn wilting and soaked, flower beds sodden. In the summer, her garden bloomed with wild flowers and roses. All of which she meticulously attended to. But now, on the precipice of winter, everything was barren. The only colours watery greens and browns.

A log snapped in the burner, sparks spattering the glass.

Abbie hurried to it, dragged the knob along the base, cutting off the oxygen. Killing it. Behind the glass the flames raged briefly and then began to ebb away.

She needed to be quick. It was a fifteen-minute drive to the school and if she didn't leave soon she'd risk getting caught in traffic.

Keys. She needed her keys. Stalking into the hallway she found them perched in the china tray dish atop the telephone stand, chunky in their delicate holder. Abbie grabbed them, clutching them tight in her palm before doubling back into the kitchen. Handbag next. This was in the centre of the dining table. Mulberry. Cream. She grabbed it, tucked it over her shoulder.

Coat. She'd need it in this rain, especially if she spied Carol and wanted to chat with her. That meant a trip upstairs. Abbie moved quickly, keys jangling in her hand as she entered the master bedroom, footsteps soft on cream carpet. She thrust open a pair of doors and stepped into her walk-in wardrobe. She quickly found her coat and placed down her handbag so she could shrug it on. Burberry. Beige. John had the matching design from the men's collection. When they both wore them, Pippa would tease that they looked like a worn-out attempt at an advert for the brand. The 'worn-out' part stung but Abbie never let on, happy to laugh along with her daughter.

Back downstairs, into the hallway, handbag on her shoulder, car keys in hand, front door in view— Ringing. Loud and urgent. Like a terrified bird. Ringing and then silence, sudden and draining. Abbie stiffened, disorientated by the sound. Then she looked to the phone resting atop the table in the hallway, its buttons glowing as a fresh burst of ringing filled the room.

'Christ's sake,' Abbie sighed, placing her bag by her feet, her keys beside the phone, 'I'm already late.' She grabbed the receiver, raised it to her ear.

'Hello, Park residence, Abigail speaking.' Her voice was smooth, with no hint of any of the irritation she was feeling for this sudden delay.

'Abbie!' Carol panted on the other end of the line. She sounded the complete opposite – breathless and urgent. 'Abbie, so glad I caught you.'

'What is it?' Abbie's fingers tightened against the plastic of the phone. 'Carol, is everything all right?'

'The girls,' Carol declared.

'The girls?' Abbie repeated as she felt her chest tighten.

'Hannah . . . Hannah sent me a text message.'

Like a reflex Abbie looked in the direction of the lounge, feeling betrayed by her own forgetfulness. Her mobile phone remained on the side table, distant and useless when it should be by her side, in her handbag. Always with her. Because that's what John had insisted it was for – emergencies. And this sounded like something urgent. If Hannah had texted her mother then Abbie had surely received such a message from Pippa. She began to move from the hallway, padding through the house, grateful for the cordless nature of her phone. If she'd answered the house phone in the kitchen, with its long spiral cord, she'd have been much more restricted.

'What did the message say?' Abbie asked tightly as she entered the living room.

'They're still on the run,' Carol told her. 'They can't leave because one of the girls is missing.'

Abbie froze. 'Missing?'

'Missing,' Carol repeated, voice high with anxiety and the delicious feeling of being the first to deliver big news. 'She just messaged me, so of course I called you.'

'Of course.'

'Have you heard from Pippa?'

Abbie scurried to her mobile phone, tapped a button to illuminate the screen.

There was nothing. No new messages.

She felt sick. 'Did . . .' She swallowed, tried to calm herself. Her nerves swirled within her, a wave cresting into a tsunami. 'Did Hannah say who is missing?'

Missing.

The word almost stuck in her throat. How could one of the girls be missing? They were flesh and bone, hairspray and lip gloss. Girls don't just evaporate into thin air. Socks go missing. Spare buttons. Not teenage daughters.

'She didn't say,' Carol's voice dropped to a near whisper. 'I think we should head to the school and find out what's happening.'

Abbie couldn't speak; she kept staring at her mobile phone, willing the screen to blink to life with a message.

'I'm sure it's not Pippa,' Carol said, sensing her friend's fear through the line.

'I'll meet you there.' Abbie managed to croak out the words and hung up before Carol could reply, sprinting back through the house.

In the conservatory the fire in the log burner had completely gone out, leaving only smouldering ash behind.

Pip Pip,

So after the park on Friday I did sneak over to Scott Williams' house. I know, I know. Dumb move, right? But we'd had all that cider and I was looking shit-hot in my boob tube and didn't want it to go waste.

I'm going to tell you a secret about something that happened at the party. And you're going to keep it, OK? Because that's what best friends do.

At the party I did some vodka shots which were GROSS. Like, drinking petrol level gross. But I had them and I was feeling woozy and next thing I know I'm upstairs in a room with Tristan. I know you think he's no good. That he's only after one thing. But Pip, he's so handsome. Those brown eyes . . . they melt me. Every time. He asked for a blow job and I don't know why but . . . I did it. And it was weird. Like . . . awkward. He kept shoving his dick down the back of my throat which made me gag and drool kept going down my chin which is NOT a good look. I did it for like, ten minutes, gagging and sucking and then he finished and it was SO RANK. Like drinking mouldy yoghurt. He left and I had to down like, four more shots, just to get rid of the taste. I was so wasted I stayed in bed all of Saturday. My mum barely noticed as she was at work most of the day. She's like your dad, always working.

*I told you he's been giving her lifts home. It's weird.
They don't even work together.*

*Oh — in History earlier did you see Mr Hall staring
at me? He's doing it a lot lately. Do you think he's
hot? I think he's hot, for an older guy. A man. Do you
think it'd be weird giving him a blow job? Do you think
his wife gives him one every night?*

*Write me back! And DON'T tell anyone about
Tristan — I'll know if you do!*

Love you,

H

xoxo

5

'Heather!'

'Heath-er!'

The wind tried to steal away their cries as they stalked the river bank.

'And you're quite sure,' said Miss Charnley, her bony fingers like needles in Pippa's elbow, 'this is the way you came?'

Pippa nodded. 'I'm sure.' Rain had soaked through her jumper and polo shirt, settled on her skin. The shiver which travelled through her extended all the way down to her bones.

The old teacher released her and drew as close to the edge of the water as she dared. The river was brown, murky and fast-moving. 'Heather Oxon!' Miss Charnley barked her call along the current. 'Heather Oxon, can you hear me?'

Hannah drew up close at Pippa's side, wet arms clamped tightly to her chest. 'I bet she's not even here.'

'Agreed.'

'Where did you last see her?'

Pippa glanced back over her shoulder, at the slick path and the angry river. 'Just there.' She dragged wet tendrils of hair off her forehead, out of her ears. 'I told her I needed to rejoin the others. She got pissed with me. You know how she is. So I just doubled back and took off.'

The girls walked in tandem, bare legs glossy with rain, each locked in a thoughtful silence.

'Heather!'

Along the river the calls kept coming, sweeping up and down the bank.

'Heather! Heather Oxon!'

Only the rain hissed in response.

They were almost at the point where the shortcut merged with the main path. Miss Charnley faced her students, face streaked with water and worry. She raised a hand as though commanding hundreds of troops instead of half a dozen drowned girls.

'We need to head back to the bus,' she informed them. Her sharp eyes flicked over each student, quickly studying them in turn. 'Daylight is getting away from us. We need to head back to the school and call it in. That is, unless Miss Rogers' endeavours have been more fortuitous.'

'Call it in?' Pippa whispered, her question turning to mist against the rain.

'Phone the police.' Hannah's arm looped through her own, linking them.

'Police?'

'Maybe she fell in the river,' another girl offered. 'Heather's a strong swimmer, she'll be fine.'

'Rivers have strong currents.' Miss Charnley looked beyond her young charges, towards the water, voice thick with distrust. 'Even the strongest swimmer can be over-whelmed by them.'

Pippa shivered so violently her knees began to knock together.

'She's just hiding somewhere.' Hannah leaned in close, smelling of rain water and Impulse body spray. 'She's waiting until she's got all of Waterbridge up in arms, then she'll turn up. You'll see.'

It sounded like vintage Heather. Always putting on a show. Pippa felt her shoulders sag with exhausted relief as they began to march back towards the shelter of the minibus.

'No sign of her.'

The teachers were conferring beside the minibus, the drumbeat of the rain on the metal roof not quite loud enough to dull their voices. Pippa leaned close to the glass, listening, every girl mirroring her position within their own seats, eager to eavesdrop.

'Nothing at all,' Miss Rogers continued, head bent as low as her mood. She was no longer bothering to keep her hood up, letting the rain fall freely against her red hair. 'No bag, no shoes, signs of a struggle. Nothing.'

Signs of a struggle.

Pippa latched onto the words, looped them around her mind, searching for more meaning. What sort of struggle was Miss Rogers searching for? Someone slipping in the mud and sliding towards the river? Or worse . . . blood. Footprints.

'We're going to return to school, tell them Heather is missing, let the authorities take over,' Miss Charnley stated with impressive stoicism. Pippa had heard through hallway whispers that the old woman had been widowed twice – first from a car crash and second time thanks to an alcoholic's failed liver. She could easily weather the storm of a runaway student.

'School already know,' Hannah said loud enough for everyone within the bus to hear.

'How's that then?' challenged Wendy Ashley, who had chosen to occupy Heather's freshly vacated seat at the back of the bus.

'I texted my mum,' Hannah announced with a smugness which irked Pippa. Competition was so fierce at Waterbridge Prep that everything was up for grabs – even bragging rights to something potentially sordid, potentially grim. Hannah had been the first informer. Ten house points. Pippa's cheeks burned. 'You know what my mum's like,' Hannah continued, 'the whole town will already know by now.'

Pippa dove a hand deep into her bag, felt for the solid weight of her mobile phone. It was off. As it always was during school hours. Her father had been very clear when he gave it to her that it was only to be turned on for emergencies. Did this count as an emergency? For Heather – yes. But what message would Pippa send? There had already been a breach in the dam of information from Hannah. What was the point of repeating old news?

'You really think they'll involve the police?' Olivia wondered, using her finger to trace initials and hearts on the fogged windows of the bus.

'I guess we'll soon find out,' Hannah replied as she raked her fingers through her hair, trying to cast the water out of it.

'Girls.' Miss Charnley was back at the end of the aisle, Miss Rogers gathered nervously behind her. All the whispers ceased. Only the rain continued to rattle overhead. 'We're going to head back to the school. It's getting dark and I can't risk losing any more of you. If anyone hears from Heather,' her wrinkle-framed eyes settled on Pippa, 'please let us know immediately.'

Pippa looked down at her knees, skin prickled from the cold.

Once the teachers were seated, the minibus shuddered away from Sefton Park, headlights burning a route down the dark country lanes. The night had crept in quickly and quietly, pressing up against the windows so that the fields were now gone. All Pippa could see in the foggy glass beside her was her own pale reflection.

6

Abbie's car always felt too big when she was alone in it. Too wide. Too high. Herself too small behind the wheel. She shoved the Range Rover into reverse, the clutch whining against her haste. The vast car slid out of her paved driveway, gates automatically parting as she passed through them.

The moment she turned out of her tree-lined street, her heart plummeted into her stomach and turned to stone, feeling hard and heavy in her gut. It was busy. Traffic was bumper to bumper, brake lights shining a vibrant red against the darkness of the wet twilight.

'Come on.' Abbie tapped her fingers against her wheel, listened to the hollow thud of her platinum wedding band connecting with plastic. She didn't have time to dawdle. Already her mind was racing ahead while her body was static within the car. She imagined arriving at the school, the place lit up blue with emergency vehicles. Someone in a uniform coming to find her, their expression grave, whispering the words, 'I'm sorry.'

A girl was missing. That's all she knew. A girl from Pippa's PE class. From her cross-country run.

Please be OK.

Abbie finger's closed around her wheel with a python-like grip, cutting off her own blood supply. The car ahead of her moved and she lurched forward, too eager, too hot on the accelerator. Her car skidded towards the roundabout taking a hard right when she should have waited. Horns blazed as she stared ahead at the rain lashing her windscreen, huge drops settling for a millisecond before being swiftly destroyed by her zealous wipers.

I'm coming, Pippa. I'm coming.

Usually Abbie drove as a nun would. Or at least, this was her husband's belief.

'Abs, you don't really need to keep your hands at ten and two,' he'd say mockingly on the rare occasions when she was the driver, his breath usually laced with the several whiskeys he'd downed at a function. Abbie was cautious. She gripped the wheel just as she'd been taught to; she kept to the speed limit. Never above or below it. Always steady. Always safe. She'd worked the graveyard shift in A&E; she knew what happened when people were reckless behind the wheel, when they decided to get in their car after one drink too many. Crushed skulls. Twisted limbs. A body is so brittle when thrown against solid metal.

But now her driving was manic, erratic. She sped through lights on amber where she'd normally wait for them to burn red. People pipped their horns at her and she didn't care. She needed to reach the school gates, to get answers.

A girl was missing.

It would be common knowledge by now. Abbie hated how she only had half the story. What if it was Pippa? What then?

In her stomach her heart remained as stone.

As she merged onto the bustling A-road which led her towards the upper end of town and the school, Abbie released one hand from the wheel to search within her handbag. Her fingers dug deep, fumbling past her long purse, a pack of tissues, some lipstick. Finally – the solid weight of her phone. She plucked it free and dropped it onto her lap.

Sweat beaded on her forehead.

There was talk that it would soon be illegal to use your phone whilst driving. She'd already seen first-hand what happened when someone was distracted at the wheel.

Severed spines.

Shattered pelvic floors.

Death.

But it wasn't illegal *yet*. So Abbie ignored her better judgement, the part of her which always looked both ways before crossing the road, and glanced down at the phone in her lap before stabbing at the buttons with her free hand.

She called Pippa.

Swerving around a car on the side of the road, hazards blinking bright, she pressed the phone to her ear and braced herself for the dull drone of a ringtone. Instead she heard the pulsing rhythm of her daughter's answerphone message where the singer Craig David smoothly instructed her to leave a message after the tone.

'Dammit.' Abbie sped up and ended the call, her hands and feet working independently of one another.

Pippa's phone was off. Why was it off? It was supposed to be on when there was an emergency. Wasn't a missing girl an emergency? Was this why Abbie hadn't received a text like Carol had? Because Pippa's phone was off? Because her daughter was parted from it? Because her daughter was in danger . . . was missing?

She was spiralling. With a strained shudder, Abbie returned both hands to the wheel and forced herself to slowly exhale. Right now she needed to focus, not fall apart. And she wouldn't know anything until she reached the school.

Her exit was up ahead. Slowing, she jabbed at her phone again, this time dialling the second most recent number in her call history.

The name 'John' glowed on her screen as the call rung out. When his answerphone message kicked in, it was the automated Orange one, lacking any personal touch. Abbie waited for the beep.

'John, I know you're probably in surgery but I needed to call as I might be back late. I'm headed over to the school to pick up Pippa . . . apparently there's been an—' She stopped talking, mouth hanging open as her words stuck in her throat. Indicating to take her exit, she considered how much she could say. *Should* say. John hated idle gossip with a passion.

'A bunch of clucking hens' was how he referred to the mothers who gathered at the school gates. And he'd never taken to Carol, feeling that she fed off the plight of others far too greedily. He didn't understand that between the mothers, gossip was their life blood. It connected them. Entertained them. And made them feel that little bit less alone. If the missing girl on the run turned out to be a fallacy then he'd be furious that Abbie had bothered him at work about it. Best to remain vague until she could confirm her source.

'There's been an incident at the school,' she quickly stated as she joined the next roundabout; two more left turns and she'd be at Waterbridge Prep. 'I'll be home as soon as I can.' Then with the press of a button she hung up. She imagined John in his scrubs and surgical gloves, brow furrowed as he performed some intricate procedure. It was a Wednesday which meant . . . Abbie searched the database of her memory, enjoying the distraction from her current thoughts.

Mondays were for major surgeries, to give patients a full week of complete in-hospital care to recover – things like a panproctocolectomy or the forming of an ilestomy. Abbie liked those surgeries; they were long but in-depth and intricate.

Wednesdays were for more routine procedures like the removal of hernias and piles. Less exciting but more copious in number and simpler to perform. John always seemed the most fatigued mid-week. By Friday the emergencies would have trickled in, which tended to rouse his spirits in time for the weekend.

Abbie took the first left and wondered if she could still successfully assist a complicated surgery. Things changed in medicine, sure, but not that quickly. She'd be rusty but she could still navigate her way through the procedure, could still—

Waterbridge Prep was aglow. Blue lights shone off the red brickwork. Abbie dragged her car up against the nearest curb, killing the engine and peering through her rain-smeared windscreen at the huge gates swinging open in the distance, the collection of police cars parked before the stone steps which led to the entrance. Above the grand arch, the emblem of the school was etched in stone.

As she stared, Abbie began to shake.

A girl was missing.

But who?

Her temple throbbed as tears pressed against the back of her eyes, desperate to fall in a tidal wave down her cheeks. Reaching for the phone in her lap she stabbed at it again, screamed in frustration as once more Craig David told her to leave a message.

7

The journey back to school was a subdued one. Theories drifted among the girls like debris from a shipwreck.

'She's fallen in the river.'

'She's hiding.'

'Some pervert carried her away, shoved her in the boot of their car.'

As the minibus entered the upper part of Waterbridge, Miss Charnley's patience snapped.

'Girls, let us try something of a respectful silence,' she shouted over their cowed heads. 'One of you is missing. If you have something to say, I suggest it be something helpful.'

'And,' added Miss Rogers, hugging the back of her seat and resting her chin atop it as she looked at her students, 'if any of you hear from Heather, please let us know. I promise she's not in trouble, we just want to know she's all right.'

Pippa idly kicked her foot against her backpack which rested on the floor, thinking of her mobile phone at the base of it. Turned off. Useless.

'Police!' The word, which heralded from Hannah Edwards, was like releasing a fox into a hen house. Seconds later the bus exploded with sound and movement, all the girls scrambling to look out their windows, frantically wiping condensation away with their sleeves, then peering at their smeared view of the world outside.

Even though it was night the school was not clad in darkness. Instead it glowed. Flashes of blue broke the dark like fireworks exploding against the main entrance. Police cars, half a dozen of them, clogging the turnaround usually solely reserved for official school vehicles.

'They already know.' Miss Rogers slowly climbed to her feet, hand gripping the headrest of her chair for support as she looked through the windscreen at the scene beyond.

'Girls!' Miss Charnley released the word like a whip over their heads, demanding order, obedience. 'Who sent a message about Heather? Who?'

'She's missing isn't she?' Olivia stated from the back of the bus, chin raised with the challenge of her comment. 'Good job someone let the school know.'

'I texted my mum,' Hannah offered smoothly. 'I was worried,' she added, almost sounding earnest.

Miss Charnley audibly scoffed. 'You girls and your phones. You're going to lose the meaning of patience, mark my words.'

The bus parked up just beyond the gates. Pippa could see uniformed police officers on the steps, by the grand double doors.

With a hiss the minibus door opened and the cold night air swept in, bringing with it the tsunami of sound from outside. So many voices. And car horns. And phones ringing.

'All right, usual departure here girls. Line up.' Miss Charnley positioned herself at the end of the aisle, extending a scrawny arm out straight, fingers stretching to the back of the bus. Even in chaos the old woman would find order.

They stood up in a line and filed their way outside, just as though it were any other day, any other return to school. Exiting just in front of the main gates, they technically weren't on school property. And it was on the steps, by the doors, that the police swarmed. Pippa stole a look at them, recognised several teachers gathering with them. All of them talking. All of them looking nervous.

'Pippa!'

She turned instinctively at the sound of her own name.

'Oh, thank God.' Her mum's arms wrapped around her shoulders, drew her in close. For a moment all Pippa could smell was the heady aroma of Chanel N°5, so thick she could taste it on her tongue.

'Mum . . .' Her voice was muffled against Burberry cloth. 'Mum!' Managing to break free, she stepped back. The rain had eased from a downpour to a mist.

'Look at you.' Her mum gripped her shoulders, assessed her. 'You're soaked to the bone. You must be freezing. Come on, we need to get you home.' She turned her daughter away from the bus, from the school gates, and began marching her in the direction of the car which Pippa now saw was parked further down the road. Other mothers were grabbing their daughters, hurrying them away.

'Wait, wait!' An officer with a thick black moustache chased after them. 'I'm afraid you girls can't go disappearing just yet. We need to ask some questions.'

'What these girls need is to get home and get dry,' Abbie fired at him, hands on Pippa's shoulders, squeezing.

'We won't take too long, we'll just—'

'We're taking our daughters home.' Carol had joined the fray, shoving Hannah along towards their waiting 4x4. 'You can ask any questions you have tomorrow. In daylight. When they're dry and warm.'

Pippa watched the officer struggle. Saw his gaze dart over the crowd he'd gathered, the lionesses all wedging themselves between him and thier cubs. It took less than thirty seconds for his shoulders to droop in defeat. Pippa understood why. If this were any other school in Waterbridge he'd be able to throw his weight around, make demands. But this was Waterbridge Prep. His bosses and their bosses sent their children here.

'Tomorrow,' he said, pointing a finger at each of the girls in his line of sight, 'be at school. Be prepared to answer questions about the run.' Now he shifted his gaze to the mothers. 'Anybody who can be spared should get over to Sefton Park to join in the search.'

Pippa began to wonder how they'd conduct a search at night over such a vast area when her mum propelled her roughly up to the car, not even pausing to make small talk with Carol. Once they were both inside, buckled up with the engine humming, she looked at her daughter, face pale. 'So who's missing, Pip? What happened?'

Instead of waiting for an answer, her mum glanced in her side mirror, saw a gap and seized it, flicking on her indicator and pulling out so fast the tyres skidded.

'Woah, Mum, take it easy.'

'I just want you home,' her mum explained, sniffing. 'I want you home and safe.'

Pippa watched the hands gripping the wheel, noticing the quake in them.

'Mum, it's OK, I'm fine.'

'But someone is missing.' Her mum was speeding down the next street, doing thirty-five in a thirty area. Pippa said nothing. 'Who, who is it, Pip?'

'Heather. She's...gone.'

Her mum had to break suddenly at a red light. They both jerked forwards in their seats.

'Heather's missing?'

Pippa tipped her chin to her chest, sunk as low as she could. Hearing the words come out of her mum's mouth made them seem too real.

Heather's missing.

And Pippa had been the last person to see her. She used her hands to tug up the wet hood of her jumper, wanting to hide any tears she might shed.

'What happened?' her mum asked. The lights turned amber to green and she sped off again, treating the route home like a Formula One track.

'She took a short cut and just . . . disappeared.'

'Just like that?'

'Just like that.' Pippa wanted to be home, to be warm, to lie under her duvet and close her eyes and forget about the entire afternoon.

'What do you think happened?'

Pippa shifted awkwardly beneath the pinning pressure of her seat belt. 'I bet she took off on purpose, for attention.'

Out of the corner of her eye she watched her mum nod in agreement. 'That certainly sounds like something Heather would do.'

'I know, right.'

'So I'm sure she's fine.' They turned into their street. Lined by grand oak trees which were now almost completely bare, solid gates concealed the long driveways and impressive homes beyond. This was Pippa's street. She'd learnt how to ride a bike here, raced out of her gate to get to the ice cream van for a 99 on hot days, used the lampposts as wickets when she played cricket with the Connor kids from two doors down. This was her home. Her safe place.

'Michelle wasn't there,' her mum continued, speaking softly, almost to herself. 'Working late I guess, or perhaps hadn't heard anything.'

'Mmm,' Pippa mumbled in agreement. Heather's mum was a GP at the local practice. Pippa had been to see her the previous spring when her acne got out of hand. Something she tried to forget.

'Some girls do struggle with acne at this age,' Heather's mum had said as she'd plastered on a thin smile.

Some girls. Not her precious, golden Heather. And her mum, Michelle, was just as glossy and tanned, only with shoulder-length blonde hair and the same piercing blue eyes.

'I don't like her mum,' Pippa declared as they approached the gates to their house.

'No,' Abbie said, clenching her jaw, 'me neither.'

The double gates parted seamlessly, revealing a black BMW already occupying half of the driveway.

'Oh, your dad beat us home,' her mum noted with surprise. 'That's a first.'

8

Abbie bustled through the front door, shaking droplets of rain from her coat onto the mat beneath her feet. Her knotted thoughts wove themselves together, tangled and messy, as she entered her home, suddenly concerned about the practicalities of dinner. Of normality.

'Go upstairs and have a bath,' she told Pippa, cupping her daughter's slim face between her palms and gazing into her soft brown eyes. 'Put on your pyjamas and get nice and warm while I sort dinner.' Pippa's cheeks felt like ice in her hands. 'I stuck the immersion on earlier, so the water will be nice and hot by now,' she continued, her focus drifting to the staircase and the lit landing above, 'as long as your father hasn't used it all showering since he came home.'

It was John's ritual – get in, place his briefcase on the walnut desk in his austere study and then disappear into the main bathroom, reappearing once his skin was pink and his curly hair flat and wet against his scalp. 'Washing off the day,' he called it. Abbie understood. Even with surgical gloves, scrubs and masks, some things still felt like they made their way to your skin. Blood. Death. They came home with you. With the release of a stiff breath she looked again to her daughter, noticed how the colour had yet to return to Pippa's face, how her eyes were streaked red and bloodshot.

'Heather is going to be fine,' she assured her, leaning down to kiss Pippa's forehead, leaving a red stain of lipstick against alabaster skin. 'Like you said, she'll be doing this for attention. I bet she turns up safe and sound before midnight.'

Pippa was silent.

'Go on then.' Abbie marked her with a final kiss before watching her slink up the stairs, leaning heavily against the oak banister.

With her daughter out of sight, Abbie headed to the kitchen. There wasn't time to carefully prepare the dinner she had planned – shepherd's pie with broccoli florets. But she knew there was some leftover lasagne in the freezer she could quickly warm up in the oven and serve with some salad. That should do. She moved quickly and urgently, preheating the oven, then delving into the freezer. Above the pipes began to wheeze and bang as Pippa began running the bath. Abbie glanced at the ceiling, comforted by the sound.

'You were late home.'

She'd been so preoccupied with sorting out dinner she hadn't heard John walk in. Gone was the suit he wore to work. Now he was casual in his pale grey cashmere jumper and jeans, hair coiled in tight curls. Abbie chewed her lip as her gaze flitted between her husband and the ceiling adorned with Aertex, hoping the water remaining in the immersion heater would be sufficient for Pippa's bath.

'Yeah.' She brushed her hand through the air in a dismissive gesture. 'Dinner will be a bit ad hoc tonight, I'm afraid.'

'Fine.' John moved past her, towards the living room. Moments later Abbie heard the brisk tone of a news reporter's voice as John took in the latest national headlines. The pipes continued to echo in the walls as Abbie tried to reheat the remains of what they had eaten yesterday.

'Feeling better?'

The table was set. Abbie insisted on them always having dinner together in the dining room, the three of them almost lost among the eight gathered seats. Abbie would light candles, always have fresh flowers as a centrepiece and the silverware had to match. Detail. She'd always had such a keen eye for detail. It was one of the first things John had complimented her on back when they worked together, back when he still towed the line of being her colleague, not even yet in the spring of their relationship.

Pippa's cheeks were now flushed. She nodded at Abbie as she settled in her usual seat, the hood of her fluffy dressing gown pulled up over her damp hair.

'Glad you've been able to warm up a bit,' Abbie smiled at her. 'Sorry dinner isn't that great tonight, didn't have time to make anything from scratch.'

'It's fine, Mum. Really.' She picked up her fork and stabbed at her lasagne, forcing some mincemeat to tumble into her pile of salad.

'Good day?' John had followed her into the room and now slid into his seat which was positioned opposite Abbie's, asking his question to no one in particular, gaze fixed on his plate.

Abbie and Pippa shared a look. 'A strange one,' she ventured gently, sensing her daughter's hesitance. Just as she'd felt on the phone earlier when leaving him a message, she wondered if discussing events from the run veered towards sharing gossip. Only now the police were involved, there was nothing idle about it. If anything it was now surely news. Abbie placed her knife and fork down, knitting her hands beneath her chin and looking at her husband, wondering why he had yet to mention the voicemail she'd left him.

'Uh-huh,' he nodded absently, shoving a forkful of pasta sheet and red sauce speared with salad leaves into his mouth.

'There was an incident at the school,' Abbie explained. Now he looked at her, blue eyes bright with interest, the lines which had appeared around them in the past decade deepening. 'It's why we were so late home.'

'An incident?' John looked between his wife and daughter. In profile Abbie always saw flashes of the young doctor she'd met with the kind eyes and the strong jawline, curly black hair forever falling across his forehead. Now the hair was streaked with silver and the jawline sagged.

'It happened when Pip was on her cross-country run.' Abbie studied her husband, selecting her words carefully. When she was a trainee nurse, the other women studying with her had always praised her ability to manage Doctor Parks.

'He's got such a temper,' they'd whisper together in the changing rooms, 'but you keep him level, handle him the right way.' It was a skill Abbie had perfected throughout the two decades of their marriage.

John stared at her across the table, brow furrowed, blue eyes weary. 'Well?' he demanded, voice loud with irritation. 'What happened on the run?'

'A girl went missing.'

Abbie looked to the end of the table, surprised to hear the answer coming from her daughter's mouth.

'A girl went missing?' John repeated in open disbelief. 'What do you mean, "missing"?'

49

'She was on the run with the rest of us. Then she went on this shortcut through the estate and just . . . disappeared.'

'Well she has to be somewhere.' John looked to Abbie for assistance.

'No one has found her yet,' Abbie told him.

'Teenage girls can be terribly flighty.' He commenced stabbing at his mound of meat and pasta, smearing his lips with red sauce. 'I'm sure she'll turn up soon. Don't trouble yourself with it, Pippa.'

'Like I was telling Mum,' Pippa said, pushing some salad leaves around her plate, 'Heather is always pulling weird stunts like this.'

'Heather?' John's cutlery was down. He swallowed what was in his mouth and then coughed uncomfortably. 'Your friend, Heather?'

'Yes, Heather,' Pippa nodded, studying her dinner intently. 'She's the girl who has gone missing.'

'And they don't come much more flighty than Heather Oxon,' Abbie said, directing her fork towards Pippa. 'I think you're right, sweetheart, that she's just—' A chair loudly scraped against the floor as it was pushed away from the table. 'I've a report I need to write.' John was grabbing his plate, backing away from them. 'I'll finish my dinner in my study.'

Abbie blinked at the suddenly vacant space before her.

'Dad's mad at me.' Pippa sank low in her chair, dropped her fork against the porcelain of her plate with a flat thud.

'He's not mad at you.'

'He is.' From beneath the hood of her dressing gown, Pippa peered towards the door her father had just departed through. 'He thinks I shouldn't hang around with Heather so much outside of school.'

'We *both* think you shouldn't hang around with Heather as much as you do.' The sense of solidarity with her husband felt good, and Abbie tried to bask in the glow of it for a few moments. 'She's always trying to lead you astray. And she is such a mean girl. You need friends who are more . . . aligned with you.'

Pippa was nodding as she hugged her arms to her chest, shivering even in her flannel pyjamas and dressing gown.

'Girls like Heather always get what's coming to them,' Abbie said with confidence.

'Do they?' Pippa narrowed her eyes at her mother, sad and questioning. 'You said Heather's mum is mean and she's in that big house on Long Lane all on her own, drives a Mercedes and goes to Saint Tropez every summer with her friends. She has everything.'

'She doesn't have a husband,' Abbie curtly corrected her.

'She *did*,' Pippa began to chew on her thumbnail, 'but she left him, remember? Told Heather he wasn't investing in the marriage anymore and made him go, that was what . . . three years ago?'

'Women like Michelle Oxon think everything and everyone is replaceable because they are vapid and shallow. We're better than that.'

Pippa glanced again at the door to the dining room. 'Maybe Heather's mum just got tired of taking shit from her husband. What's so wrong with that?'

'Watch your mouth!' Abbie scolded her, face heating with anger. 'You're lucky your father isn't here to hear such language.'

'He's never here,' Pippa continued, 'he's always working at the hospital, or in his study doing some report.'

'Your father is very important, he's a prominent surgeon. He has responsibilities. Duties to uphold.'

51

'I'm not having a dig at him,' Pippa sighed, looking tired as she dropped her thumbnail from between her teeth, hand falling into her lap. 'Sometimes I just think that . . .' She sighed and shook her head as though she was trying and failing to capture what she wanted to say.

'It's been a long day, let's go and have our dessert in the front room under a blanket watching TV. I've got some Viennetta in the freezer.'

'Mum, I think you deserve better.'

The sincerity of Pippa's words made Abbie's breath catch in her throat. 'Well.' She coughed, long fingers fluttering to her slender neck. With another loud cough she managed to clear her airway. 'Be that as it may, he's the man I married. And marriage means something to me. Loyalty should never be underrated.'

'Even if someone is mean to you?' Pippa was rubbing at her eyes.

'Even if someone is mean to you.' Abbie rose and began gathering up their plates, noting how Pippa had failed to eat hardly anything.

'What if they did something really awful?'

'A vow is a vow,' Abbie said, as she took what was left of dinner back into the kitchen, Pippa following close behind, 'and marriage is "til death do us part".'

'And what about me?' her daughter wondered from behind her.

'What about you?' Abbie put the plates on the island and turned around, confused.

'What if you deserve better than me? You're not bound to me by a vow.' Within her dressing gown Pippa began to shake. And then cry. It overwhelmed her, tears cascading down pale cheeks as her body shuddered. Abbie instantly swept her up, pulled her close, letting her sorrow soak into the shoulder of her jumper, breathing in the sickly sweet scent of the bubble bath Pippa was so fond of.

'I am bound to you by something much, much stronger than any vow,' Abbie whispered against her daughter's wet hair. 'I am bound to you by a mother's love, and that, my darling, is utterly unbreakable.'

'Promise?' Pippa sobbed as she gripped tightly to her mother. 'Promise you'll always love me?'

'Promise.' Abbie said it without an ounce of hesitation. As she clutched her weeping daughter, her thoughts strayed to her husband, locked away working on yet another report. He was so important, so valued. So absent.

9

Two thousand, eight hundred and eighty minutes. That's how long it had been since Heather had failed to cross the finish line at Sefton Park. Forty-eight hours. Two days. Pippa ran the numbers over and over in her mind. It was Friday afternoon, history class. But she wasn't paying attention. None of the girls were.

Uniformed officers were in the hallways. At the dining tables at lunch. And they had questions. So many questions.

The headmistress, Miss Archibald, had braced her students for the inquisition that morning.

'Answer all questions asked of you honestly and thoroughly,' she had instructed in her clipped voice, grey hair drawn back severely in a tight bun. 'Even if you feel something is unimportant, it might prove to be crucial in helping to find Heather Oxon. I know we all continue to pray for her safe return.'

The mood within the school had fizzled from nervous excitement to simmering anxiety. With each passing hour, the girls stooped a little lower as they walked, all too aware that the longer Heather remained missing, the more likely that any news they received about her would be bad.

During class, girls kept being called away, Pippa noticed in alphabetical order by surname. A methodical approach.

She'd already spoken with a kind-faced female police officer the day before, told her all she knew.

'Girls, if we could try and focus.' Mr Hall was standing at the front of the classroom, tapping his pen against the whiteboard. 'I know it's hard at the moment but we need to distract ourselves as much as we can as there's nothing more we can do for Heather right now.' Behind him were scrawled dates detailing the rise of the Tudor dynasty. Dates Pippa already knew, had already studied. It was a period of history which genuinely interested her so she readily raced through all the assigned textbooks and reading materials. Heather had been the same. The previous term they'd devoured so much about the Tudors.

'It's all so scandalous,' she'd declared, eyes wide and wild. 'All the sex. The affairs.' Heather had peered at Pippa over the top of the book she was reading, *The Other Boleyn Girl* by Philippa Gregory. It was their latest shared obsession. Each had a copy where the spine was so bent from over reading the title was barely legible.

'It does make things more interesting,' Pippa agreed, trying to sound nonchalant. But she had to admit, it made things more than interesting, it made them thrilling. The divorces, the beheadings. History more than came alive when they studied the Tudors, it became *real*. Pippa would lie awake at night wondering about the lives they led, how tumultuous it all was, especially compared to her cocoon of normality.

'I guess some things never change,' Heather studied Pippa intently as she spoke. 'All the sex. The affairs.'

Pippa had always hated it when Heather spoke like this, brandishing her wealth of experience about like a badge of honour. While in contrast, Pippa had never even been kissed.

At the back of the classroom Pippa turned from the window to peer at the vacant chair beside her. The chair where Heather usually sat, doubled over her notebook, protecting her words with her arms as though she were so committed to her work, so afraid of it being stolen from her. In reality she was writing notes, usually for Pippa. Usually about Mr Hall. Notes which, Pippa felt, had the sole intention of making her face burn.

What do you think he looks like naked?
How big do you think his dick is?

Little tufts of paper would land in Pippa's lap and as she discreetly unfurled them beneath the desk she'd feel sick, sweat streaking down her back and gathering in her armpits as she imagined Mr Hall noticing the contraband note, taking it from her, reading it aloud, humiliating her before the entire class as beside her Heather dissolved in a fit of hysterics.

'Pippa Parks.'

Hearing her name was like a starting gun. Pippa turned to the front of the class, heart racing, ready to bolt.

'Pippa.' Mr Hall smiled wanly at her and gestured to the open door where the same kind-faced uniformed officer from yesterday stood. Her name had been Officer Simons. . . Simmons. Pippa couldn't recall. 'I think the police have a few more questions for you.'

'OK, yeah, sure.' Pippa slid back her chair, the metal legs grating against the floor. She eased away from the table, palms growing clammy.

'Best take your bag,' the officer commented, watching her, 'in case we're a while.'

The collective intake of breath from the other girls made Pippa's blood run cold. She knew the second the door closed behind her they'd be whispering among themselves, writing fresh notes. Wondering what she knew.

Head down, Pippa followed the officer towards a vacant science lab which was being used for interviews. Miss Rogers waved limply from the back of the room where she was playing chaperone. Once again Pippa settled herself on a wooden stool, backpack propped by her ankles, elbows resting on the bench.

'Hi, Pippa.' The officer smiled at her, lips ruby red, hair the colour of fresh snow. 'I know we met yesterday, but I'm being joined today by Officer Richards.' She nodded to the man beside her – handsome in a squared-off, chiselled way. With his thick arms and smooth skin he was just Heather's type. Pippa looked down at her lap, willing herself not to cry. 'We just have a few more questions,' the blonde officer explained.

Pippa nodded numbly, daring to lift her gaze to peek at the bench and its raised gas taps, onto which the tubing of Bunsen burners would be attached. She used to fear the flame the burners would produce, how you were supposed to twist them from blue to orange, marvelling at the power of fire. Heather wasn't afraid. She'd singe the tip of her tie and laugh as the smoke curled away from the fabric. And she passed her boldness over to Pippa in the form of a plastic purple lighter. 'You shouldn't fear it,' she had told her with a wolfish grin, 'fire can be exciting, mesmerising.'

'We gather that you were the last person to see Heather,' Officer Richards stated. Pippa wondered why he was even there. Was he superior to the other officer or had he been brought in as some kind of incentive to get her to open up more, because of his set jawline and frosted tips? Pippa closed her eyes, trying to calm her nerves. Fear and despair were playing cat and mouse in her chest and it was nauseating. She just wanted to go home, for it to be the weekend.

'Like I said,' she explained quietly, eyes darting upwards to briefly glance at the female officer, 'we took the shortcut and then I changed my mind and doubled back.'

'And how was Heather when you left her?' As Officer Richards asked the questions, the other officer wrote in her small notebook, biro scratching against soft paper.

'She was . . .' Pippa gathered her hands in a ball in her lap and tightly clenched them together. 'Annoyed.'

'Why was she annoyed?'

'Because I was leaving. She wanted me to stay on the shortcut.'

'But you didn't want to?'

'No.' Pippa drew in a ragged breath, wondering how long until the bell to mark the end of the day rang and she could leave. Unless they wanted to keep questioning here, to hold her in the lab, or worse, take her to the police station. 'I needed . . . I needed a good time.'

'From the run?'

'Yeah, from the run.'

The female officer leafed through her notebook, sourcing a previous page. 'For someone who deviated from the route you ended up having an impressive time.'

'I'm a strong runner.' Pippa forced herself to raise her chin, to return the woman's stare. The warmth from the officer's face the previous day seemed to have drained overnight. The girls at school had already speculated this would happen. Especially Hannah.

'The longer this goes on,' she had warned over lunch earlier that day, 'the more desperate the police will become. And that means they'll get shittier with us. A lot shittier.

Because we were there when she went missing. So in their eyes, we're all complicit in her disappearance.'

Pippa's stomach gurgled loudly. She'd failed to eat any of her jacket potato and cheese as she listened to Hannah ruminate on how bad things might potentially get.

'I'm the second-best runner in my class,' she told the officer. She wasn't being boastful, only factual. On her best day she could almost catch Hannah Edwards. But on her worst she'd be miles behind.

'Did Heather ever mention if she was dating anyone? Any men she might be chatting with?' Officer Richards was asking the questions now.

His delivery caught Pippa off guard. 'Men?' She frowned at him. There were definitely boys. Heather would smear names across the vanity mirror in her bedroom in thick lipstick, declaring whoever she was crushing on that current week. But the names were ever changing, turning to pink smears and then greasy stains. Had she mentioned a Tristan over at the boys' school? Pippa was struggling to think. Were the police even over at the partner school, quizzing the boys who would host house parties where Heather would get drunk and do things they promised to never speak about, but always did? 'I mean there were some boys, but it wasn't like, you know, serious.'

'Boys like who?' the blonde officer asked, and Pippa felt her face burn. Did it matter about Tristan? If she uttered his name, was she placing a target on his back that didn't deserve to be there?

'Tristan Jenkins.' She said it quickly, banishing his name from her mouth as though it burned.

'I see.' Officer Richards nodded as his pen moved across the surface of his notepad. 'And was she speaking with anyone online?'

Pippa shook her head, tightened her grip on her hands. 'Heather likes things to be real. She says only losers hide behind a screen.' Her cheeks were starting to turn from pink to red.

'And how were things at home for Heather?' the female officer wondered, voice softening. 'Did she see much of her father?'

Maxwell Oxon was gone. Off living in the city. 'He loves being divorced,' Heather had declared. 'Now he gets to fuck every tart in London and forget about being a family man.'

That left just Heather and her mother, Michelle, in their grand house. Their whole life sounded like an episode of *Gilmore Girls*. At least the version Heather would tell, where it was all late nights gossiping and mornings drinking too-strong coffee. Pippa knew the truth. How Heather was often alone while her mum worked late. How she lived off microwave meals and oven chips.

Pippa began to cry. All this thinking about Heather, investigating her life, it was too much. Her shoulders shook as the female officer plucked a tissue from a nearby box and handed it to her. With trembling fingers Pippa took it, sniffed out a 'thank you' and tried to mop up the deluge that was running down her cheeks.

'I know this is hard.' The blonde officer rubbed Pippa's upper arm. 'You must be so terribly worried about Heather, especially as you two are best friends. But we need to ask questions, lots of them, to help us try and find her.'

'Did she ever talk about running away?' Officer Richards asked, keen to press on. But Pippa couldn't answer. Like water down a drain, she couldn't help but swirl towards the previous comment.

Especially as you two are best friends.

Was that what the girls at her school were saying? Was that what people thought? Pippa couldn't breathe. Her tears were too much, trying to drown her. As she gulped for air, face pink and pinched, the female officer continued to try and soothe her.

'Don't worry,' she said over and over, voice gentle and nurturing, as though trying to calm a baby, 'we're going to find your friend. We're going to find Heather.'

'My best friend,' Pippa coughed through sore lips, tasting the salt of her sorrow. And she wondered if Heather were there, what she'd say, if she'd agree with the statement or laugh so loudly she'd nearly deafen them all.

P Parks,

Why the hell have you been ignoring me all day? Is it because of what I said at lunch about your dad? Because he HAS been to my house. I'm not making it up. I promise. My mum tarts herself up, full make-up, the works. And he comes round. She tells me some crap about he's checking the leaking tap in the bathroom but I know they're doing it. For one – we don't have a leaky tap!

My mum thinks I'm so stupid. Always has. She's the dumb one.

But you need to stop ignoring me! I don't like it.

Tristan has been texting again. I need to show you the messages. In the last one he said we should hang out sometime. What do you think that means? Because I don't want a boyfriend. I suppose if I did, it probably would be Tristan. Do you think he likes me like that?

STOP IGNORING ME.

I'll call you later. House phone so you have to speak to me.

Love you,

H

xoxo

10

Abbie loitered in the doorway to her daughter's bedroom. The air in the room felt thick, curtains drawn tight against the autumnal sun burning bright outside.

'I don't have to go,' Abbie said for the third time.

'Mum, I said it's fine, go,' came the mumbled response from beneath the duvet. The television on the adjacent chest of drawers was paused with a blurred image of a handsome boy crossing a street.

'I can stay home,' Abbie offered, 'we could watch . . .' She frowned at the screen, trying to decipher what the programme was. 'We could watch your show together.' She hated how this made her sound, like she was disconnected and uninformed. As her own mother had been.

'Mum, go see your friends,' Pippa ordered from under her canopy, the lilac fabric bearing the design of Groovy Chick tented over her. 'I just want to have a duvet day.'

Normally, Abbie would fight. She'd haul the duvet off her teenager, throw open the curtains and let the sunlight blast in, declaring that it was a beautiful day and not to be wasted. But things were not normal. Heather Oxon was still missing. Yet normality yearned to be preserved, which was why her weekly lunch with her friends from the school had not been cancelled. Their reservation at the gastro pub in the next village over held. She was expected there by noon. Already it was half-past eleven.

'Well, I'll be home by the three at the absolute latest.'

'Uh-huh.'

'And if you need me *call*.'

'Uh-huh.'

'I'll have my mobile with me.'

'Uh-huh.'

Defeated, Abbie withdrew onto the landing, the silence from the rest of the house already pressing in on her. John had long left for work since he was yet again on call for the weekend. At the top of the stairs Abbie hesitated, fingers clasped around the edge of the banister. 'Love you,' she offered towards the bedroom. She heard a distant rustle as Pippa remodelled her bed fort.

'Love you.'

Abbie exhaled with relief and felt several inches taller as she descended towards the hallway and the glowing morning outside.

'Still missing.' Carol alternated between sipping from her glass of white wine and shaking her head as she looked round at her friends. 'Can you even believe it?'

They were nestled in a quiet corner of the Wenlock, an old pub renovated almost a decade ago. Their table was wedged against bare stone walls, close to a vast fireplace in which a few golden flames burned. Abbie looked at the bubbles rising and popping against the surface of her white wine spritzer.

'Where can she even be?' Ashley Jenkins wondered, overly plucked brows lifting up her forehead as far as her recent Botox treatment would permit. 'It's new,' she'd previously informed the group, 'my beautician told me about it. Apparently it can take decades off you.'

So far all it had taken from Ashley was her ability to form facial expressions.

'I've heard the police have combed every inch of Sefton Park,' Carol continued. She puckered her lips, which made the old chicken-pox scars upon her cheeks more prominent. 'No sign of her. Not a trace.'

'Even her sports backpack was gone,' Ashley added. 'You know, the ones the girls keep their water in during long runs.'

'I know the one,' Abbie noted mildly. She'd filled Pippa's water bottle the morning of the now infamous run and shoved it inside her backpack, reminding her daughter as she dropped her off to take it with her, to make sure she stayed hydrated.

'If it was Hannah missing I would be going out of my mind.' Carol raised a hand to massage her forehead.

'Same if it was Pip,' Abbie agreed.

'Boys are different,' Ashley said, draining the last of her red wine which had already stained her lips burgundy. 'If Tristan or Jasper went missing I'd assume they'd done something bad, not that something bad had happened to them. You know?'

The other mothers nodded, muttering their under-standing. Carol also had Harry, three years younger than Hannah and Pippa. But for Abbie there was just Pippa.

'Wasn't Pippa with her?' Carol asked, lowering her voice as their lunches arrived via a young waitress.

Abbie looked down at her Caesar salad, feeling her appetite ebbing away.

'Just before she disappeared?' Carol added, as though Abbie needed further explanation. 'Hannah says she's the last person to have seen Heather.'

'Has she said anything?' Ashley leaned forward eagerly, placing a thick chip between her teeth and biting down.

'She . . .' Abbie looked at her plate, stabbed at some lettuce with her fork. The Ted Baker blouse she was wearing began to feel too tight, pulling against her chest. Releasing her fork she fumbled with her top button, neat nails wrestling between the smooth surface and the slickness of the silk of the blouse. Finally it opened and she breathed a little easier. 'She's so worried about Heather. Understandably.' She offered her friends a prim smile.

'Of course.' Carol was biting down into her tuna melt sandwich.

'Mmm.' Ashley was eating chips, nodding.

Abbie focused on her own lunch, replaying what little Pippa had told her. Stomach lurching at the scarcity of the information, she still forced her salad down, refusing to show even an ounce of discomfort, thinking of Pippa's account. 'She was mad at me because I was leaving.'

'You were leaving?'

'The shortcut.' Pippa looked so exhausted when Abbie was questioning her. She peered up at her mother, brown eyes glossy with sadness and fear. 'Mum, we've been over this.'

The events from Wednesday had left Pippa so shaken, so fragile, that Abbie didn't dare press too hard and risk shattering her daughter's already delicate exterior.

'I've been trying to give Pippa some space,' Abbie told her friends. 'She's so upset by it all.'

'It's so upsetting,' Carol agreed zealously, placing down her sandwich to reach for her wine. 'Who knows where Heather could be? Or if she'll even turn up alive at this point.'

They all bent their heads as though unable to fight against the gravity of the comment.

For a minute no one spoke. Mumbled conversations floated in from the tables nearby, punctuated by hearty laughter.

'Geoff says the first forty-eight hours are crucial.' Ashley spoke quietly, reverently. And Abbie and Carol listened. Ashley's husband, Geoff, was a police chief and no doubt working on the case. 'After that, the chances of finding a missing person alive drop significantly.'

Abbie grabbed her glass, wishing she'd been bolder and opted for a full-on wine, not just a spritzer. She drank deeply as Carol dared to pump for more information.

'Has he said anything?'

'You know I can't answer that,' Ashley chided her, pursing her lips.

'Doesn't mean you won't,' Carol challenged, eyebrows lifting in expectation.

Ashley puffed up her cheeks and then exhaled loudly, as though battling a desire to say more. 'Fine,' she said, rolling her eyes and putting a hand to her chest as though they'd worn her down. Abbie blinked, aware it had barely been ten seconds since Carol asked for information. 'No leads at all, nothing.' Ashely shrugged wearily. 'I think the next step is to go through her phone, logs on her computer, that kind of thing.'

'Have they found her phone?' Carol asked.

Ashley mused on this, sipping from her drink. 'If it was in her regular bag, then yes. But if it was in the sports bag she had with her on the run, then no. As I think that's still missing.'

'I bet she's run away with some boy.' Carol held her half-empty glass in her hand and used it to gesture to her friends.

'Or a *man*,' Ashley added. 'Would explain the need for secrecy.'

'Wasn't there something about Mr Hall?' Carol drank more, using the wine to fuel her memory. 'You know . . . the history teacher.' As she thought, she drummed her long nails, painted a vivid shade of red, against the table.

'I think that was just a rumour,' Abbie interjected. One they'd all heard and mostly dismissed. Because Mr Hall was young and blonde with a trendy beard. He wore waistcoats and trainers to school. He was going to attract rumours, especially at a girl's school. But being young and fashionable didn't mean anything.

'He's still at school, though,' Ashley said, swatting the suggestion away. 'He can't be involved else he'd have disappeared too, surely.'

'Does Pippa know anything?' Carol pinned Abbie with an intense gaze. 'Her and Heather are usually thick as thieves.'

'She doesn't know any more than the rest of us.' Abbie felt regret swirl with the spritzer in her stomach. She should have stayed home. Pippa needed her, was fearing for her friend. What sort of mother goes out to a social engagement at such a time?

'You know Michelle has been turning up for work,' Ashley announced with a smug smirk.

'She has?' Carol openly gasped. 'That can't be!'

'Heard Geoff discussing it on the phone last night. She's been at the practice Thursday and Friday. Says her patients need her.'

'That –' Carol's hand slapped against the table making the other women jump '– is truly preposterous. If my Hannah was missing I'd be out combing the streets looking for her, screaming her name until there was no breath left in me.'

'Absolutely,' Abbie agreed, growing animated. 'I wouldn't eat, wouldn't sleep, until Pip was returned home safe and sound.'

'She must know something.' Ashley's dark eyes narrowed as she leaned back in her seat. 'I bet she's protecting her.'

'Do you think so?' Abbie wondered, failing to understand in what scenario that would ever be plausible.

'Makes sense to me,' Carol declared after swallowing down the last of her sandwich. 'She's always been a funny one, that Michelle. Never participates in any school events, always *too busy*. I bet she knows more than she's letting on.'

Drinking even a spritzer on an empty stomach was never a good idea, and Abbie began to wish she'd eaten more of her salad. Her thoughts were pushing too hard against her temple, falling too easily onto her tongue and from her mouth. 'Maybe she's protecting her.'

'From what?' Carol demanded hotly.

'I . . .' Abbie massaged her throat, feeling hot. John used to tell her she had a swan's neck – slim and slender. Now her long nails scratched against it, leaving pink marks. 'I don't know.' She glanced helplessly between her friends. 'But if it were either of you . . . wouldn't you do anything to protect your child? Even lie to the police?'

Unanimous nodding.

'But –' Ashley clicked a finger and then pointed at Abbie '– with Michelle I'd wager she's protecting herself more than she's protecting Heather.'

'Get Geoff to press her,' Carol urged. 'She must know more than she's letting on.'

'Time will tell.' Ashley glanced deeper into the surrounding pub, searching for their waitress now that her glass and plate were both empty. 'Because the clock is ticking, and if Heather doesn't turn up soon it's likely something bad happened to her.'

Abbie felt cold even though the fire beside her crackled and spat. 'She'll turn up.'

The others were silent.

'She'll turn up and she'll be fine,' she added. Because bad things just didn't happen in Waterbridge. It was a good town, a sought-after town. People moved there for the prestigious schools, the elite shopping district. And together they watched scandal from afar, so very safe in their ivory towers.

'As soon as Geoff hears anything,' Ashley whispered across the table, 'I'll tell you.' And they all nodded solemnly, the pact made. Abbie didn't like how Ashley's gaze lingered on her for a beat too long, as though she knew something.

The wink of sunlight off the polished black body of John's car, glistening like an exotic beetle as it pulled into the driveway, told her that he'd got her text message. What a way to end an already awful weekend. Abbie released a fluttery breath and withdrew from her vigil at the window. Her husband's key was barely in the door when she thrust it open, cheeks like apples. 'The *police,* John,' she whimpered as she ushered him inside, peering nervously down the length of the drive. 'Coming *here.* Whatever do they want with us?'

'Settle down,' he ordered stiffly, leaving his briefcase in its usual spot beneath the coat hooks. As though this were any ordinary Sunday afternoon. 'They'll just want to talk with Pippa, that's all.'

'But they've spoken with her already,' Abbie said, walking in tandem with him, towards the kitchen. 'At school.'

This made him pivot. He was smart in his suit, dark eyes shining as he studied his wife. 'They did?'

'Pip mentioned it. . .' Her hand nervously darted about her face as she spoke, like an anxious bird trying to reclaim all her harassed words. 'But she . . . I don't know, John. They called and said they'd like to speak to us here. At home. Today.'

'OK.' He smoothly turned away from her, busied himself making a cup of tea. The action irked Abbie.

71

'Here,' she said, and pushed him aside, unable to bear that he was reaching for the wrong set of mugs, the ones that were reserved solely for guests. 'Let me.'

'Who was with her?' John grazed his chin with his fingertips as he waited for his drink to be made for him.

'When?' Abbie snapped, pouring scolding water onto a teabag, watching it deflate and stain the milk.

'At school, when the police spoke to her?'

'I don't . . .' Abbie shook her head, swirled a small silver spoon around the rim of the cup.

'Because we weren't informed,' he said in that haughty, annoyed voice of his, the one he chastised young residents with.

'She mentioned something about a teacher being there.' With a gasp of despair, Abbie handed John his fresh mug of tea. 'Can you focus, please? They'll be here any minute.' Her eyes darted about the kitchen, assessing the sides. Were they clean enough? Free of clutter? Or were they too clean? Nervously she hurried to the front room, began plumping cushions. Did she need to light a candle? Would it help if it smelt of vanilla? Or perhaps orange? She still had that citrus candle from— The doorbell rang like an alarm. Abbie straightened, inhaled, smoothed down the emerald blouse she'd put on barely ten minutes ago. She moved to the hallway with elegant restraint, pausing to call up the stairs, 'Pippa, can you come down here, please?' Through the glass in the door she saw the blur of neon and blue and nearly retched.

'It'll be fine.' John's hand, warm on her lower back, eased past her, opened the door, applied his brightest smile. 'Good afternoon,' he greeted them, 'come on in.'

★

The officers, one male, one female, both young, bookended the sofa. Pippa was in an armchair, knees pressed to her chests, Abbie hovering nervously behind her. John lingered by the fireplace, one hand resting on the mantle.

'Like we were saying,' the female officer smiled at Pippa, 'we just wanted to run some more things by you.'

'But you've already spoken with her,' John frowned, one hand in his trouser pocket.

'Indeed,' the woman nodded, 'but we just have a few more questions, if that's all right with you?'

John watched her, jaw tight. 'You didn't check if it was all right with us when she was at school.'

'Excuse my husband,' Abbie breathily intervened, forcing a bubble of laughter. 'He's just tired from being on call this weekend.'

'And I'll be due back at the hospital imminently,' John confirmed, making a show of checking the time on his Rolex.

'OK, right.' The female officer flipped open her little notebook, leaned forward. 'Well, Pippa, we talked to you about your friendship with Heather, if you knew anywhere she might go. But did you see anyone else when you were with her? Anyone . . . hanging about? Waiting for her perhaps?'

'Someone might have given her a lift,' the man – Richards, had he said his name was? – chimed in. 'Helped her get away from the parkland.'

'I didn't see anyone.' Pippa pressed her chin into her knees. 'Other than the girls from school.'

'OK,' the woman said, and scribbled a note. Abbie strained to see it but the paper was frustratingly tilted at an angle to prevent any snooping. 'And as a family you're close to Heather?' She looked between Abbie and John.

'We know her well, yes,' Abbie confirmed, fingering the gold necklace around her neck. 'She and Pippa . . . they've basically grown up together.'

'And her mother?'

The question landed like an axe in Abbie's back. She pushed back her shoulders, kept her poise and smile in place. Golden Michelle Oxon who was always glorious, always gorgeous. Beloved GP. Abbie inhaled sharply when she felt something snag behind her back; lowering her hand she saw the broken chain of her necklace hanging limply between her fingers.

'What about Heather's mother?' John interjected. Whilst eyes were upon him, Abbie hastily closed her hand around her broken necklace.

'She says she has no idea where her daughter might be,' the officer continued. 'We wondered how you'd describe her relationship with Heather?'

'As a loving mother,' John said, narrowing his eyes.

Abbie felt a flush creep up from her chest.

As a loving mother. Were those the words he'd use to describe his own wife? 'She works a lot,' Abbie informed the officers, 'so we often have to step in for Heather. For school pick-ups, dinners, that sort of thing.'

More notes in the book. Abbie swelled with satisfaction.

'Look,' John checked his watch again, 'I really am going to be needed back at the hospital. I'm one of only two consultants on call this afternoon.'

'Right, of course.' The female officer slapped her notebook closed. 'We appreciate you taking the time to speak with us.'

'Absolutely.' Abbie eagerly guided them back towards the hallway, keen to have them gone, to reclaim her home.

'And if you remember any details –' now the woman's gaze was pinned on Pippa, who was hanging back in the shadows of the kitchen '– no matter how small they seem, call us right away, OK?'

'She will,' John said icily as he opened the front door for the officers, waving politely as they departed.

Once they were gone from the driveway, Abbie peered at her husband. 'Do you really have to go back to the hospital?'

'Yes.' He moved to grab his briefcase. 'I wouldn't have said it if it wasn't true.'

'Right, yes, of course.' Abbie tried to smile at him but felt it wilting upon her face.

'I'll be back as soon as I can.' He left a dry kiss on her cheek and then left.

Abbie withdrew back into the house, joining Pippa in the kitchen. 'I've told them everything,' her daughter sniffed, pulling on the sleeves of her hooded jumper.

'I know, sweetheart, I know. They're just doing due diligence, that's all.'

'Why would they ask about Michelle?'

Abbie pouted, one hand on her hip, the links of her broken necklace digging into her palm. 'Clearly, they think she's involved somehow. Which wouldn't surprise me one bit.'

'You've never liked her, have you?'

'No,' Abbie admitted, stony-faced, 'I haven't.'

'Why?'

She shrugged lightly. 'In my experience, people who seem too good to be true, they are never what they seem.'

Abbie felt Pippa's gaze on her. 'It is because she's so pretty?'

Shoulders set, Abbie couldn't, wouldn't slump at this. 'There's more to life than being pretty,' she reminded her daughter.

'I know.' Pippa was looking into the distance, attention drifting away. 'But it really helps.'

12

Sunday arrived, the closing act of a stressful weekend. Abbie was in the living room, fabric swatches in hand. Needing something, anything, to distract herself. In turn she held them against the sofa, trying to imagine the little patch of soft plaid wider. Larger. Inhabiting most of the room. She switched them out, changed the angle of her grip. She felt she was growing closer to a shortlist when the music playing in the kitchen hooked her attention. She'd left the radio playing to itself while a lamb shank cooked in the oven. Abbie liked having the radio on, the music a pleasant murmur when she was alone in the house. But *this* song, she didn't like.

Quickly she stormed back to the kitchen, dropping the collection of swatches. Swiftly she clicked off the radio, plunging herself into a jarring silence, disturbed only by the soft hum of the cooker. Abbie frowned at the dormant radio, hating how her heart now raced.

The song, an upbeat pop number from the late nineties by some band who had an eye blind. It used to be played on the radio *all the time*. And it was playing the day she walked away from Sunnycroft Care Home for the last time and slammed her car door shut.

'Will we see you next week?' a short nurse with rosy cheeks and frizzy blonde curls had asked as Abbie strutted towards the exit.

Abbie had thrown her reply over her shoulder: 'No'. She wouldn't be returning. She'd continue to sign the cheques, but that was it. Once inside her car she realised she was shaking. Turning on the engine, the song erupted around her and she wept as it played.

For so long Abbie had done her duty, had been a good daughter. As soon as her mother became too enfeebled to look after herself at home, Abbie found the best care home she could within a twenty-minute drive and sent her there. She returned her mother's house over to the council, hoping that the memories new tenants made there would be happier than her own. And she footed the bill for her mother's care, or at least, John did. But marriage was about equal assets, right? What's mine is yours? John had been more than kind.

'Get your mother whatever she needs,' he'd said. But he never offered to visit. And Abbie didn't blame him. Her mother had never liked him, had never even bothered to hide her disdain. It was the reason Abbie and John married abroad on a beach in Mexico. She'd told people it was so it could be an intimate affair but really it was so she didn't have the suffer the humiliation of her mother drunkenly telling everyone she didn't approve of the union.

After all their long years of marriage, still her mother belittled him. Moaned about him. And on her final visit to Sunnycroft, Abbie had had enough. She was in her mother's room, far too hot in her cashmere jumper thanks to the radiator that blared beneath the window. Her mother was in a stiff-backed armchair, facing the lawn outside, grass still dappled with dew.

'How are you feeling today, Mother?' Abbie had asked as she tucked in a blanket across the old woman's knees and studied the room for signs that anything was amiss. But all was in its place, including the framed picture of Pippa on the bedside table. Abbie frowned at it, feeling that it really needed updating. In it Pippa was gap-toothed and peppered with freckles. 'Are you doing OK?' She raised her voice so the old crone could hear and reminded herself how selfless she was to keep up her visits.

'I want to go home,' the old woman muttered angrily.

'You know you can't do that,' Abbie sweetly informed her, as she did at every visit. 'Someone else lives in your old house now.'

'It's *my* house.' She shook with brittle fury as she spoke, spittle flying from her mouth.

'Not anymore,' Abbie smiled at her.

'Tell him to let me live with you then. Just don't leave me here, alone.'

'Mum, you know I can't do that.' Abbie placed an empty cup of tea upon a tray for the nurses to come and tidy away, frowning at their tardiness over such tasks. 'We simply don't have the room.'

'Your house is huge.'

'Not really.'

'He doesn't want me there, does he?'

Abbie sighed and looked beyond her mother, to the window and the sea of green grass. She doubted John would even notice if she moved her mother in, the amount of time he was home lately. But she wasn't about to reveal that.

'Grown tired of you, has he?'

Abbie snapped her attention towards the old woman who was eyeing her shrewdly, wrinkled face turned up, eyes narrowed. Where once Abbie's mother had been large – tall and broad, with a plump face and brown curls – she was now withered, like a grape dying on a vine. Gone was her vibrancy, the power her arms could muster when

79

delivering a slap. Her skin was grey, hair thin and sparse so that Abbie could see the mottled design of moles upon her scalp. Inhaling sharply, Abbie met her mother's stare. When she was sober she'd been astute, sharp of mind. But most days had begun with a shot of cheap whiskey, at least when she was in her old council house.

'Sorry?' Abbie enquired sweetly, refusing to let her mother know that the question had rattled her.

'You have the look of a woman who is worried about her husband.' The old woman continued to stare up at her. 'I should know. It's a face I wore enough times.'

'How dare you even insinuate such a thing,' Abbie said quietly, breathing hard through her nose. 'John is an exemplary husband. You owe him everything.' She gestured around the room, at the brown carpet and matching curtains.

'I always said he'd tire of you,' her mother scowled. 'A man like that . . . he wanted you to be a *role,* Abigail. Wife, then mother. He never wanted *you.*'

'Please,' Abbie heard the shrillness of her awkward laugh, 'what do you know about marriage, Mum? Dad left you and never once looked back.'

'You used to have fire,' the old woman continued. 'You were so like him. But now you're just . . . a puppet.'

'It's called growing up.'

'Working late, is he?' Her mother raised an ashen eyebrow, bony fingers tightly clasping the edge of the blanket Abbie had placed so neatly against her. 'That's what he tells you?'

'He's a prominent surgeon at—'

'Each time you walk in here I see a ghost,' her mother snapped. 'You treat that man like the sun but now he's warming someone else and you're dying in the darkness.'

A hand pressed to Abbie's chest. 'I will not listen to such—'

'The old Abigail, the daughter I fought with, the daughter I loved in spite of everything she did, she wouldn't have been any man's doormat.'

'I am no one's *doormat*.'

'The day he put a ring on your finger, it was a noose about your neck.' Her mother's lips puckered with displeasure at the memory of it all. 'You were wild, like your father, and you let him break you down. Tame you.'

'And where did Dad's wildness get him?' Abbie asked, voice high, cheeks flushed. 'He wasn't a responsible father, a good husband!'

'True,' the old woman nodded, looking down at her lap and the plaid pattern spread across it. Then she peered at her daughter, face crumpling with sadness. 'But he was happy.'

'I'm done with this discussion.' Abbie reached for her coat which was hanging on the back of the closed door and began pulling it on.

'I'll bet she's pretty,' her mother continued, 'whoever he's spending his nights with.'

'He's *working*,' Abbie snapped, almost hysterical. Panting, she leaned against the door, remembering herself. What if someone had heard? What if someone burst in to ask if everything was all right? What would she say? How would it look?

'You don't really believe that, do you?' the old woman asked with disdain. 'I didn't raise a fool, Abigail.'

Abbie had heard enough. 'Goodbye, Mother.' And it was. Her marriage was fine. Just fine. She left the care home, powered over to her car, arms swishing at her sides, fell into the driver's seat and turned on the engine. On came the song. So mockingly merry in tone. But as Abbie listened to the lyrics she felt there was more there. That it wasn't describing something happy at all. It just sounded like it was. And that made her feel so much worse.

Standing in the kitchen, Abbie absorbed the quiet, focused only on the hum of the oven. How long had it been since she'd had to send a cheque over to Sunnycroft to cover her mother's care? Twelve months? It had to be. Exhaling a trembling breath, she stretched out a hand and turned on the radio. A new song was playing. Abbie returned to the living room, scooped up her abandoned swatches and carried on testing them against her sofa.

13

The weekend was nearly over. And Heather Oxon was still missing. In her bedroom, facing her small TV, a cushion pressed against her stomach, Pippa curled on her side and tried to lose herself in a succession of American dramas.

Smallville . . .

The OC . . .

Dawson's Creek . . .

She watched box set after box set, episodes and seasons blurring together. When night came, her DVD player continued to whir. Beyond her bedroom door she heard her parents as they separately crept up to bed. Heard their steps again come the morning. Two whole days drifted by in a strange blur. Her mum brought her meals to her, a quiet understanding shared between them that Pippa needed to be alone.

During a break from her solitude to go to the toilet, Pippa heard her parents' voices drifting up the stairs from the kitchen just below. Creeping close to the spindles of the banister, Pippa knelt beside them, wrapping cold hands around the varnished wood and peering down into the darkness of the hallway, just as she had done when she small, desperate to catch snippets of the exciting adult world that existed after she'd been dismissed to bed.

'You shouldn't just let her stay in her room.' Her father's voice, stern with judgement.

'She needs space.'

'She's been holed up in there all weekend.'

'John, she's processing things. Her best friend is missing. We have no idea what she must be going through. Right now we need to be supportive.' There was a steeliness to her mum's voice which warmed the pit of Pippa's stomach. A soldier downstairs fighting her battles, defending her. It felt good to be so protected.

'Abigail, it isn't healthy to just hide away.'

'Don't start throwing your opinion around when you haven't even bothered to be here all weekend.'

Pippa began to withdraw from the staircase, not liking where the conversation was going. It was a twisted path she'd followed her parents down too many times.

'I'm needed at the hospital.' Her father spoke with a lofty anger.

'You're *needed* here.'

Pippa had heard enough. She darted back to her bedroom, her duvet, her DVDs. As the next episode loaded she did her best to escape, but could still hear the murmur of an argument carrying through the floorboards. Closing her eyes and pressing her face into her pillow, she permitted herself to cry.

Monday arrived too quickly. The limbo of the weekend immediately banished to memory as a knocking tapped against her bedroom door. The sound pulled Pippa out of her dream. Skin clammy, she wiped at her eyes, did her best to shield them as the door cracked ajar and the light from the landing singed against her tired gaze.

'Morning, sweetheart.' Her mum came in, already fully dressed in white jeans and an emerald turtleneck jumper, dark hair pulled back in a low ponytail. She looked both elegant and effortless, both things which Pippa would never pull off. Groaning, she rolled onto her side.

'Come on,' her mum said, peeling back the edge of the duvet, 'time to get showered and ready for school.' Pippa stretched out a hand and snatched back the fabric, returning it to fully cover her.

'I don't feel well,' she mumbled into her pillow. It was true. She felt tired and empty, as though over the weekend someone had turned her upside down and tipped out all of her essence, her mirth. And now she was just hollow. And so desperately tired. She longed to roll over and slip off the cliff of consciousness into a deep, dreamless sleep.

'What's wrong?' A cold hand was instantly pressed against her forehead. Her mum's hand smelt of Body Shop dewberry lotion.

'I'm just . . .' Pippa sniffed, wondering how to explain it. She continued to rub at her eyes, at the damp tendrils of hair that had fallen into them as she slept. 'I'm not feeling well.'

'Are you sick? Feverish?' More touching of her forehead. Then the cold hand pressed against her upper back. 'You don't feel hot.'

'Mum . . .' She peered out from her duvet shroud, voice raw.

'They're going to find Heather.' Her mum was using the soothing sing-song voice she adopted whenever Pippa was ill or afraid. 'Today will be the day, just you wait and see.' She stroked Pippa's forehead, then cupped her cheek.

'I'm just so tired.'

'I bet.' Her mum wore her own exhaustion in the dark circles beneath her eyes but she concealed them well with

85

foundation and mascara. Pulling her ruby lips into a smile, she gazed down at her daughter from where she neatly perched on the edge of the bed. 'I know you haven't slept this weekend.'

'You do?'

'I'm your mum,' she said, her smile widening. 'I know everything.'

Pippa sank heavily against her pillow, limbs feeling as though the marrow in her bones had been replaced with dense iron. She longed to just lie there, to slowly sink into the soft surface of her mattress.

'Why don't you take today, spend it in bed, catch up on some sleep?'

Pippa nodded at the suggestion with as much enthusiasm as her fatigued body could muster.

'I'll phone the school and say you're unwell.' Her mum planted a soft kiss on her forehead. 'It will be OK, sweetheart. Try not to worry too much. The police are doing all they can to find Heather.'

'And what if they don't find her? Will they just stop looking?' Pippa wondered anxiously.

'No.' A crease appeared between her mum's neat eyebrows as she answered. 'They'll just . . . cast a wider net.'

'And if they still can't find her?'

'Stop. Worrying.' Another kiss on her temple. 'Go back to sleep, shout me when you wake up again and I'll fix you some breakfast, OK?'

'OK.'

The bedroom door closed and the darkness returned but Pippa did not succumb to sleep. She peered into the dense shadows, wide awake.

*

'What do you mean, not going in?'

Barely ten minutes had passed since her mum had left the room. Pippa crept to her door and crouched beside it, listening to the argument flare several feet below in the hallway. She imagined her father in his suit, briefcase in hand, about to step outside into the lingering night, dawn still an hour away.

'She feels unwell.' Her mum's voice was measured, calm.

'This is ridiculous,' her father lamented. 'She needs to get outside, to be with her friends.'

'She *needs* to rest.'

'Honestly, Abigail, I truly can't talk to you sometimes.' The front door opened with a flourish. 'You give in to her too much. You always have.'

'What time will you be home?'

'Late.' His voice was growing more distant; Pippa wondered if he was now on the driveway, close to his car. 'I'm on call.'

'Again?'

Her father's response didn't reach her. Pippa scurried back to her bed, pausing to turn on her television as she passed it by and grab the large remote control. She knew her father was a gifted surgeon, he told her often enough, but she wished, just sometimes, he'd focus on fixing things closer to home instead of devoting all his time to strangers. But then . . . tucking herself up in bed she pressed a button and the DVD player whirred back into life. It was better this way. Being her and her mum. They were a team. They understood one another.

The sound of the front door slamming closed echoed through the house, telling Pippa that her parents had not parted on good terms.

14

They had a cleaner who came every Tuesday and
Thursday. She hoovered, polished, scrubbed the bathrooms, emptied the bins. But it still wasn't enough for
Abbie. As she moved from the hallway to the kitchen
she saw specks of dusk on window sills, marks on the
carpet, stains on tiles. Which is why by 10 a.m. that
Monday morning she was sweeping her Dyson around
the lower floor of the house. First the kitchen, then the
dining room, switching attachments. Finally she was in
the living room, the hoover droning in her grip as she
pushed it back and forth. Back and forth. She matched
her breathing to the rhythm. Felt some of her internal
tension begin to ease.

A girl is missing.

She made her strokes across the floor more aggressive.
Bringing up carpet fibres along with dust.

A girl is missing.

She could feel sweat pooling beneath her armpits and
still she pressed on.

Back and forth.

Back.

And.

Forth.

Panting, she reached the edge of the room and the
double glass doors which opened onto the large garden.

The grass was wilted with dew. If the mornings dropped a few degrees lower, Waterbridge would have its first frost of the season. Abbie liked frost-laced mornings. They were crisp. Clean.

Clicking off the Dyson, the silence that piled in around her was suffocating, like suddenly entering a sandstorm, the air too thick. Abbie looked at her reflection in the doors. Hoovering in couture. What would Carol say? Would she laugh? And John . . .

Abbie's chin touched her chest and the softness of her green sweater.

'You can take the girl out of Dunsten but you can't take Dunsten out of the girl.' It was one of his favourite sayings. And he said it with a fondness which almost made it sound endearing. He'd make the remark when Abbie complained about hiring a cleaner, insisting she should do it. And when she insisted on mending well-worn pairs of Levi's jeans with holes in the knees, instead of just replacing them. Abbie blinked at the woman in the doorway. She looked so proper. Wedding band sparkling even in the dim November morning light.

A creak overhead. Abbie's hand dashed to her throat, pulse instantly racing. She didn't dare move as she strained to listen, trying to chart her daughter's movements by sound alone. Another creak from a floorboard, this one more distant. Pippa was going to the bathroom. Abbie stalked to the centre of the living room and suddenly froze, unsure what was required of her, what to do next.

Should she go upstairs to check on her? Or was that being too pushy? Would she be guilty of doing the interfering John was always accusing her of?

Mothering a teenager was a tricky path to tread. Every misstep risked placing her on a landmine.

'I'll wait,' Abbie decided quietly. Pippa knew where she was, that she only had to shout if she needed her mother.

But the waiting was excruciating. By eleven Abbie was perched on a stool at the kitchen island, hating that it was still too early to go upstairs and make enquiries about lunch. Mobile phone in hand she tapped out a message to John.

> I'm worried about Pippa. She's going through so much right now I think we need to show a more unified front of support. Could you get home early tonight? I think a family dinner would be a good idea. I'm making chicken in red wine sauce with dauphinoise potatoes. Love A xxx

It was John's favourite meal, though Abbie neither expected him to reply or to be home before seven. Mondays were notoriously busy days in theatre. And she knew from glancing in his Filofax that he had a complete large bowel resection at nine. On a fifteen-year-old. When she saw the scrawled note she felt her own insides clench. She thought of the girl's mother, of the day she would now be having waiting for her daughter to wake up, how her daughter would be forever altered by what happened in theatre.

Thinking of mothers in despair drew Abbie's thoughts to dwell on Michelle Oxon. She was the kind of natural beauty who always drew appreciative glares but when she deemed to dress up, wear make-up and thick lashes like the other mothers did on a daily basis, she elevated herself to Hollywood levels of beauty. Diminishing everyone else around her without even trying.

Abbie spun her phone on the sleek surface of the island. It was never good to think about Michelle Oxon. Even though her thoughts were now pitying ones.

I'm glad I'm not her.

She must be terrified.

But she was still at work. Ashley had said so.

Abbie had told John the previous night as they were sitting side by side, propped against their pillows, respective books open in their laps. 'She's still going in, you know.'

'Mmm?' He was reading some Russian oligarch's biography.

'Michelle Oxon,' she'd continued, her own book failing to hold her interest. There was something about reading about murder when a girl they knew was missing which just felt distasteful. Abbie hoped that the next choice for their book club might be something a bit more genteel, more akin to their usual pace of Austen over Bronte. 'She's still turning up at work, even with Heather missing, can you believe it?'

'I imagine,' John replied, aggressively turning the page in his hardback, 'that being home alone in that big house is simply unbearable. And she has people who rely on her, patients who need her.'

'I know but if it were Pippa and—'

'You should be *applauding* her,' John thundered, glaring at his wife. 'That's the problem with you women, always so quick to tear one another down when you're jealous.'

'Jealous?' The word lodged in her throat like a barbed seed trying to choke her. 'J-jealous? John, are you serious?'

'She's a beautiful, accomplished woman. I'd be surprised if you weren't jealous of her.'

Abbie wasn't sure which stung more. That her husband found Michelle beautiful or that he thought her accomplished. She felt her chin tremble, the familiar rush of heat to her cheeks which meant that she needed to cry. But she wasn't about to reward his remark with her tears. Climbing out of bed she made for the bathroom.

'Oh, Abigail, don't now sulk,' he wearily called after her. 'It'd be nice if for once we could have a serious conversation without you getting so emotional.'

At the kitchen island Abbie alternated between watching her phone and watching the clock. There was beauty in her dark eyes and high cheekbones. John had once told her as much. And she was *accomplished*. She'd raised their daughter and before that . . . Eyes shuddering closed, she permitted old memories to surface. Hedonistic days at university, her hung over to hell as she stood over a mannequin trying to remember how to give someone CPR while the other student nurses giggled around her. Weekends spent studying textbooks thick enough to prop a door open. And all the while, as she attended lectures, went to class and workshop after workshop, Abbie worked at the market stall in Dunsten selling flowers. Funding her own future.

Even once she was qualified and working shifts at the hospital, she still had to keep up her weekend shifts on the stall, needing the extra money to help cover rent.

When John had found her there one Saturday, he bought every rose they had and once they were bunched up he handed them over to Abbie. 'When you're my wife,' he told her lavishly, 'you'll never have to work again. I'll take care of you, always.' Exhausted by the constant grind of it all, Abbie swooned at his words. John with his fancy education, expensive upbringing. He was a doorway into a

92

whole other world. One where her hands wouldn't always smell of bleach, where she wouldn't spend the last days of the month in darkness because there were no pound coins left to slot into the electricity meter.

'Be careful,' her late mother had warned her, 'don't just fall for the money.'

How easily Abbie had scoffed, had dismissed her mother's comment as jealousy from the old woman perched at the kitchen table in her small council house. For Abbie it had always been about escape. Escape from the life she didn't want to lead. First college, then university, she was always climbing, always trying to elevate herself away from her roots. And then she met John. And accepting his hand in marriage was like stepping into a lift and immediately ascending to the penthouse.

Atop the island her phone whirred, vibrating erratically away from her. Abbie grabbed it, the screen blinking with the new message icon. Pressing it she saw Carol's name and hated that her stomach dipped; that even now, two decades into her marriage, she could still be so needy with John, so desperate, yearning for every message to be from him. But what she read filled her with a new fire. Shoulders tensing, she looked to the ceiling, listening for any fresh signs of movement.

15

French. That's what Pippa was currently missing. She'd normally sit beside Hannah as Mrs Willoughy waxed lyrical to them about the difference between *vous* and *tu* while the musky of her heavy Dior perfume fused with the musty dustiness of the room. Wedged at the back of the school like an afterthought, the language rooms never felt the glow of direct sunlight. There was a dampness that lingered among the desks and textbooks that even the peak of summer couldn't pierce.

Twisting beneath her covers, Pippa was glad to be home, in her sanctuary, instead of a stuffy old classroom. There'd be work she'd have to catch up on later, she knew that. But it was an acceptable price to pay for her absence. Staring dully at her television, she watched one episode roll into another as a beautiful brunette told a tall blonde how she'd fallen for his best friend. Pippa normally lived for this level of drama. She'd watch and wonder if one day she'd get to live out a moment like this – get to feel the fragility of a boy's heart in her hand, delicate like glass, liable to shatter. Heather had wielded this kind of power with frightening regularity.

Moving herself so that she was no longer lying down but sitting up, back pressed against her headboard and slumped pillows, Pippa dragged her hands through her hair, tried to clear her thoughts.

Out of the corner of her eye she saw the pictures tacked to the noticeboard above her desk, just by her window. Pippa on a beach. Pippa holding their deceased dog, Milo, when he was a puppy. Pippa and Hannah smiling broadly at the camera, cheeks smeared with birthday cake. And in the top right, Pippa and Heather, arms wrapped around each other's shoulders. Heather had one hand on her hip which she jutted out, lips slick with gloss and drawn into a pout, blonde hair ironed poker-straight. She'd been thirteen there and more woman than girl. Beside her Pippa was an ironing board: straight up and down. Her eyebrows seemed bushy, untamed, and her cheeks were peppered with freckles given to her by the sun. While there were notable differences between them, both girls wore identical smiles – wide and bright, cheeks pushed to bursting point. Pippa remembered her mum taking the picture in their garden after she and Heather had returned from the fair that had shown up in the local park. Lifting her Kodak camera, her mum had asked them to smile and it had been so easy. Pippa was high on sugar from candy floss and the giddy excitement of walking around on Heather's arm, attracting glances and waves from boys, sour looks from girls. It had been so intoxicating.

Climbing out of bed, Pippa powered over to her desk, stretched up and snatched the picture from the noticeboard. It was so flimsy in her hand, so thin. She looked down at the smiling pair of girls, let them almost disappear as tears gathered in her eyes, blurring her vision.

Something juddered.

Her phone. Pippa recognised the sound. Dropping the picture onto the neat, organised surface of her desk, she withdrew back to her bed, pulling the duvet almost completely off to reveal her mobile resting in the centre of the mattress, vibrating gently against the sheets. Dragging the back of her hand across her eyes, she inhaled shakily, took a second to compose herself. Then the phone was in her possession, screen aglow with a new message. Frowning Pippa opened it, seeing Hannah's name.

> So apparently you're off sick today. Lame. Now I have to suffer through French alone x

The message had been sent an hour ago and had previously gone unnoticed by Pippa. Her phone had been buzzing away to itself to update her about the newest message, again from Hannah, sent less than a minute ago.

> *OK so something is definitely going down at school. Suddenly A LOT more police here. And Mrs W just got called out of the room. Think they've found H? x*

Staring at the phone, the message, Pippa lowered herself against her bed. Had Heather been found? Just thinking about her made her fingers work from memory to open her contacts list, press down until Heather's name was highlighted and then she was calling her. There were no long, drawn-out rings. It went straight to voicemail. Heather's voice was suddenly in her ear, bright and viscous.

'Bitch, I can't answer the phone right now because I'm busy having *a life*. Text or call me back and *maybe* I'll get back to you.' Her personal answerphone ended abruptly on her shrill giggle. Pippa withdrew her mobile from her ear and threw it back against the bed, feeling betrayed by it. Where even was Heather's phone? Turned off and useless, lying somewhere like a lifeless brick. Would the police be tracing it, like Pippa had heard them do in the Huntley case that was all over the television? And if they found the phone, would they find Heather . . .?

16

Abbie was hoovering, certain the cleaner had done a sub-standard job, when she saw something out of the corner of her eye. A flash of fur. White and bronze. Clamping a hand to her chest she breathed heavily, retraced her steps to switch off the vacuum with the tip of her toe. The room fell into an eerie silence. Dropping the extendable hose she edged forward to the corner the creature would have bolted to, peering around the back of John's favoured armchair. There was nothing behind it. Only the crease of the skirting board and a couple of dust motes.

'Damn.' Abbie pressed a hand to her forehead. She was tired, that's all. Seeing things. But the memory had stirred now, risen to the forefront of her thoughts like curdled milk, leaving a sour taste in her mouth.

Mr Nibbles.

That flash of fur, that scurry of paws. It used to haunt most corners of their home. Mr Nibbles had been Pippa's eighth birthday present. How delighted she had been when she came down that bright morning to discover a cage on the kitchen island and beside it a little box dotted with holes. The small hamster earned his name. He nipped anyone who came near him, drawing juicy red droplets of blood from well-meaning fingertips.

'It's a good lesson for her.' John had been keen on the gift. 'It'll teach her about responsibility.'

And every Saturday morning he and Pippa would clean the cage together, filling it with fresh sawdust and soft, new bedding. Bedding which Mr Nibbles would always resentfully pull out of his little plastic home every Saturday evening. Abbie almost envied the ritual of it all; her only part in it was to buy all the things the hamster needed. To surreptitiously fill up the water bottle when Pippa forgot.

He'd been in their home almost six months when Abbie found Pippa weeping in her bedroom one weekend.

She'd rushed to her daughter's side, knelt beside her, the fibres of the carpet digging into her bare knees. A sticky summer meant that Abbie had been almost solely in tea and tennis dresses the last few weeks. 'Sweetheart, what's wrong?'

Pippa was shaking, her little body unsteady even crouched upon the floor. Slowly she raised her head, revealing hands cupped within her lap.

'Oh no.' Abbie stroked Pippa's crown in understanding. 'Don't worry, sweetheart, these things happen. Pets don't live forever.' In her mind she pragmatically began a list of what would need to be done that morning. A burial first. In a Tupperware box, in case next door's cat tried to get at the corpse. Then she'd need— But as Pippa's hands unfurled she saw there was something off about the bundle of fur her daughter was clasping. 'I didn't mean to,' Pippa blurted, voice wobbling. 'I held him too tight and he . . . he . . .'

'Don't worry.' Abbie adopted her most genial voice, relieving the little girl of the deceased rodent and clasping him within her own hands. 'We'll give Mr Nibbles a nice burial.'

'I just wanted him to know how much I love him.' Pippa looked up at her mother with water-clogged eyes. 'I just wanted to show him.'

'I know.' Abbie smiled sadly, closing her hands over the hamster. 'But sometimes we can hurt those we love, without meaning to, by holding on too tight.'

'Don't tell Daddy,' Pippa requested in a whimper, 'we're meant to clean him out when we gets home and—'

'It will be our little secret,' Abbie replied.

And it was. Abbie told John that the hamster had escaped his cage. John spent weeks setting humane traps about the house, calling out for the little ball of fur. And sometimes Abbie swore she almost saw Mr Nibbles scurrying across the floor, as if her lies had somehow become truth.

She clicked on the vacuum cleaner, filling the living with its droning sound, and resumed hoovering. She didn't have time to worry about old ghosts. Not when there was a house to be cleaned, dinner to be made.

Abbie stirred the baked beans in the saucepan as they simmered, still dwelling on the text message she'd received from Carol over an hour ago:

Hannah says increased police presence at school. Wonder if there's been an update on Heather? X

As the days dragged on, the people of Waterbridge had grown more desperate. Heather's face was now plastered on almost every lamp post in town.

Have you seen this girl?

Had someone come forward? Had someone seen something?

Abbie stirred more furiously as behind her the toaster popped. It was just past midday and lunch was almost ready. Working methodically, Abbie buttered the toast, placed it on the two white porcelain plates trimmed with pale blue which she'd laid on the kitchen island. She cut Pippa's toast into small triangles but left her own whole. She was about to reach for the pan when the landline attached to the nearby wall began to ring, shrill and insistent. Abandoning the half-prepared lunch, Abbie smoothed her hands from the front of her jeans and grabbed the handset from the wall, letting its curled cable gather at her feet.

'Good morning, Parks residence, Abigail speaking.'

Shit. She winced at her error, realising that it was now the afternoon. Not that the caller cared about her faux pas.

'Abbie.' Ashley sounded breathless.

'Ashley?' Abbie protectively placed both hands around the phone which was against her ear, leaning into it. 'Are you all right?'

'Oh, Abbie.'

There was an uneasiness to her friend's voice which made Abbie's spine straighten and shiver. 'Ashley, what's wrong?'

'They've found her.' The words were delivered in a desperate whisper. 'They've found Heather.'

Abbie exhaled with a shudder. 'Right . . . well, that's wonderful! Where was she? Is she OK?'

She imagined the jubilation coursing through the police force which would soon bleed into the community. Tomorrow the headlines would declare: *Local Girl Found.* All would once again be right with the world.

'They found her just outside of Clapton,' Ashley explained, voice quiet.

'Clapton?' Abbie frowned. It was the next town over to Waterbridge but smaller, with houses adorned with thatched roofs and wattle-and-daub walls. It attracted a lot of tourists who found the whole set up 'quaint'. But

Clapton lacked the sleekness of its neighbour, the modern town centre filled with high street stores, the large library and enviable school system. 'What was she doing over in Clapton?' People went there to walk the aged cobbled streets, enjoy afternoon tea in tiny cafes and stroll through the dusty corridors of antique stores. There was little there for a sixteen-year-old. Waterbridge had the cinema. The bowling alley. The ice rink.

'They . . .' Ashley took a long pause and Abbie heard ice knock against glass. Was her friend day drinking? The thought felt absurd but it flashed hot and challenging in Abbie's mind. She knew ice in whiskey when she heard it, had to listen to the gentle clink on the evenings when John was home, as he carried his nightcap up to bed and then sipped from it between turning the pages of his book. 'They found her on the side of the river.'

'On the side of it? Doing what?' Abbie released a hand from the phone to massage her temple. Perhaps Ashley really was drunk. It would explain why she was making so little sense.

'Abbie . . .' Ashley sighed out her name, then there was the unmistakeable sound of her sipping a drink, and her delivery hardened: 'They found her on the side of the river.'

'I . . .don't . . .' But Abbie did. She just didn't want to let it in, let it sour the pristine interior of her kitchen, her home, her life. She couldn't steal away to the liquor cabinet with Pippa upstairs, couldn't dull the pain which now pulsed through her.

'They say it looks like she drowned,' Ashley confirmed.

'Christ.' Abbie leaned her forehead against the wall, tried to hide against it. 'That's . . .' She *knew* Heather. Had given her lifts home, had her over for play dates. She thought of her bloated on the riverbank, barely recognisable, and whimpered. How easily that could have been her daughter. Her child. The thought left her breathless.

'They've informed her family, the police are letting the girls at school know today.' Ashley began to sound distant, her tone mechanical.

Abbie's gaze instantly lifted to the ceiling. Pippa. 'I'll. . .' She closed her eyes, enjoying the brief moment spent in darkness. 'I'll let Pip know.'

'They say she must have had a seizure or bumped her head. They won't know for sure until they conduct the post-mortem.'

'Christ,' Abbie repeated, not knowing what else to say.

'I really thought they'd find her alive,' Ashley said, pausing to drink some more. 'But Geoff called to confirm it all earlier and well, with Pippa being so close to her, I thought you should know.'

'Yes . . . yes, thank you. I'll talk to her now.'

'Sixteen,' Ashley sighed. 'Fucking sixteen.'

It was the first time Abbie had heard the 'f' word come out of her friend's mouth. 'It's a tragedy,' she agreed.

'I keep thinking about her poor mother.'

'Mmm.' But Abbie didn't want to think about Michelle Oxon, not even now. The air in the kitchen began to sour. The baked beans on the stove were burning.

As Abbie climbed the staircase, she wished she'd had the foresight to seize her daughter's phone that morning, to cut off her line of communication with the outside world. What if she already knew? What if she'd had to read the awful news over a text message? It wasn't right. None of it was.

Abbie's progress was slow, her steps sluggish. In the kitchen she'd opened the windows wide to air the room, binned the charred remains of the beans and now carried a plate bearing only cold buttered toast. It was a meagre offering but she knew Pippa wouldn't be able to eat. Abbie was almost at the long landing where oak doors peeled away to bedrooms and the main bathroom. She wondered how long it would until any of them could eat normally again. Until the shock wore off.

With a shake of her shoulders, Abbie forced herself to ascend the final step and approach Pippa's bedroom door. Stickers of ponies and unicorns traced the moulding of the wood, attached half a decade ago and still sparkling. Making a fist, Abbie rapped against the door. As she returned her hand to her side she realised she'd never done that before. She always just walked straight in.

'Shit,' she uttered through clenched teeth, pushing on the handle and letting herself in, hating that she'd already revealed that something was wrong. The room was dark, the air thick.

'Pip?' she called to the mound beneath the duvet. 'Pip, sweetheart.'

Slowly the covers were pulled down to reveal the flushed cheeks of her daughter, dark hair bunched messily at the back of her head.

'Hey, how are you feeling?' Abbie placed the plate of toast on the dresser closest to her, beside framed pictures of Milo and a collection of Cherished Teddies ornaments. 'You doing OK?'

Pippa nodded sleepily and Abbie came to sit beside her on the bed, pulling her daughter into a tight embrace and breathing her in. The sweetness of her Herbal Essences shampoo lingered in her messy hair, as did the medicinal scent of the Clearasil she bathed her face in each morning. 'Oh, Pip,' Abbie mumbled, not wanting to let go, to break the moment, to shatter what remained of her daughter's childhood and innocence with this awful truth. Entangled together, they lingered on the precipice of change.

'Mum, you're hurting me,' Pippa eventually complained, breaking free of the embrace.

'Sorry.' Abbie bowed her head, mildly wounded. She'd endure slingshots and arrows if it meant she could hold onto her baby girl for even a second longer.

'Is that lunch?' Pippa glanced behind her mum, at the plate of toast.

'Yes.' Abbie touched her daughter's cheek, so warm to the touch, and felt tears swell in her eyes as she considered how Heather's cheeks must now feel. They'd be cold. Waxy. 'Pippa.' She summoned up the courage she needed and looked her daughter square in the eye. It was always a strange magic, seeing that same depth of brown that she'd stared into for a lifetime whenever she looked in the mirror. 'Sweetheart, I need to tell you something.'

Pippa Longstocking,

I am so OVER Hannah. Where does she get off telling me to shut up in front of everyone? Just because after PE I happened to mention that her pants had blood on. Why the hell isn't she using tampons like a normal person? Who uses period PADS? They're for like, OAPs. Dumb bitch. Then she went and told Miss Rogers I was picking on her and I got a warning. Whatever. She needs to stop being so sensitive. I hate her. Don't you? She thinks she's so smart.

It wasn't all bad though. After History, Mr Hall asked me to hang back. Remember – you left with the others and I stayed behind? He said I looked upset and asked what was wrong. Like, he actually cares about me. Notices when I'm upset. Tristan hasn't even texted me back for a whole week. Prick. Mr Hall wouldn't do that to someone. He's a gentleman. I bet he's the kind of guy who buys his girlfriend roses and opens the car door for her. I like how he's wearing his hair lately, don't you? And that short beard he's got going on, it's hot. I told him I was fine as I'm NOT Hannah and I'm not about to start bitching to teachers. Although it is different with Mr Hall. Talking to him doesn't feel like talking to a teacher. It feels more . . . intimate. Not that you'd understand. Boys, or men, don't notice you. WEAR

THE BRA.
   And start sneaking some make-up on in the mornings.
You need it.
   Love you,
   H
   xoxo

17

Pippa recognised the slant of her mum's shoulders, the way she held her mouth in a hard line. It was like looking to the horizon and seeing grey clouds in the distance. She knew bad news was coming.

'I've just been on the phone with Ashley.' Her mum rested a warm hand on Pippa's shoulder.

'It's about Heather, isn't it?' she said, her stomach beginning to curdle with understanding.

'It is. Yes.'

'Have they –' Pippa swallowed, her voice beginning to fail '– found her?'

A nod from her mum. Expression grim. 'They have sweetheart, yes.' Suddenly Pippa was swept into a strong embrace, held tight and close as her mum whispered: 'She was in the river.'

'So . . . she'd . . .' Pippa pulled back from her mum, blinking furiously as her temple began to pound.

'They think she drowned.'

'They *think*?' Pippa demanded, suddenly indignant. 'Don't they *know*?'

'Well, yes,' her mum floundered as she tried to back-pedal, eyes searching the distant corners of the room as though she might find the answers she sought in their depths. 'They know she drowned. They just don't know why.'

108

The pounding in Pippa's head switched up from loud to offensive. She closed her eyes and pressed the heels of her hands against them.

'It's OK.' Her mum pulled her close again, began to rub a hand up and down her back, rocking her slightly. 'I know this is all so much, and so terrible.'

'She drowned.' Pippa shook her head, hands still against her eyes. 'She drowned, she drowned.' She kept repeating the final verdict on Heather's life. *She drowned*. She thought of water filling lungs, final desperate breaths. Sliding beneath the murky surface of the river. What was the last thing Heather saw before her lights completely went out? Was it the slate sky above or the muddy surface of the river below?

'The police think she either had a seizure on the river bank, fell in and then failed to swim, or suffered a concussion when falling in. Either way, it is a truly, truly awful accident.'

'An accident,' Pippa echoed with a loud sniff. But accidents were things like tripping over a raised curb, falling off your bike. Not sliding down into a river and never getting back up.

'All the girls at school are being told today,' her mum continued, voice gentle with reverence, as though they were seated in a church, not on a Groovy Chick duvet. 'I know this is such an awful shock for you, Pip. Please know that I'm here for you.'

'So they think she just . . . fell into the river?' Pippa lowered her trembling hands, trying to recall her last moments with Heather. The mud had been slick on the riverbank. And the rain had been falling hard and fast.

'That's what they think, yes,' her mum replied, one hand still charting circles against her daughter's back. 'It's why you must always be so very careful by the river. The Severn is deeper than it looks, with fast-moving, hidden currents.'

Pippa already knew this. A boy whose cousin had gone to primary school had suffered an epileptic fit whilst fishing on the banks of the river. He'd fallen in, rod and all, and by the time he was lucid again the current had him, was hungrily carrying him away to his doom. There had been assemblies on it. On the importance of keeping away from the river. Never jumping into it. Never swimming in it. It was dangerous and to be avoided. As her mum had said, the currents in it ran strong especially when rainy weather made the river burst its banks and run high. Like it did every November and February.

'Are you all right?' Her mum leaned close to kiss her forehead. 'Stupid question.' She eased away, pressing her free hand to her temple. 'I know you're not all right, sweetheart. And I don't know how to make you feel all right. This . . . this is going to hurt. And for some time. I wish I could take that away for you.'

'Heather deserves me to hurt.' Pippa shuffled across the bed, forging her own slice of space where she lay down, turned away from her mum, towards the television.

'Look, I know things seem strange and awful right now but—'

'I'd like to be alone.'

She heard the breath that her mum drew in, couldn't bear to roll over and see the shock which was surely etched across that pretty face. Out of any other teenager's mouth the remark would make sense. But not Pippa. She never asked for her mum to leave, for there to be a divide between them. They weathered all their storms together, as an impenetrable unit. Drawing her duvet up to her chin, Pippa could smell the Persil from when it had been washed over the weekend. She waited for her mum to fight her, to insist that she shouldn't be alone. But instead the weight on the mattress shifted as her mum stood up.

'I'll be downstairs if you need me,' she said quietly. Her footsteps whispered across the carpet, pausing briefly to glance back once she reached the door. 'I'll come back in a bit to check on you, OK?'

'OK, yeah.' Pippa fumbled under the duvet for the discarded television remote and wondered where her mobile phone was. She imagined it'd soon be crammed full of messages as news about Heather spread through the school. And it'd move quick – like a virus entering a nervous system.

'I love you, Pip.'

This made her cease searching. Pippa folded back the bedspread to look across the room at where her mum lingered in the doorway. 'Love you too, Mum.'

The pounding in her head only worsened. Grief, it seemed, was like a sledgehammer, keen to crack through her skull. Pippa took some ibuprofen she found in the bathroom cabinet and then returned to her bed, her duvet. When sleep took her, it felt like drowning – all-consuming and sudden. One moment she was staring with unseeing eyes at her television, the next there was only darkness.

When she awoke the darkness extended beyond her bed and covered her entire room. Rubbing her eyes, Pippa wondered how long she'd been asleep. The low growl in her stomach told her it had been quite some time. Drawn downstairs by hunger she headed to the kitchen, flicking lights on throughout the house as she moved. Every room was swathed in shadow and the house was surprisingly silent.

No distant murmur of a TV or pipes banging in the walls as someone ran a bath. There was nothing.

Flicking on the kitchen light, Pippa gave a shriek of surprise. Her mum was sitting on a stool at the island, slim body concealed by her silk dressing gown which reached down to the tiled floor. Before her stood an empty wine glass and bottle. Her long fingers kept spinning her mobile phone against the sleek surface of the island. Round and round it went.

'Mum!' Pippa exclaimed from where she stood barefoot at the threshold to the room.

'Pip!' Her mum lifted her head to smile at her, lips stained red with Merlot. 'You feeling better? I came to check on you earlier and you were fast asleep.'

'What time is it?' Pippa padded over to the island, struggling to understand why her mum was drinking alone in the dark. It took a second for her brain to catch up and release her thoughts from the foggy prison of sleep.

Heather.

Her mum had also known her. Seen her grow up. She'd be mourning too, wouldn't she? Just because her mum hadn't particularly liked Heather didn't mean she wouldn't feel pain over her death. Pippa felt embarrassed at her lack of consideration.

'Sorry.' She groggily rubbed at her eyes. 'You OK, Mum?'

'I'm . . .' Another twist of the phone. It spun so effortlessly, so easily. 'I'm fine.'

'OK . . .' Pippa moved past her, towards the double-door fridge. She opened it and peered inside, looking at containers of olives and numerous cheeses, the remains of a roast chicken tucked beneath tin foil, bottles of milk, containers of juice, grapes, a punnet of strawberries. Pippa grabbed a particularly ripe one and shoved it into her mouth. Still chewing, she glanced back at her mum. 'Have I missed dinner?' Then she glanced at the clock. One in the morning.

Shit. She had slept for a long time.

'I made bolognese,' her mum said, and swept her long fingers in the direction of the microwave. 'Want me to heat yours up for you?'

'Please.' Pippa was starving. Which given the circumstances felt strange, like her body was betraying her. She should have no appetite, just be crying until her whole body felt raw, right? Because that was how people grieved. That was the right way to do it.

'I'll sort that for you now, sweetheart.' The silk of her mum's dressing gown rustled quietly as she moved.

'Thanks.' Pippa stole her position at the island, glancing enviably at the empty bottle of wine. Then again she tipped her head up to the clock, the time marked in bold roman numerals around the edge of its face. 'Mum?'

The pinged notes of the microwave being set were followed by the whir of it working. 'Hmm?' Her mum moved and spoke as though she were in a dream, which Pippa supposed was the result of the wine.

'Mum, is Dad home yet?'

'Not yet, no.'

'OK,' Pippa nodded but kept looking at the clock, and the positions of the big and small hands. It was really late. And her dad had been gone since half-seven that morning. He was no longer a young man; these kinds of long days surely had to be taking a toll on him. 'I guess he's working over, again.'

'Uh-huh,' her mum nodded, watching the plate of spaghetti spin behind the glass, getting hotter and hotter.

'Do you think he'll be home soon?' Pippa wondered. She was expecting the usual comforting platitudes.

Of course.

Any minute now.

Don't worry, he'll be back in the next hour.

Instead her mum shrugged in a nonchalant manner and said, in a deadpan voice, 'I have no idea.'

18

3 a.m. The spaghetti Abbie had shared with her daughter a few hours earlier felt like lead in the pit of her stomach – heavy and hard. The wine she washed it down with had left her in the awkward limbo between sleep and restlessness. She longed to close her eyes and disappear into darkness but her mind refused to settle. She felt like she was pacing the room, even though she was curled on the armchair beside the fireplace in the front room, an empty glass in her hands.

3 a.m. Upstairs, her daughter was sleeping. Abbie waited at her bedside until Pippa's eyelids drooped low, until her breathing slowed. There, next to her in the darkness, it was so easy to pretend Pippa was still young enough to need her, to always want her there. Some mothers despaired at the newborn and toddler stages, at the sheer physical exhaustion they brought, along with the various other trials. But Abbie had been almost infuriatingly upbeat. She enjoyed the night feeds, savoured the chance to comfort her daughter. And whilst her body did ache, and she had yearned for a moment's respite, one look at Pippa's cherubic face had always made any negative thoughts melt away.

3 a.m. and her daughter was safe. She was tucked up beneath her duvet, right where Abbie had put her. Behind a closed door, within a locked house, behind a high gate

and brick-wall-lined gardens. Abbie looked down at her empty glass and wondered what Michelle Oxon was doing. How her 3 a.m. looked. Was she sleeping? Comatose from the draining shock of losing her daughter? Or was she sitting red-eyed beside her own grand fireplace just a few streets over?

A girl is missing.

But it wasn't Pippa. Pippa was home. Pippa was alive. It was Heather who was gone, who was taken away by the river.

'Like an act of God,' had been Carol's words when she called earlier that evening, her usual clipped voice softened by the vodka she'd no doubt been drinking. 'You can't . . . can't predict something like that. Seizure. Bump on the head. Freak accident. Horrific, truly.'

'Truly,' Abbie had mumbled into her phone she held to her ear, glancing between the ceiling and the door which led to the hallway, wondering which would omit a creak first. John was already late home. She hated him working late at the best of times but now she needed him, needed to breathe him in, be held in his arms. Grief and shock were not things Abbie wanted to treat alone.

'I remember that boy with the epilepsy in the Severn.'

'Yes, same.'

'Strong, strong currents.'

'Indeed.'

'And remember Hazel Davies when we were young?' Carol continued, music playing gently in the background. Abbie tried to listen in, to catch on what her friend was doing to distract herself from this latest tragedy.

'I remember.'

'Tripped over that rock on Emral Street, fell from standing height, clean broke her neck and died on the spot.'

Abbie remembered Hazel, with her gap teeth, wide forehead and eyes such a pale blue they almost seemed translucent. Hazel who would be forever fourteen. Hazel, who became a cautionary tale for why you should always look where you're going.

'Just another act of God,' Carol continued to lament, her words drifting soft and then louder as though she were rocking on a boat. Abbie tried to focus on the chords behind the voice, coming from the CD player she knew her friend kept in her kitchen. In the past they'd play Abba and Rod Stewart on it while drinking champagne and pretending they were young and carefree once again. Even though they were girls no longer. They were women. Wives. Mothers.

'The Corrs,' Abbie blurted.

'Sorry?'

'Oh.' Embarrassed, Abbie touched her temple, shaking her head. 'The music you're listening to, I was trying to figure it out.'

'Oh, the Corrs. Yes. Not sure if this is mine or Hannah's CD.'

Abbie's gaze again tipped the ceiling, a smile of under-standing pulling on her lips. Pippa liked her modern music, sure, but she shared some tastes with her mother. Together they'd listen to Dolly Parton and Kirsty MacColl. Together they'd sing along so loudly their throats hurt.

'Imagine if it'd been one of our girls.' Carol's voice was suddenly a whisper, delivered sharply into the phone so that her words reached Abbie like a hiss.

'No,' Abbie instantly replied, raising a hand to massage the back of her neck, the diamonds of her eternity band scratching against her skin. 'I can't imagine. Because that would just destroy me. Utterly destroy me.'

'Same, same.'

For a moment the old friends were silent, as the Corrs launched into their rendition of Fleetwood Mac's 'Dreams'. It was an upbeat interpretation full of hearty strings. But Abbie had never heard the song that way – to her it was always sad. About a man yearning for escape, for freedom, not realising what he has, not understanding the hole which would open up within him if he were to act on his whims.

'You know Michelle will be just fine.' A steely edge crept into Carol's voice as she spoke and Abbie felt it transfer along the phone line and stiffen her own spine.

'Absolutely,' she agreed.

'I bet she'll be back at work before the month is out.'

'Because she's so *needed*.' Abbie felt her skin crawl as John's previous remarks came from her own mouth. 'So *important* to this community.'

'If I'd lost Hannah I wouldn't be able to get out of bed let alone leave the house,' Carol grunted as she unscrewed a bottle cap and then Abbie heard the gentle tinkle of liquid landing on ice within a glass. Leaded, of course.

'One hundred per cent,' Abbie agreed, nodding. But moving her head that way made it throb, made the wine she'd already drunk begin to pound against her skull. She knew the only remedy was another glass.

3 a.m. and the front door had yet to creak open. Tyres had yet to crunch against the driveway, headlights had not cast their beams through the living room's bay window. Abbie shifted her gaze to peer at the gas flames dancing behind glass a few feet away. How they twisted and moved with a restrained regularity. Fire wanted to break free, to run

wild, to burn. But behind the glass, amidst the faux piece of coal, it was contained and pretty. Something to look at, to admire. Its sole purpose to warm the house.

Abbie kept staring until the orange of the flames blurred in her vision and her eyes began to ache.

3 a.m. and John was not yet home. She could text but what would be the point? She'd already sent him over a dozen messages, all asking a variation of the same question:

When will you be home?

There must have been an emergency surgery. A life hanging on the line. Someone John had to save. John with his skilled hands and years of expertise. She used to watch him from the front lines with such admiration. How a ruptured artery wouldn't derail him, not even for a second. Keeping calm, delivering his orders clearly, he'd clamp the offending vein and then swiftly suture the wound. He was quick. He was diligent. And within the hospital he was a god.

Abbie felt herself drifting off to sleep, her limbs becoming heavy yet slack as she sunk into the armchair, the warmth of the fire curling around her like a welcome embrace.

A missing girl.

An act of God.

An absent husband.

She tried and failed to the cling to the questions which were struggling to form in her mind, the wine and the heat making every thought too dense with fog. Her drop into sleep was sudden. One moment there was fire. The next only darkness.

19

The news of Heather's death hit the school like a freight train, powering through and obliterating every other slip of conversation and dragging every student and faculty member along for the ride. As soon as Pippa passed through the gates on Tuesday morning, shivering in her oversized silver parka, the momentum of it grabbed her, pulled her along. First it was Hannah at her side, clasping her elbow.

'You've heard,' she said, drawing in close, leaving barely an inch between them. 'Of course you've heard.'

Pippa nodded grimly. Around them all the other girls marched slowly towards the front stone steps in the same tight clusters, holding onto their friends as though they were all that was stopping them sinking just like Heather had.

'Drowned.' Hannah stopped moving as she said the word, forcing Pippa to mirror her standstill. 'Like maybe a seizure or something.' She looked directly into Pippa's face. Without her usual coating of beige foundation, Hannah's skin was heavily cratered and blotchy, blonde hair blowing into her eyes which she didn't bother to bat away. 'It just doesn't make sense.' She stared at her friend, let other students drift past them as they remained linked at the arm. 'Does it?'

Before Pippa could attempt to answer, the peal of the bell rang out, shrill and indifferent to the recent tragedy, calling them all inside like cattle to the feed. But that was where the usual daily routine ended.

On normal days the girls assembled in their form classrooms and confirmed that they were present before waiting on another bell and dispersing around the school for their first lesson of the day. Everything was timetabled, even lunch and study breaks. But this day was different.

'You'll go straight to the main hall,' Pippa's form tutor, Miss Rogers, informed their class, her pale lips drooping with sadness, eyes wide and distressed, all of her usual energy completely drained out of her. Pippa furtively looked at her classmates, a dozen heads either bowed or craned towards their neighbour's seat, bent low in a conspiratorial whisper.

The whispers were like rats, speeding down every corridor, gathering in every corner. Pippa heard them as she moved to her form room and then to the main hall, keeping in step with the other girls, keeping her head low.

'No way she drowned.'

'Like a seizure.'

'Did she have epilepsy?'

'I bet she jumped in.'

'She was pushed.'

'I heard she was swimming and got her foot trapped under a rock.'

'I heard that history teacher did it.'

Whole school assemblies meant that every girl from every year gathered beneath a high vaulted ceiling, perched on cheap plastic chairs and listened to the headmistress speak from a wooden podium on which the school's emblem had been seared like a brand. Normally they'd all pull their voices together to sing the school's song and chant in Latin the words beneath the emblem.

Scientia vero.

In truth there is knowledge.

Pippa scratched at her arms, the fibres of her blazer feeling too coarse against her skin. Knees tightly locked together, she focused on the back of the chair in front of her, at the knobbly row of nails forced into plastic at the seams. She felt woefully tired. Her entire body yearned for rest, for darkness, even though she'd slept away most of the previous day.

'Move,' came a hissed instruction to her left. The chair beside her squeaked as the girl sitting on it got up and allowed Hannah to take her place. Pippa glanced up, surprised. Normally such behaviour would be heavily repri-manded. The girls had to be in their assigned chairs, in their assigned order. But raising her gaze even higher, over all the heads gathered around her, Pippa saw that none of the teachers were watching the students. They were whispering among themselves, shooting glances to the rear of the hall where four uniformed police officers were gathered, their neon bright against the walnut walls adorned with trophies and banners from past school victories.

'Hey,' Hannah whispered in a brief greeting. 'How you holding up?'

Pippa managed to raise her shoulders a few centimetres then promptly let them fall.

'You look like shit,' Hannah remarked with brutal honestly. 'But then I guess we all do.'

It was true. Usually the sea of girls shimmered. Despite all the rules and regulations, they each broke them in their own subtle way – a slick of mascara here, a sheen of lip gloss there. But now, hair that was usually clamped between a pair of straighteners for half an hour was kinked. Acne was left on display. No one had primped or preened that morning. Grief had left them all in their rawest forms.

'I just keep thinking she can't really be gone,' Hannah continued, 'like this is all just some sick joke.'

'Yeah,' Pippa agreed, her throat aching as she spoke. She wanted that more than anything, for none of this to be true.

The assembly lasted for an arduous hour. Pippa zoned in and out, catching snippets of what was being discussed. She already knew the headlines, she couldn't stomach reading the entire article.

'We are all deeply saddened by the loss of one of our own, one of our brightest, Heather Oxon.'

Some girls began to cry. Their sniffles and whimpers carried through the crowd like a current, pulling in others.

'She'd love this, you know,' Hannah whispered, using her fingertips to smart away her own shed tears. 'Everyone here talking about her, an assembly in her honour.'

'Yeah.' It was all Pippa seemed able to say. Over and over.

Yeah.

Yeah.

Yeah.

Like she'd lost her ability to engage in any kind of meaningful conversation.

The headmistress talked of Heather's achievements (over-embellishing them to a great extent) and then went on to describe how she was beloved by all around her. Finally the discussion turned to how to deal with grief.

'If any of you want to talk, my office is always open.'

Pippa imagined it, walking along the corridor where the grave faces of previous headmistresses peered down haughtily from photographed portraits. Then at the end a door which she'd never seen open, not even ajar. She'd knock, wait for a curt 'come in' and then enter the office with its maroon drapes and back wall covered in bookshelves whose purpose seemed only to be to gather dust since no student had access to them. From behind her grand desk the headmistress would rise up, just slightly, to nod in greeting and then settle again in her leather chair, legs crossed neatly at the ankles (never at the knees). Pippa pictured herself across from her own, opening her mouth, breathing in the aroma of old books and furniture polish mixed with ink. What would she even say?

'And the police are here with additional questions.'

She snapped back into the moment and blinked, feeling hot and dizzy. 'Questions?' She glanced to her side, to Hannah who'd tugged her sleeve over her wrist to mop up the last of her tears.

'Oh, yeah.' Hannah cleared her throat, composing herself, before throwing a not very subtle look over her shoulder, at the gathered officers who stood two feet apart from one another, stern and silent, like chess pieces waiting to make their move. 'They're back in today.'

'What questions?' Pippa pressed. 'If Heather . . . you know . . .' She didn't want to say it – the word felt ugly and awkward on her tongue. 'Drowned,' she finally managed, her own distaste twisted her features, making her eyes glisten with the tears she'd failed to shed during the assembly. 'If that's true, what questions could they have?'

Hannah gave a quick shrug and sighed. 'I guess . . . why? I mean, if she didn't fall in. If it was like a deliberate thing.'

'You think she killed herself?'

Around them girls were beginning to be dismissed row by row. When their turn came they stood up, pressing close together so they could whisper as they moved towards the long corridor beyond.

'Absolutely not,' Hannah replied, with so much heat Pippa felt it burn against her uniform. 'This is Heather we're talking about. She'd hurt someone else, sure. But not herself. *Never* herself.'

'Hmm.'

'But the police don't know that.' They were at the door to Pippa's form room, due to part ways, but Hannah slipped inside. It was surreal. Like the rules no longer applied. A move which Heather would have pulled off without thinking twice. 'They're looking for reasons she'd have done this to herself. Why else would they be here?'

'I . . .' Pippa cautiously eyed her form mates returning to their chairs, too preoccupied with their own conversations to even notice Hannah. 'I guess you're right.'

'I think all fingers point to Mr Hall.'

'Mr Hall?'

Pippa liked her history teacher. He was kind. Funny. Passionate about the subject, which made the time spent in his classroom pass more easily.

'He was always eyeing Heather up.'

Pippa frowned. Was he? The other way around, sure. Heather was drawn to a handsome face like a magpie was drawn to anything that glittered. But had that attention ever been returned?

'All right now girls.' Miss Rogers entered, raising her voice but lacking the stern edge of her colleagues.

'I'm telling you –' Hannah poked Pippa's arm, emphasising her theory '– that's why the police are here. That's what they'll be asking questions about.'

'Hannah Edwards, run along to your own form please,' Miss Rogers sighed her command.

'All right, Miss.' Hannah rolled her eyes and then darted back into the corridor.

'How are you?' Miss Rogers asked, her eyes full of concern. Pippa remained by the door, close to her form tutor, pinned like a fish on a hook. Opening her mouth, she tried to draw in breath, wishing she hadn't lingered in the doorway, was already back in the safety of her seat, far away from Miss Rogers and her kindness.

'I'm . . .'

A mess.

Broken.

Falling apart.

She was all those things and more.

'It must be so very hard for you.' Miss Rogers gave a sympathetic tilt of the head as she continued to study Pippa.

'Because we were best friends,' Pippa nodded, feeling her face growing hot. Everything in the past tense now.

Were best friends. Nothing current. Nothing present. Heather was gone.

'Yes,' Miss Rogers nodded, but her expression remained strained with interest, eyes never leaving Pippa's face. 'And because, well –' she stepped a little closer and lowered her voice '– you were the last person to see her alive.'

Pippa's chest clenched so tight she feared she might stop breathing and just fall to the hard wood floor.

'You're doing so well,' she offered with a sad smile, 'you're being so strong. Heather would be proud.'

Pippa pushed past her as she sprinted for the corridor and beyond it the girl's bathrooms. Once she was locked behind a stall door she doubled forwards, knees pressed against the cold tiled floor, clutched the porcelain of the toilet and vomited up the spaghetti she'd eaten the night before.

20

Abbie never liked seeing Michelle Oxon. She was thankful that Michelle's long hours at the local practice meant she rarely lingered at the gates during the school run. But on the occasions she was there, Abbie would sense her before she saw her. Like the electrical feeling you get in the air before a storm.

Michelle Oxon was like the sun. Golden. Warm. People just gravitated to her. She'd throw them a soft, easy smile, raise a hand as a procession of sleek, silver bangles slid down her arm. She was the human equivalent of a Labrador. Everyone loved her.

Everyone except Abbie. She wasn't entirely sure when the seed of her resentment had been planted but she suspected John had been involved, had made some passing comment back when Pippa was toddler and Abbie was exhausted and run ragged from chasing her around all day, saying how impressed he was that Michelle had chosen to go back to work. Those feelings of admiration would be mentioned every few years, like an eclipse, plunging Abbie into darkness.

'*Michelle balances work and motherhood so well.*'

'*Michelle gives so much to her community.*'

'*Michelle is an exceptional doctor, Waterbridge is lucky to have her.*'

He'd throw these comments across the dinner table Abbie had carefully laid out, using the silver she'd furiously polished, swallowing down the roast turkey she'd spent the better part of three hours basting.

Fucking Michelle Oxon and her halo.

When her husband Maxwell finally had the good sense to leave her, Abbie had glowed with that terrible feeling of delighting in someone's downfall. She liked to imagine Michelle weeping, begging for him to stay, pretty face blotched and swollen. She had thought it would bring John to his senses, make him realise that in being a good doctor, Michelle had failed to be a good wife. Women could not have it all. Instead, she was a victim in his eyes. And to Abbie's despair, in everyone else's.

'Clearly, he didn't support her decision to work,' John had lamented as he chewed on shepherd's pie. 'Such a backwards view.'

Abbie had nearly choked on her own dinner but said nothing. Because she *was* a good wife. She kept a beautiful home, had raised a bright, determined daughter. She was doing everything *right*.

'She should have focused on her home life more,' Abbie told him coldly. 'Perhaps then Heather wouldn't be so wayward.'

'Some children just have a rebellious nature.'

When it came to Michelle Oxon, John always had a retort, a positive spin. Each time he defended her, complimented her, the beast of Abbie's loathing grew larger, fiercer, angrier.

Abbie felt like a wash cloth that had been used one too many times. Her skin was too coarse, her muscles too wrung out. Wilted within the armchair beside the fire, she stroked a finger around the lip of her now empty wine glass.

Tuesday was about to become Wednesday, the clock on the mantelpiece poised to strike midnight. On a regular Tuesday evening Abbie would cook the fresh pasta she'd spent the afternoon making. Often ravioli stuffed with crab. But her stomach was now bloated with pizza which she'd ordered as a takeaway as this was no regular Tuesday. Pippa had looked so broken as she approached her mum's car after school that day. So utterly exhausted.

'Pizza,' Abbie had announced before she'd even eased away from the curb.

'But it's Tuesday.'

'Doesn't matter. I think you deserve a pick-me-up. So we'll do pizza and ice cream. Deal?'

'Deal.'

Pippa hadn't brightened on the car journey home but at least her shade of grey hadn't deepened. Abbie had decided to take that as a win.

And so rather than sit at the dining room table, they ate their pizza straight out of the takeaway box in front of the plasma TV watching several episodes of *Friends*. Pippa even cracked a smile when the group were using an elaborate poking stick to check on a neighbour. But her mirth didn't last long.

'Will Dad be back late again?'

Abbie struggled to swallow down the bite of pizza she'd been chewing. 'Um . . .' She coughed, hand clamped to her mouth. Did her daughter even know he'd yet to return home since the previous morning? The hospital had become a Tardis into which her husband stepped into but rarely came out of. A quick glance at the clock told Abbie it was already half-past seven. 'Yes,' she replied with complete confidence, 'he'll be back late again.'

★

She hadn't wagered just how late that would be. And now, as midnight slipped by, Abbie wondered if perhaps she'd again be sleeping alone in their queen-sized bed. The fire that had previously danced over the faux coals in the hearth was now out and the living room was growing ever colder. Abbie shuddered, wondering if she should wrap a blanket over her knees or just abandon her vigil and go up to bed.

A car in the driveway.

The sound was unmistakable. Like a dog, Abbie was attuned to it.

A key in the latch.

These were the sounds she raced against. Raced to smooth down her clothes, straighten her hair, reapply lipstick if she had a few seconds to spare and spritz some perfume across her body, against her inner wrists.

The front door opening. A briefcase being placed on the floor. Footsteps.

Abbie rose up to meet him, her body moving on memory and instinct.

'John?' When she reached the hallway she found him halfway up the stairs, body hunched and creeping like a teenager who was returning home far too late. With the glow of the kitchen lights behind her, she peered up at her husband, her brows furrowed in confusion. This was not the routine. Normally he would find her in the kitchen where he'd place a kiss on her forehead and ask about her day, enquire about dinner. It was all very civil yet comfortable. Had he forgotten the steps to their marital dance?

'Abs.' Her name escaped from his lips sounding like a weary sigh. He doubled back down the stairs. 'Sorry, I thought you'd already be in bed.'

Abbie put on her most welcoming smile. 'I was waiting up for you.' She took in her husband. His shirt was crisp, tie smooth against it. He must have sent his clothes out to be dry-cleaned whilst he spent a day in scrubs.

A day and a night, Abbie reminded herself. But in John's face there were considerable creases. Deep lines were etched against the corners of his mouth and eyes. And his bright, usually overtly alert eyes seemed dull and bloodshot.

'You should have told me you'd be back so late,' she told him, struggling to keep her voice even.

'I'm . . . I'm sorry.' He raised his left hand to rake it through his curls. 'It's just been one emergency after another so I grabbed a few hours in the On Call room as it didn't make sense to come home.'

'Ten minutes.'

'What?' He shook his head at her, one hand still ruffling his hair.

'It takes ten minutes to drive home.'

'Oh, Abs, come on.' He turned his back on her and continued his ascent up the stairs.

'It was why we moved here, to this house, remember?' Abbie followed after him, angrily snapping at him like a neglected Jack Russell. 'It's close to the hospital, close to the grammar schools. You said it was perfect because you hate sleeping in the On Call room.'

'Abigail.' Now they were standing in their bedroom as he hurled her name at her like it was a weighted brick. 'I'm not doing this now. I'm knackered. I've had a day, OK?'

'A day?' Abbie clasped a hand to her chest. Behind them their bed was neatly made, Egyptian cotton sheets beneath a smooth silk duvet and woollen comforter, all in a soft shade of grey. The large headboard rose halfway up the wall, upholstered in silver velvet. 'John, I've had *a day.* Mainly because I was up all last night waiting on you to come home!'

'I was needed at the hospital.' He was loosening his tie, angrily yanking it free from his neck.

'John, you were needed here. Pippa is in pain.'

Tie removed and thrust to the floor, he perched on the edge of the bed and began fighting with the buttons of his shirt.

'John, her best friend is dead. Heather Oxon is dead. You must have heard.'

'I heard.' His focus was on his buttons and the crisp pale blue cotton they were attached to. 'The whole of Waterbridge heard.'

'And you didn't think to come home to comfort your daughter?'

With a loud grunt of exasperation, John abandoned his half-undone shirt and twisted to stare up at his wife who loomed large on the far side of the room, hands placed on her hips.

'You've been drinking,' he scolded, staring at her for a long beat and then returning his attention to getting undressed.

'That's not the—'

'Your lips are bloody stained red with it. How many times, Abigail – try and limit the weeknight drinking.'

'Heather Oxon is dead.' Abbie released the statement in a strained whisper. 'I mourn her. Your daughter mourns her.'

'And what about Heather's mother?' John raged angrily, cheeks turning pink. 'Do you think she is in mourning? Do you think she is drinking herself into a stupor?'

'I don't care what—'

'There's no talking to you when you're drunk.' Finally free of his shirt, clad in just a white vest, John stalked over to the bathroom.

'I'm not drunk!'

The bathroom door slammed shut in response. Abbie slowly approached the bed and sank onto it, legs beginning to shake. She wasn't drunk, far from it. But she knew there was no arguing with her husband, not when his mood was so sour. Spreading her hands against the wool comforter beneath her, Abbie reminded herself of the hardships found within the walls of the hospital. Of the burdens she used to have to manage when she worked there. Heather was dead. Yes. But given John's distemper, Abbie was sure he'd had someone die on his table, perhaps that very day. And he was a good surgeon, he cared. He had a notebook in the top drawer of his desk, a small navy Moleskin one in which were names and dates. Every time he lost someone in surgery he wrote down their name.

'So I never forget,' he had explained to Abbie when she found the notebook, when they first lived together. 'I take the names home with me, write them down, so that I'll always remember the stakes involved. Every time I go into theatre, it is life and death. I can't ever let that get away from me.'

Abbie looked forlornly at the closed bathroom door, hearing the drone of the electric toothbrush beyond it. She sensed how much her husband needed her. So she got up, pulled back the duvet and cast off her own clothes and pulled on her pyjamas. She switched off the main light and turned on the two bedside lamps.

After ten long minutes John emerged from the bathroom in his olive green pyjamas.

'I'm sorry you've had a hard day,' Abbie told him earnestly as he climbed into his side of the bed.

He moved to switch off his lamp and then paused. 'Pippa is lucky to have you.' He studied her in the gentle light.

Abbie smiled softly at him.

'She'll be OK,' he continued. 'She'll get over losing Heather, because she has you.' He leant across the vast space of their bed and planted a kiss upon Abbie's cheek. And then he turned to switch off his lamp, casting his side into darkness as he slid down beneath the covers, planted his head upon the pillow and turned away from her.

Abbie's fingers lifted to touch her cheek, skin still damp from his kiss. That night she was smiling as she fell asleep.

21

The night had barely tipped into day. Pippa was in the kitchen, swathed in her dressing gown, bare feet cold against the tiles. It was dark outside, the house was quiet. In the glow of hob light she paced around the island, a glass of water chilling her palms.

Her body sagged with the need to sleep, to rest, but her mind forbade it. She felt like a faulty appliance, one that would usually just get tossed out. Pippa needed to sleep, to keep herself sharp. The next day she needed to study. And if the police came around again with more of their questions, she'd need answers. They'd wouldn't want her sallow-faced and unresponsive.

Creaking. Overhead. Pippa sipped on her water, pushing down the sigh that almost escaped from her.

'Pip?' Her mum was sweeping into the kitchen, silk dressing gown whispering with each step. 'Sweetheart, are you all right?'

'I'm fine,' Pippa mumbled her stock response. To the teachers. The other girls at school. She was *fine*.

Heather was gone and she was *fucking fine*. OK?

'I thought I heard someone pottering around down here.'

'God, Mum, you've got the hearing of a bat.' Pippa rolled her eyes, but then noticed how her mum's briefly crinkled in sadness. Her guilt sucker-punched her in the gut and Pippa wished she could take back the comment. She knew why her mum was up, was attuned to the nocturnal sounds of the house. Clearly, her dad was not yet home. Some emergency at the hospital, she assumed. Again.

'When it comes to you it is purely instinct.' Her mum came over and rubbed Pippa's upper arms. 'When you're not happy, I'm not happy.'

'Who says I'm not happy?' Pippa cast her eyes down in embarrassment. It was a stupid thing to say. Of course she wasn't happy. How could she be?

'Want to talk about it?' Her mum released her and settled onto a nearby stool, hands neatly clasped atop the island. Pippa envied her mum's easy grace. Her own body always felt too long, too awkward. No matter how many times her mum reassured her that things would get better, that one day she'd feel at home in her skin, she feared it'd never happen. That she'd always be clumsy. Feel poorly put together.

Not like Heather.

Pippa winced at the thought of her. Heather, who seemed to have been spun from gold and sunlight. Just the right curves, lips just plump enough. She moved like she was underwater – gliding, weightless.

Not anymore.

Pippa wondered what state Heather's dewy skin had been in when they pulled her from the river. Was she already covered in grave wax? Pippa had read about that in a book in the school library. When a body was submerged for a long time, such as a corpse found at sea, it started to get covered in a grey, waxy substance. It was hard to imagine Heather that way, dull and devoid of her usual lustre.

'I'm finding it hard to sleep,' Pippa admitted, claiming the stool beside her mother.

'Oh, honey.' Her mum's long fingers swept her cheek, pushing back a lock of her unruly hair. 'I can only imagine what is going through your mind right now. But if you need to talk, I'm here.'

'I keep thinking.' Pippa studied her hands in the dim light, the length of her fingers, the bare nails and messy cuticles, the callus on her right index finger caused by how she held her pen. So many imperfections in such a small space. 'Can you love and hate something equally?' she asked as she closed her hand into a fist.

'I mean, I suppose so, yes,' her mum replied, nodding thoughtfully. 'Love and hate run pretty close together as emotions. One can often lead to the other.'

'But at the same time?' Pippa demanded.

'I. . .' Her mum began to twirl her wedding band, the gold dulled by years of wear. 'I guess you can, yes.'

'Can you control that?'

'I—'

'Because I want to take control of things.' Pippa shoved her hands into the soft pockets of her dressing gown, unable to stand the sight of them any longer.

'Well, be careful,' her mother warned smoothly. 'Sometimes in trying to *take* control, you can lose it. Love, hate, they can so often be at war with one another. It's about balance.'

A distant grumble from beyond them. Pippa's dad was home. When she'd left her bedroom to creep downstairs, the digital clock on her bedside table had read just past midnight.

'Some days there is hate, some days there is love.' Her mum's hand was now rubbing her back. Pippa smiled up at her, eyelids beginning to grow heavy.

'What if there is more hate than love?'

Her mum paused, her mouth dipping at the corners. 'Then your feelings are no longer equal. No longer in balance.'

'So what should—'

'Oh, hey.' Her dad walked in, the crisp night air tight on his heels. She shivered even within her dressing gown as he placed down his briefcase, locked the front door and strode through the hallway towards the kitchen and the glow of the hob light. 'What are you two doing up so late?'

'Girl talk,' her mum explained, hand still pressed to her daughter's back.

'Well, I'm exhausted –' his mouth gaped open with a yawn '– so I'm heading straight up to bed.'

'Busy one at the hospital, Dad?' Pippa called after him.

'Yes, terrible,' he replied as he began ascending the stairs. 'Night.'

Pippa peered at her mum, waiting for the tell-tale creaks overhead. 'Mum,' she said, keeping her voice low. 'Are you in balance?'

Her mum nodded, pulled her lips into a tight line. 'Yes, I am.' She left her stool and kissed the crown of Pippa's head. 'At least for now.'

Sleep was clawing at Pippa. Unable to fight it any longer, she followed her mum back upstairs, keen to drop onto her bed and fall into the vast darkness of a dreamless sleep.

22

That week rumours swirled through the school like a maelstrom and by Friday Pippa felt as though she might drown in them. Everyone had a theory. A conspiracy. The chatter of it all silenced the school's plans for a memorial. Students weren't talking of how they missed Heather, of the gap she'd left behind in their lives. They talked only of her drowning. Of the strangeness of it all. The mystery.

'I mean,' said Hannah, plucking a chip laden with salt and vinegar from her plate and snapping it between her teeth before continuing, 'none of it makes sense. None of it. Heather had never had a seizure before. Ever. She was the picture of health,' she swallowed down another chip, 'save for her nut allergy.'

Pippa gazed down at her own plate loaded with starchy carbs. Usually she looked forward to Friday lunchtime and the junk food on offer as a treat. She'd opt for chips along with her friends and together they'd plunge them into small pools of ketchup as they gathered around a table dissecting the previous week. It was only Heather who would abstain from them.

'Moment on the lips, forever on the hips,' she'd declare with a lift of her perfect eyebrows.

At lunch she ate what she always had — salad. There were variations on it: sometimes a tuna salad, sometimes a Caesar. Freshly prepared by her mother every morning. 'Because, you know, I can't risk contamination for the school food,' she'd acknowledge with a brief shrug. Not that there were ever any nuts in sight within the canteen. And it was a fair-weather policy that Heather adopted as and when it suited her. Pippa recalled the times at the cinema her friend would happily add fudge to her pick-and-mix bag even though the label on the little glass container told nut allergy sufferers to steer clear. 'My allergy isn't even that bad,' was Heather's excuse.

'I think,' Hannah leaned in close, her breath smelling like a day at the seaside, 'Mr Hall knows something. I mean, he's been off all week.'

'With his IBS,' Olivia offered from further down the table.

'As if,' Hannah scoffed. 'He's hiding away, can't face being here, can't face his own guilt.'

'That's what my mum says anyway,' Olivia declared defensively.

'Is your mum suddenly a doctor?' Hannah asked as a smug smile pulled on her lips. In the chair beside her, Pippa shrunk, felt her shoulders press down against her. Once again, she was at the queen bee's side. How quickly and effortlessly Hannah had stepped into the role. It chilled her. But no one else seemed to care, too happy to have someone to guide their captain-less ship.

'I'm just saying—'

'Absence is guilt,' Hannah savagely cut Olivia off by raising her voice, gaze darting about the rest of her gathered audience. 'If he was innocent, he'd be here. Right?'

Nods of agreement rippled through the girls.

'What do you even think he's guilty of?' Pippa asked, peering up with hooded eyes. With each passing day it became harder and harder to sleep. At night in the darkness she'd swear she could hear Heather's gulping last breaths, like water stuck in a plug. 'The police said it was an accident. Nothing more.'

'Someone like Heather Oxon doesn't just have an *accident*.' Hannah turned to face her, expression stony and serious. 'Do you really think she just *fell* into the river? You don't reckon she was pushed?'

'I . . .' Pippa looked at her mountain of chips, at the pool of ketchup beside them smeared like a bloodstain.

'You were there,' Olivia chimed in, eyes wide with the animalistic urge to tear apart a peer. 'Did you see anyone? You must have seen something!'

'Yeah.' Another voice, just as direct, as challenging. 'You were the last person to see her alive.'

Pippa hung her head. It had been like this since Heather disappeared, ramping up once it had been discovered that she'd died. It was as though the space Heather used to inhabit – that cruel area where spite was the steel rod which kept the rest of the girls in line, gave the school a backbone – was suddenly a vacuum which just had to be filled. Everyone was meaner, angrier. Pippa wondered if it was grief or something else at work. Like wild dogs, were they now sparring for the chance to be leader of the pack?

'I told you guys what I told the police,' she muttered quietly, lacking the energy to match the level of the voices around her. 'We argued, I went back along the shortcut, rejoined the race. Heather was alone when I left her.'

This was the thought she kept circling back to in the small hours, the part of her statement she resented the most. *Heather was alone when I left her.*

And she stayed alone. Would now be alone for all eternity. What sort of person does that? Walks out on someone who you call a friend?

But what if that person deserved to be alone, kept pushing everyone away until they were all alone. What if they had it coming?

'Mr Hall knew she'd be there,' Olivia stated, nodding aggressively. 'He could easily have followed you all out for the run.'

'Sefton Park is a big place,' Hannah agreed. 'Open to the public. He could have parked on a side road, jumped the outer walls to get in.'

'And what?' Pippa asked of the group, feeling her stomach begin to churn. 'He followed Heather, waited until she was alone and then pushed her in the river? That's ridiculous.'

'Is it?' Hannah snapped another chip between her polished teeth.

'The police said there was no sign of a struggle.'

'The rain would have washed it away,' Olivia stated. More nodding.

Pippa groaned and looked again at her plate. It had been like this all week; every rumour, every theory starting as a snowflake but gathering so much weight, so much momentum, that now there were vast snowballs all over the place, large enough to take down a wall. An entire school.

And Mr Hall with his bad stomach, was he at home fretting over such worries? Had the police knocked on his door, asked him to answer some questions?

'He'd have been teaching,' Pippa realised aloud, 'when Heather went missing. He'd have an airtight alibi.' It was something she'd heard people say on TV in the American crime shows her parents sometimes watched. It felt strange to say it, to be part of an actual, real-world drama. She and her friends were supposed to be discussing the latest episode of *The OC*, boys and NSYNC. They weren't supposed to be speculating on murder suspects.

'Free period.' Hannah slapped her hand against the table as though playing a particularly rowdy game of snap. 'I checked.' She clicked her fingers at Olivia who was nodding manically now.

'So he'd have been in his office,' Olivia continued, growing an inch taller, emboldened. 'Alone.'

'He'd easily have had time to drive over to Sefton, do the deed and be back by final bell.'

Pippa felt that this wasn't actually true but stayed silent. Her friends' plotting had become a juggernaut she didn't want to get crushed by.

'Maybe he isn't at home sick at all.' Olivia eyed all those around her. 'Maybe he's in police custody and the school is keeping it from us for fear of what it will do to its reputation when it comes out.'

'I heard from Tristan,' Hannah said, her tone lifting from scandalous to conversational, 'that the police are going to search every locker here at school and might even do home searches.'

'Home searches?' Olivia blinked, confused. 'Looking for . . . what?'

A shrug from Hannah. 'Tristan didn't know. He thought maybe old notes sent during class, that kind of thing. Anything that can help pin Mr Hall to the murder. Did you know they went to his house?'

'Mr Hall's?'

'No,' Hannah corrected with a tut, 'Tristan's. The officers working the case showed up the other night and his parents were pissed. He got asked all sorts of questions about his relationship with Heather.'

'What did he say?' Pippa pressed, feeling light-headed.

'Just . . .' Hannah shrugged, 'that they kind of dated I guess. But if you ask me, it's Mr Hall's house they should be going to.'

'But . . .' Pippa's objection caught in her throat and she had to cough the rest of it out: 'Why all the sudden questioning? The police aren't saying she's been murdered.'

'Not yet,' Hannah agreed with a lofty sigh. She tucked a short strand of her blonde hair behind her ear, revealing that she was wearing diamond studs. Something that was forbidden. Something which the teachers would normally shit a brick over. But things were different now. Pippa wasn't sure if the world was upside down or if it was burning. Either way, she longed for the day when she could look at blue skies without her eyes smarting. 'But there's a reason they're still all over this.' She dramatically nodded towards the far end of the canteen where a uniformed officer was positioned, impassively surveying the students as they ate dinner. It was the handsome officer, Officer Richards, who had been present for Pippa's second interview.

'Miss Rogers said they're here to help with grief management,' Pippa said, reciting what her form had been told at the start of the week.

'And you believed her?' Olivia was appalled.

'Like, when have you ever heard of that happening before?' Hannah asked, tone slightly more sensitive. 'I know you and Heather were close,' she reached for Pippa's hand and gave it a squeeze, 'and I know it can't be easy being the last person to have seen her. But you're not thinking straight. Don't worry, though. We are. And we can see that there is more to this, Pip. Heather didn't just drown.'

'My money is on someone pushing her,' Olivia added, shifting in her chair to glance back at the officer. 'And the police aren't going to leave here until they've got some more answers.'

'It'll be Hall,' Hannah told the group. 'It's the only thing that makes sense.'

Pippa often thought on how she liked Mr Hall. He was friendly and kind and didn't smell musty like so many of the other teachers did. He smelt of cologne and mint. And when he talked about the Tudors he made them come alive, his passion contagious. But she didn't want the police poking around him too much, risking him sharing things that Heather had confided in him. Or maybe he was smart enough to know that if he shared being privy to such information, it'd make his friendship with her look more than unprofessional, verging on inappropriate. And what young male teacher at the start of his career would want to be dealing with that?

'It's a witch hunt is what it is,' said Carey Simmons, positioned just beyond the group at the far end of the table, mousey with large glasses. Her plate of chips was empty, Carey having eagerly gnawed on them as she listened in. 'Ironic that our beloved history teacher is at the centre of it, don't you think?'

No one answered her.

'This weekend,' Hannah announced grandly, 'that's when Tristan says they'll search the school and maybe our homes too. He heard it from his dad.'

'Don't you need like, a warrant for that?' Olivia wondered.

Hannah considered this, then gave a stern nod. 'Homes, yes.'

'But not the school,' Carey replied, determined to be heard. 'The school is public ground and therefore fair game. So I hope none of you have any skeletons lurking in your closets.' When she was again met with a wall of silence, Carey picked up her empty plate and walked away.

'Square bitch,' Hannah sneered as Carey departed from the canteen. Pippa straightened with a jolt. For a second it was like hearing a voice from beyond the grave, like being right beside Heather.

Pipsqueak,

I actually can't BELIEVE your last letter. Did you seriously write that my words will 'catch up with me?' Pip — what are you ON? I most certainly was not being a bitch with Hannah. She needed to know about the stain. Needed to know that if her flow is so fucking heavy to properly protect herself. The rest of us don't want to be subjected to the sight of her bloodstained pants after we've been playing netball in the rain for an hour. Christ — I was doing her a FAVOUR! I thought you of all people would understand that.

I am not 'deliberately being mean to people', whatever the hell that means. I'm being honest. I'm only ever honest with people. So no, to your other point, I'm not making it up that your dad is over my house all the time. He's there. Next time I'll take a Polaroid if you need me to. Though as my best friend it is your duty to believe me. You might want to remind yourself of that.

Write back when you've cooled down from being such a bitch. See you at the park at eight. I'll bring the cider.

Love you,

H

xoxo

23

It was at night, on the cusp of sleep, that Pippa thought of Heather most. Of the sleepovers where they'd lie side by side on the living room floor, swathed in brightly coloured sleeping bags like exotic caterpillars, daring one another to sit through one more horror film. Neither girl was willing to show fear, so they'd watch monsters with needles poking from their faces, demons covered in bees, pretending it was all fine. That they weren't afraid.

Everything was a game with Heather. And she usually always won. Pippa used to like how, during the sleepovers, when drunk on exhaustion, Heather would lower her guard. Say something true, something real.

'You're so smart you could rule the world if you wanted one day,' she'd tell Pippa. 'You're going to be like my mum, with a career, a life all of your own.' The comments cocooned Pippa in a warmth that lulled her to sleep, but come the morning, in the cold light of reflection, she'd often wonder if Heather thought her path would lead her to be like her own mother. Was she destined to be kept? A trophy left to gather dust on a shelf?

'What will you do when you're older?' Pippa would ask. But she never chose her moment wisely, she always caught Heather when she was 'on' and her answers were always grandiose.

'I'm going to be a Vegas showgirl.'

'Hollywood superstar.'

'I'm going to join a girl band and tour the world.'

Nothing concrete. Nothing real. All just part of the show.

'We're like that yin and yang thing,' Heather had once muttered, tucked tight in her sleeping bag adorned with moon and stars, the credits for *Scream* playing on the nearby TV. 'One half light, one dark. Only . . .' Her pretty mouth gaped wide in a yawn as Pippa rolled onto her side to study her friend's profile. 'I look like the light one, being blonde. But I'm actually dark. And you've got the dark hair, but you're actually light.'

'We're like good cop, bad cop?' Pippa smiled.

'Exactly.' Heather yawned again, longer this time. 'That's why we're best friends, because we're a good fit. And, you know. . .' She turned to face her Pippa, her eyes bright even in the dim light. 'Even though I can be bad, you see the good. And even though you're good, I see the bad.'

Pippa's smile fell. 'Wait, what?'

But Heather's eyes were closed, she was sleeping. Forever leaving on a dramatic, unsatisfying note. With a grunt of annoyance, Pippa rolled onto her back and stared up at the light fitting above her. An ugly thing with too many arms and bulbs. Were they best friends because they suited one another, as Heather believed? Or were they best friends because it was all they'd ever known? A habit they couldn't break? Pippa considered this until her breathing slowed and sleep took her too. The credits on the television stopped, replaced by a blank screen.

24

Abbie lingered in her car, watching dry auburn leaves skitter along the path beside her. It was a day that threatened rain. When she'd left, Pippa was still tucked up in bed, sleeping, making the most of her Saturday lie-in. The text that had pinged through to Abbie's phone the previous evening had been curt in its instruction.

We need to go and see Michelle tomorrow.
Love C x

Carol, ever politically minded, knew it was time to call in on the grieving mother. To offer baked goods along with condolences.

Won't she be working? Xx

Abbie had tapped out her reply as beside her John turned a page in his hardback, brow furrowed, thoughts distant. Carol's response came back with brisk efficiency.

No, she'll be home. I checked x

Of course she did. Carol was always thorough. Abbie had struggled to fall asleep after that, tossing and turning as though her mattress had become the deck of a ship, lost on stormy seas.

Knuckles rapped against her passenger window, causing her to jump.

'Come on.' Carol was beside the car, gesturing impatiently for Abbie to get out, her hair tangling in the wind. Abbie tightened her grip against her wheel, flexed her fingers so hard they started to ache. Then with a grunt she released them, grabbed the cling film-covered lasagne in a glass dish from the seat beside her and climbed out. Her beige coat flapped behind her in the wind as she hurried along the pavement to catch up with Carol. Ashley was already at the end of the grand gated driveway, iron bars preventing them from going any further.

'I'll get us buzzed in.' Carol searched the brickwork beside her, stepping towards a silver intercom. Abbie held her lasagne against her chest, cradled it from the wind. Ashley had a domed serving dish under which was surely her famous lemon meringue. And Carol had bought along bread and butter pudding. All three together were enough to easily feed a dozen people instead of just the one mouth. As Carol waited by the intercom Abbie peered through the bars, at the sweeping driveway which led to an impressive two-storey faux-Georgian house. The front door bordered by two stone columns, all the windows long and edged in white. A beautiful home.

A voice crackled through the intercom: 'Hello?'

'Michelle!' Carol said her name as though it were the most wondrous thing she'd ever held in her mouth. 'How are you my darling? I'm just here with some of the girls and we wanted to pop by and see how you were.'

Silence punctured with static. Then: 'Come on up.'

'I hope she's a little more grateful in person,' Ashley muttered as together the trio walked through the opening gates.

Michelle's house was a testament to elegant style. Every room filled with clean, smooth lines. All walls white, all floors polished wood. It was so sleek. Almost like a show home. They were led through the lower floor towards the back of the property and the grand conservatory, which looked out on a garden that pressed against the back of a golf course. Beyond the fence Abbie could see the mani-cured curve that led to the seventh hole. It was a course John often frequented.

Michelle moved with an easy grace, like a dancer accus-tomed to being on stage, eyes forever on her. Her cheeks were not speckled with red, nor were her eyes blotchy. To Abbie, she did not look the part of a grieving mother.

'I'm sorry.' Michelle perched across from them on the arm of a wicker chair, the slightest crinkles appearing in the corners of her eyes as she coolly studied her guests. Her slender frame was almost lost in the large cable knit jumper she was wearing over a pair of leggings, her golden hair piled atop her head in a messy bun. Her cheekbones were more pronounced than usual. Had she lost weight? 'I'm not really set up for visitors at the moment.' Her tone was brisk, busi-nesslike, as though the other women were patients, not peers.

'Oh, we understand,' Carol said gravely. 'I could always go into the kitchen and make some cups of tea if you like or—'

'No.' Michelle's response was sharp. Twisting her long fingers together, nails tipped white, she glanced anxiously between her guests and the garden beyond. 'I mean, I'm sorry. But I'm due to go out soon.'

'Out?' Carol's interest was instantly piqued. 'To work?'

'No.' Michelle tucked a strand of hair behind her ear, smiling weakly. It was the colour of straw that had been out in the sun, soaking up all of its yellow goodness. 'I'm . . . seeing family.'

'Ah.' A nod of approval from Carol. 'Family are so very important at times like this.'

'How are you holding up?' Ashley leaned forward as she spoke, hands resting on her knees. They were all still in their coats, hair still tossed from the wind.

'I'm . . .' Michelle attempted to answer, looked again to the garden, blue eyes glistening. She shrugged helplessly, the corners of her mouth turning down. 'I don't know. I'm just . . . I don't know.'

'We're all so impressed that you're still managing to go into work,' Ashely enthused.

'Oh yes.' Carol eagerly jumped on the bandwagon. 'An amazing feat. One I definitely couldn't manage.'

'Nor I,' Ashley placed a hand to her chest.

'It makes for a good distraction.' Michelle glanced at the women from the corner of her eye, foot tapping anxiously against the tiles on the floor. 'Being here,' now she looked beyond them, towards the kitchen they'd previously walked through, a trio of offerings now resting on the island as though she'd just been visited by the three wise men. 'The house seems so empty now.'

The wind brushed against the glass of the conservatory, carrying leaves which peppered the class. Abbie was listening, watching the grass upon the lawn flickering, wondering how busy the golf course was on such a blustery, cold day. She didn't notice Michelle's blue eyes settle on her, the tapping of her foot grow faster, more pronounced. 'Pippa was the last person to see Heather.'

Hearing her daughter's name from Michelle made her entire body sharpen as though it were a starting gun. 'Pippa?' Abbie frowned, tried to focus on what was being said in the room. 'Yes . . . yes, she was with her on the run.'

'And she didn't see anything?'

The wicker of Abbie's chair creaked as she stiffened against it, spine suddenly poker straight. 'No,' she said, looking between her friends and Michelle, 'she didn't see anything. The girls had a brief disagreement and then Pippa left to join the others.'

'A brief disagreement?' Michelle's blue eyes narrowed.

'All of this has been relayed to the police.' Abbie heard her voice hardening, the words forged in the furnace of the anger which now boiled in her belly and travelled up her throat. 'Heather wanted to cheat, to take a shortcut. Pippa did not.'

'So Pippa just left her?'

'So Pippa *returned to the race*.' Abbie smoothed her hands down her knees, pushing creases out of her coat. She had to do something with them to resist the urge to place them around Michelle's perfect neck. A vein was pulsating as she spoke, and at the nape a single diamond was attached to a delicate chain.

'Did she say if Heather was acting strangely or—'

'She's told the police all she knows.' Abbie was on her feet. 'I came here to pass on my condolences, not to be interrogated.'

'Interrogated?' Michelle followed her into the kitchen, their footsteps echoing as Carol and Ashely eagerly looked on from the safety of their chairs back in the conservatory. When she reached the island Abbie spun around, cheeks hot.

'If you have questions about Pippa's statement you should ask the police not me, you should—'

'My daughter is dead.' Michelle laid it out so plainly, one hand gripping the island. The reality of it forged a canyon between the two women as they stared across one another at it. 'And I just want to know what happened.'

'You know what happened.' Abbie raised her chin. 'Heather fell into the water. A terrible accident for which you have our utmost sympathies.'

'Fuck your sympathies.' Michelle edged closer to the precipice of the canyon, blue eyes suddenly wide. 'And fuck your false signs of concern.' She gestured to the food on the island.

'Well.' Carol's voice was sharp behind them. Now Michelle had gone too far. She and Ashley stalked over to stand with Abbie. 'We were only being kind.'

'I just want the truth.' Michelle's chin wobbled and for one awful moment Abbie thought she might break down. Her elbow buckled but she steadied herself, cleared her throat. 'What else did Heather say to Pippa?' She was staring so hard at Abbie, gaze piercing and cold.

'What else?' Abbie found herself repeating the question, lips puckered with confusion. 'I've told you. They argued about the run. Pippa left. That's it.'

'That's it?' Michelle looked at Abbie as though she were the only person in the room, as though the other women weren't even there. 'They didn't talk about anything else?'

'That's it,' Abbie confirmed, drawing on the lapels of her coat to tighten them against her chest.

'Well, I hope you're right.' Michelle fumbled with her golden hair, rustled her fingers through her bun.

Abbie turned her back on her unwilling host and began to march from the kitchen, her friends in step with her. But at the doorway she spun around, the fire that was stoked within her reaching boiling point.

'You know, children from *unstable* homes can do sudden, desperate things.'

Michelle eyed her coolly, though Abbie swore she saw the woman's jaw clench. 'I don't appreciate what you're trying to allude to.' Her face was marble – pretty and hard.

'I'm merely—'

'An absent father is so much better than an inadequate one, don't you think?'

The way she stared at Abbie, like she *knew* about her past. But that was impossible. Abbie bristled, making a show of feeling cold and rubbing her arms, least Michelle know she had gotten to her.

'I'm so sorry for your loss,' Abbie stated with a regal raise of her chin, determined to leave the unpleasant interaction on the moral high ground. She fled before Michelle could respond, made for the front door and almost tumbled out through it in her desperation to leave. Only once the iron gates were closing behind them did she exhale.

'What. A. Bitch,' Ashley lamented, shaking her head and scowling back up the length of the driveway.

'We were merely being kind.' Carol turned up the collar of her coat even though her face was flushed. 'Shows you what kind of woman she is.'

'Agreed,' Ashley raged as they walked back to their parked cars.

'Clearly, now she has no stake in the school, she doesn't care about her relationships with other parents,' Carol huffed. 'Always thought she was terribly shallow.'

'Still . . .' Ashley had reached her Mercedes, a hand resting on the bonnet as she plunged the other into her coat pocket to search for her keys. 'It's a hell of a thing to go through. To lose your only daughter. She's in a bad place.'

'You wouldn't think it to look at her.' Carol dusted hair from her eyes, red lips pouting. 'I'd be in my dressing gown for *months* if it were me, if I'd lost my Hannah.'

Abbie drifted out of the conversation as she edged back to peer again up the long driveway, seeing the shift of a curtain at a window. 'Pippa tells me everything,' she said to her friends.

'Of course.'

'Absolutely.'

Their agreement was swift.

'She's just bitter,' Abbie concluded, pressing a hand to her chest to keep her lapels from flapping, 'that she's the one who lost a daughter, not me.'

Her friends were silent.

'Don't take it personally.' Carol came close to rest a hand on her shoulder. 'As Ashley said, Michelle is grieving. She's saying things she doesn't mean.'

'Besides,' Ashley added from where she was about to climb into her car, peering at her friends over the open door, 'the autopsy report will be back this coming week. Once the suspected seizure is confirmed she'll get the closure she so clearly needs.'

'Exactly.' Carol gave Abbie's shoulder a squeeze and then leaned in close to kiss her on the cheek, her lips leaving a warm crimson smear. 'Go home, forget about it. You stood up for yourself, as any mother would have done.'

Abbie could only nod. Once she was back in her car and her friends had driven away, she noticed how terribly her legs were shaking. And as she sat there the shaking spread to her arms, her hands, even her teeth, which clattered in her mouth as outside the wind blew, spraying her windscreen with dried leaves.

25

The police. In their homes. Searching for something. For secrets.

That was the threat which had passed through the students quicker than chicken pox. Pippa wanted to believe it was just idle gossip, senseless speculation. But as she turned back and forth beneath her duvet on Friday night she couldn't dismiss two glaring truths: the police were still at her school.

The report of the autopsy had yet to come in.

Heather's death remained a guessing game. Did she drown? Was she pushed? And the police were hunting for answers. Of course they were. Heather was sixteen, blonde and beautiful. How could someone so stunning, so spectacular, have a simple, mundane death?

Pippa stared wide-eyed into the darkness, listening to the deafening drum of her heartbeat in her ears. What exactly were the police looking for? Old notes and letters? Cryptic texts on phones? Rolling onto her side, she pressed herself against her mattress and thought of the space beneath her bed, of all the dark, distant corners. When morning came she'd search every inch of it.

Where there should have been dust and disorder, shoe boxes crammed full of slips of paper and old photographs, there were neat cardboard towers, clean stretches of clear carpet. Pippa looked down at the space where her bed usually stood. It was now pulled back to the far side of the room, her back still damp with the effort of moving it. In her pink Jane Norman pyjamas she crouched against the floor, studying the boxes in more detail. One by one she picked them up, emptied their contents and frantically sifted through them like a squirrel desperately counting its nuts. Photo booth images, Polaroids, scrawled notes, old party invitations, the detritus of her early teenage years assembled around her in a haphazard collage. Notes about boys, about teachers, about friends, about enemies, about friends who became enemies. So many written in Heather's familiar looping hand, the i's dotted with large circles.

Pippa remained on her hands and knees until she'd searched every box. Every inch of space beneath her bed. But they weren't all there. Some of her letters were gone.

It was almost midday when Pippa thundered downstairs, feet bare, still in her pyjamas. Her mum had not disturbed her, probably assuming incorrectly she was having a lie-in.

She found her standing at the kitchen island, staring at the clock on the wall with a distant look on her face. 'Mum?' she said.

'Yeah?' Startled, she rubbed her cheeks, which were mottled, and looked over at Pippa. 'You all right, sweetheart? You want some breakfast?'

Pippa frowned at her and then nodded to the clock. 'Maybe more like lunch.'

'Oh, right, sure.' Her mum sounded weary. 'Guess the morning got away from me.'

'Has someone been in my room?' Pippa fought to keep her voice level, managing to deliver her question in a reasonable manner.

'In your . . .' Her mum gently shook her head as though her thoughts were clouds that were slipping away from her with quiet ease. 'Sorry, darling. You want some lunch?'

'My room. Has someone been in it?'

'Let's have soup.' She watched her mother drift over to the double doors of the fridge and pull them open, the light within instantly illuminating her. 'I've got some fresh leek and soup in here somewhere that I—'

'Has someone been cleaning, under my bed?' Pippa stepped towards her, hands clenched in fists by her sides.

'You tell me everything, right, Pip?' Her mother spun around so suddenly that the action rustled the air. One hand on her hip, the other still holding open the fridge door, she stared at her daughter. 'I mean, you've told me everything that happened that day with . . . with Heather?'

'W-what?' Pippa's throat was tight. 'Yes.' She threw the word out like a grenade, fingers scratching against her neck. She coughed, the sound spluttering from her.

'I know we're always honest with each other so—'

'Who has been in my room?' Pippa was shouting. She saw the surprise on her mum's face and felt it mirrored in herself. She never shouted. She was a calm teenager. A good teenager. But now she was shouting. She was thinking of the tidied space beneath her bed and her heart began to beat faster and faster.

'Pippa, don't take that tone with me—'

'Someone has been *under my bed*. Someone has moved something. Someone has—' She couldn't finish the statement as the tears arrived, hot and heavy and vast in number. Gasping against the sudden strength of them, she tasted salt on her lips and then felt arms around her, the familiar smell of her mum's perfume as she hugged her close, held her tight until the sobs eventually subsided.

'Sweetheart, hey, it's OK, it's OK.' She kept whispering the words over and over as she stroked Pippa's hair and they stood locked together in the centre of the kitchen, as though caught in the eye of a tornado.

'I . . .' Pippa tried to catch her breath, her entire face now slick with tears.

'If someone moved anything, it would have been Jeanette when she came in to clean during the week. If you've lost something let me know and I'll ask her about it.'

'No, no.' Pippa recoiled from her mum's embrace, dragging the back of her hand across the base of her nose. 'It's fine, really, it's—'

'What have you lost?' Her mum planted a hand on either of her shoulders and looked into her eyes. There was so much history in her gaze. So much safety.

Pippa tried to find the words. This was the face that was there when she'd scream out in the night about the monsters she'd heard scratching in the wardrobe. The face that would smile as it picked her up from a fall and applied kisses and plasters to cuts and scrapes. She knew this face. She knew her mother. 'It's all right, Pip.' Abbie plucked a tissue from her pocket and dabbed at her daughter's wet cheeks. 'You can tell me anything. You know that. What have you lost?'

Pippa shuddered as she drew in a breath. Her bedroom was now a mess, her bed shoved to the far side, boxes scattered across the floor, the carpet littered with pictures and the back catalogue of her youth. Notes from Heather listing all the boys she fancied, names being crossed out on a daily basis. Pictures of her and Heather, their faces squashed together in a stiflingly hot photo booth, eyes too dark from all the kohl liner they'd spent an entire morning applying.

'My friend,' she spluttered as she pressed herself against her mum's shoulder, welcomed the fresh embrace which gathered around her. 'I've lost my friend.'

26

Abbie had drunk too much Merlot at dinner, keen to wash away the memory of her unpleasant interaction with Michelle Oxon that morning.

'Don't worry,' Carol had consoled her during a phone call as Abbie's potatoes boiled over behind her. 'Michelle is projecting, that's all.'

'I don't like how she asked about Pip.'

'I know.'

'She's already told the police all she knows.'

'I know.'

Carol was being so calm, so patient. Abbie threw a glance at the hob of her stove, noticing a pan lid beginning to shift. Her attention was supposed to be on dinner, not parental politics.

'So you think it was nothing?' she heard herself asking again, needing to hear Carol say it, confirm it, that Michelle's probing was nothing more than the rants of a broken woman. Only she didn't appear broken at all, not even cracked.

'It was nothing,' Carol insisted. 'Now go enjoy your Saturday night with that handsome husband of yours and stop stressing, OK?'

'OK.' Abbie had swallowed down two huge gulps of wine along with her compliance. She didn't point out to Carol that John had yet to return home from work. And she didn't ask her friend if the words of support she offered down the phone were the truth. Because Abbie bet if she had Carol's mobile phone in her hand she'd find texts to the contrary. Texts sent to Ashley and God knows who else. Texts asking if they too thought Pippa knew more than she was saying.

Curled up in an armchair beside the fire, Abbie clutched a fresh glass of wine in one hand and eyed its contents distrustfully. Was the crimson liquid the cause of her paranoia? Focusing on the flames in the hearth, Abbie reminded herself that Carol was being honest with her, being kind. That her husband was merely working late. But as the clock crept closer to midnight, she began to doubt all that she held to be true. How many nights could he really be needed so late? Weren't there other doctors available? The questions curdled in her stomach, flooding her throat with a sour taste.

When a car did pull into the driveway, Abbie had crossed over from tipsy to drunk. But she managed to stay within the lounge, wait for him to come through the house to find her.

'You're still up?' he noted from the doorway, tie loose around his neck.

'Waiting for you,' she grinned a little too wide.

'You've been drinking.' He turned his back and stalked towards the kitchen, searching for any remains of the dinner he'd missed.

'I've had a rough day.' Abbie stood up and followed him, sensing how light her footsteps felt, how distant all the walls seemed. How much wine had she had? One bottle? Two? It was always so easy to lose count after the third glass.

'Abigail, just go up to bed.'

'You know I got shouted at today.'

John was leaning into the fridge and he suddenly stopped, straightening and turning to face her. 'By Pippa?'

'By Michelle Oxon.' The name blurred together on her tongue.

'Wait.' John slammed the fridge shut, narrowed his eyes at his wife. 'You went to see Michelle Oxon?'

'Uh-huh.' Abbie placed her glass on the island, not caring about the red ring it would surely leave against the polished surface. 'With Carol and Ashley. We took food. We were being *nice*.'

'You went to her house?'

'No, we went to Sainsbury's.' Abbie laughed and rolled her eyes. She really was so very drunk. 'Of course we went to her house.'

'You should leave her in peace.'

'We took food,' Abbie repeated, hands manoeuvring wildly in front of her as she gestured towards an invisible dish which was now inside Michelle Oxon's kitchen. A dish which Abbie knew she'd never see again. 'John, we were being good neighbours. Good friends.'

'You were being busybodies. What's for dinner?'

'And she had the nerve, the *nerve* . . .' Abbie felt her body tightening just at the memory of it.

'To what? Did she tell you to fuck off?' John wondered, an amused smile pulling on his lips. Abbie blinked, took a beat, in no mood for her husband's brand of humour. 'It's what I'd have done,' he mumbled as he returned to searching the shelves of the fridge.

'She asked me about Pippa.' Raising her chin, Abbie placed a hand upon the island, needing to grasp it to cease the room from listing from left to right.

'About Pippa?' His attention was back on her.

'She asked if Pippa had told me everything, about what happened when she was last with Heather.'

'OK.' His jaw was set in a hard line. 'What did you say?'

Abbie's hand found her empty glass of wine, closed around its slim stem.

'I said Pippa's told me all she knows.'

'Which she has.' John studied her and she wondered if it was a statement or a question.

'I don't like her prying about our daughter,' Abbie fumed, not enjoying being under his spotlight.

'Me neither,' he agreed hotly.

'She asked if Pippa had told me everything, about her last moments with Heather.'

'And has she?' Staring at her husband in disbelief, Abbie made her hand into a fist, the glass cracking against her fingers, digging into her skin. 'Jesus, Abs.' At the sight of blood he shifted into surgeon mode, yanking open cupboards until he found the first-aid kit, grabbing his wife by the wrist and pulling her towards the kitchen sink where he ran the tap and placed her hand beneath it. Abbie watched, bemused, as the water turned red. 'You need to be more careful,' he scolded her. 'You're always so damn accident-prone when you've been drinking.'

'You think Pippa knows something?' Abbie looked at her husband, studied him. Beneath the wrinkles and the grey flecks in his curls, the handsome man she'd married was still there. He was more weary, more jaded, but in his eyes his younger self lingered. Those eyes now settled on her, always sharp, always alert.

'I think Heather was a healthy sixteen-year-old girl with no pre-existing medical condition,' he said. 'She may well have suffered a seizure beside the river and fallen in.'

Abbie couldn't breathe. The water kept running from the tap, kept mingling with her own blood and disappearing down the drain.

'She may also have been hit over the head and pushed in.' John released Abbie's hand and turned off the tap, plunging them into a tense silence.

'And you think—'

'No, no.' He sharply shook his head. 'I don't think for a second that Pippa would do such a thing. Heather was her best friend. They had their differences, sure. All teenage girls do. But I think that she may have seen something, seen some*one*, and be too scared to speak out.'

Abbie placed her hand to her chest, felt the pulse of her own heartbeat in her fresh wounds. She eyed him suspiciously, wondering how it was possible for him to not know their daughter at all. Pippa and Heather were far from best friends. Abbie knew that. On the surface, yes, to an outsider they were thick as thieves. But Abbie had seen the way Pippa wilted when in Heather's shadow. It was why she had kept urging them apart. She understood the complicated dynamics of teenage relationships. At sixteen, a friend and a foe could look the same from a certain distance. It was only when you got close that you could see the difference.

'I think Pippa is afraid.' John extended a plaster towards his wife. With clenched teeth Abbie accepted the olive branch. 'I think if she did see someone that day, if it was someone she knew, she may well, understandably, be too scared to say anything.'

'Someone like who?' Abbie queried, voice low.

'I've heard the rumours about that history teacher. Mr . . . Mr . . .' He clicked his fingers, trying to connect the memory to a name.

'Mr Hall.' The wine was loosening its grip on Abbie's senses.

'That's the one,' John nodded at her. 'And Pippa likes him, doesn't she?'

'So you think she's protecting Mr Hall?'

'I think until the autopsy comes back, nothing is certain.'

Abbie placed the plaster around the cut on her finger. 'The police think it was nothing more than a freak accident.'

'Then why are they still at the school?'

Looking at her finger, Abbie watched the dark stain of blood spread against the fabric of the plaster. 'You need to stop working so late.' She looked at her husband, searched his gaze for the man who'd kissed her beneath a sky of stars, offered her a diamond on a golden beach. 'We need you here.'

He cupped her face with his hands, drew her close and kissed her forehead. 'I'm needed elsewhere too.' His breath was hot against her. 'And stay away from Michelle Oxon.' His thumb stroked her cheek. 'I don't like her asking so many questions about Pippa. I know she's grieving; best leave her to do it in peace.'

Abbie said nothing, let him think that her silence was acceptance. But she knew full well that grief and peace did not go together. And that left undisturbed, Michelle would bring the wolves to their door.

27

The call came in just after 7 a.m. on a Sunday morning, pulling Abbie from a dream in which she was running down an endless corridor, doors slamming closed all around her. Disorientated, mind still foggy, she reached out from beneath the duvet, fumbling for the landline resting on the bedside table. Each ring was a sledgehammer through the sleepy silence of the bedroom.

'H-hello?' Voice hoarse, she pressed the receiver against her ear, propped herself up on an elbow as beside her John grunted his disapproval and rolled over.

'Abbie.' Ashley was surprisingly alert at such an early hour.

'Ash.' With her free hand Abbie rubbed furiously at her eyes, trying to scrub any lingering sleep from them. 'Is everything all right?' Her mind raced through possible reasons for the call.

Was she late for something?

Did Pippa have an early class somewhere she'd forgotten about? A netball match? A cross-country run? But calls for tardiness didn't come before dawn on a weekend morning.

Abbie felt her stomach clench. This was something more serious. More dire.

'I wanted to call you first.' Ashley was speaking quietly, tentatively.

'Me first? About . . . about what?'

'Abigail, it's too early for chit-chat,' John groaned from his side of the bed.

'About the autopsy report.'

Abbie froze, felt the air around her suddenly plummet to freezing. 'W-what about it?'

'I shouldn't be telling you.' A tight sigh on the other end of the line. 'I heard Geoff get the call about a half hour ago and then he had to dash into work.'

'What did it say?'

Abbie sensed the stillness beside her as John held his breath beneath the covers.

'Please, Abbie, don't repeat this to anyone.' Ashley was speaking quickly, urgently. On her end of the call came the click of a door closing, of her hiding herself away from any potential eavesdroppers. 'I'm telling you and Carol because you're my friends and because, well –' a deep breath, a pause '– as mothers of girls the same age, at the same school, I think we deserve to know right away.'

'Ashley, what did it say?'

'Heather didn't drown.'

'Right.' Abbie cleared her throat, picked her words carefully. 'Because something happened prior to her falling into the river. Like a seizure or . . . a knock on the head?'

'Abbie . . . Christ, Geoff will actually kill me if he knows I'm telling people.'

'What did the report say?'

'The report says that Heather was already dead before she entered the water.'

Abbie absorbed this information though she had no idea how to interpret it. John was now sitting up beside her, listening just as intently.

'I don't understand,' Abbie admitted.

An accident. A horrible accident. That was the truth they'd all been fed. A fatal slip in the mud, a head smacking against a rock. Wrong place at the wrong time, nothing more.

'They're treating her death as suspicious,' Ashley declared.

'I don't—'

'Abbie, they're saying she was murdered.'

The statement slammed against Abbie like a brick wall. *Murdered*.

No slip. No fall. Just malice. Just danger.

'Jesus.' The word fell from Abbie's lips in a whisper.

'I know, I know.' Ashley was breathing quickly. 'It's seriously fucked up and seriously fucking scary. I didn't pick up anything else, only that the investigation has changed because of the report.'

'So how did she actually . . .'

'I don't know yet. But it'll come out now the report is back.'

'Oh my God.' Abbie cupped a hand against her mouth. Heather Oxon didn't just die. She was killed. There was a killer in Waterbridge. A killer who no one had been trying to find. A killer who had been walking freely among them all for over a week. Her gaze focused on her bedroom door, thinking of Pippa sleeping just a few feet away in her own room, in her own bed. 'What do we . . . I mean . . .'

'You need to talk to Pippa,' Ashley declared with sudden urgency. 'She was the last person to see Heather. She *must* have seen something.'

'She's told them all she knows.'

And me too, Abbie thought.

'What if . . . what if she's protecting someone?'

'I don't . . .' Abbie could feel her temple starting to pound with the promise of an imminent migraine. 'If that was the case she'd tell me.'

'I hope so.' Ashley released a shaky breath. 'Because right now, she's not safe.' Then, she added as a swift afterthought, 'No one is. Not when there's . . . Not while whoever did it is still loose.'

Ashley couldn't say *murderer* and Abbie didn't blame her. Such words didn't belong on their tongues, in their world. To kill, to murder, was ugly. And Waterbridge was all beauty. Neat driveways and manicured lawns. Bad things weren't supposed to happen in good places.

'So what do we do?' Abbie queried weakly. Were they to hide in their homes, lock the front doors and windows and wait until the guilty party was caught?

'I need to call Carol.'

'OK . . . well. Thank you for letting me know.'

'Of course.' There was a pause in which the two women would have embraced had the news been delivered in person. 'Stay safe.'

When the dial tone came Abbie didn't hang up the receiver, merely stared at it in her hand, a part of her wondering if she were still caught in a dream.

'Don't tell Pippa.' John's voice from across the bed brought her back to reality.

'What?' Abbie shifted to face him. His hair was crumpled, his left cheek creased from the pillow. He scratched at it with his left hand, eyebrows drawn in a tight, thoughtful line.

'Don't tell her. Not yet.'

'She needs to know,' Abbie declared with fervour.

'No point scaring her until you have all the facts.' John swung his legs out of bed and perched on the edge, elbows resting against his thighs, staring towards the curtains ahead of him as though they were open and he could see the sweeping view of their garden, the barren arms of the oak tree that grew too close to the house.

'I'm telling her.'

'Don't be a fool.' He rose to his feet, the mattress shifting as it released him. He padded over towards the bathroom door, running his fingers through his curls, loosening them.

The door closed behind him and Abbie heard the hiss of the shower, the moan of the pipes within the walls. Her body yearned for more sleep, to curl up beneath her duvet and disappear into another dream. But there were fireworks exploding in her mind, wild and loud enough to shake her bones. So many thoughts. All igniting at once.

Heather was dead.

She didn't just fall into the river.

Someone had killed her.

And Pippa had been the last person to see Heather alive.

With a shaking hand pressed to her temple, Abbie tried to stand. She needed ibuprofen and she needed it fast if she was going to make it through the morning. Walking down the stairs towards the kitchen, her thoughts kept her company, growing more anxious and more dangerous with each step.

What if Ashley was right? What if Pippa was protecting someone? The police had asked if she'd *seen* someone, but perhaps they weren't asking the right questions in the right way. Pippa might be withholding the identity of the killer out of fear for her own safety.

The possibility drained the colour from Abbie's face. She felt fingers knit into a fist in the base of her gut and punch her from within. The sensation reminded her of those internal kicks Pippa had once given her. From gentle stirrings like the wings of a butterfly to a thrust against her abdomen sharp enough to make Abbie's eyes mist, to make the breath still in her lungs.

If that was the truth, if Pippa was protecting someone
. . . Abbie winced at it all, her head pounding, mouth dry.
If Pippa was protecting someone, the question was *who*?

28

The mood within the school had changed. Pippa sensed it the moment she passed through the open gates. Officers lurked in the car park, the neon flashes of their uniforms garishly bright against the ancient, ornate brickwork of the main building. Students huddled together in twos and threes, linked tightly at the arms like otters adrift in the sea, scared of floating away. Fear. That was the change. It was so sharp in the air Pippa could almost taste it. Waterbridge Preparatory was drenched in it.

'Murder.' Hannah had found her, and fell in step with her, hooking onto Pippa's arm. 'Can you believe it?'

Murder.

Pippa didn't dare repeat the word out loud. Murders happened on the television, in the cinema. Held at a safe distance on a faraway screen. Not here. Not at home. Not at school. She swallowed, felt the cornflakes she'd forced down that morning swirl unsteadily in her gut.

'I mean . . .' Hannah craned her neck to glance at the officers gathered behind them, out on the stone steps as they entered the school. 'Are we even safe to be here?'

'I don't think—' Pippa was about to point out that one death, however tragic, did not instantly mean they were all potential victims of a serial killer. They were hardly on the set of *Scream*. But as they entered the corridor, the shock of the scene that met her hit her hard in her chest, knocking her words from her in a startled gasp.

So many police. They outnumbered the students. Their faces stern as they swarmed among them, severing the tight links, setting every girl alone, using brisk arms to break up groups. To divide and conquer. 'Now, girls.' Miss Rogers was amidst the fray, raising her voice to be heard over the nervous whispers which buzzed along the corridor. The hive was anxious. As it had been since the departure of its queen. 'Please, just go in single file to your form rooms. No talking *please*. Everything will be all right.'

'Divide and conquer, eh?' Hannah whispered to Pippa as they began to be directed to opposite sides of the corridor. 'Someone here knows something.' She nodded at the officer guiding her away with a smug smile of confirmation.

'This way please, Miss.' Another officer was gesturing for Pippa to follow along behind some first years who were on the brink of tears, their eyes glassy and lips quivering. She walked the length of the corridor with her head bowed, turning off swiftly at her form room.

'I've heard the increased police presence is for our protection.' Olivia was holding court, addressing the three girls already in their seats. Pippa slid into her own, wishing she could believe her. But she sensed that Hannah was right. The police were out in force at the school because they thought they'd find answers within the old, revered walls. 'I for one feel much safer with them here,' Olivia prattled on. 'Especially when there is a madman out there.'

Second period on a Monday morning should have been English Literature. Pippa had been quietly excited to get lost in the drama of *Othello*, but instead her name was called out by Miss Rogers before the first bell for the day had even tolled. Another interview. The same vacant classroom. Same smell of stale dust and old chalk in the air. Different officers. These were older, shrewder, and plain-clothed.

'We're interviewing all the students a second time,' the man who'd introduced himself as Inspector Marlin explained. He had a snow-white moustache and eyes the colour of a muddy puddle.

'Especially those who were present at the run,' added Inspector Thomas, a woman with a pinched face and mousy hair flecked with grey.

'I know the school wanted to close following the . . . update,' Marlin stated, moustache twitching, 'but we asked them to keep the doors open, at least for today, to aid in our investigation.'

Pippa nodded and remained silent, hands clasped tight together in her lap. The stool she was sitting on squeaked every time she moved, even to breathe, as though she were a frightened mouse.

'We want to conduct as much of our investigation ahead of Wednesday as we can,' Marlin continued, 'since the school will then close for the remainder of the week.'

Wednesday. Heather's funeral. Now that the autopsy had returned, she could be committed to the ground. Left in a varnished box to rot. Pippa knew her friend would rather have been finished in flame, a final blaze for the phoenix she believed herself to be. But she was to be buried at St. Peter's, beside her grandparents, following a service at the small church. The last time Heather had even set foot in there was the day she was christened.

'Can you recall what happened when you were with Heather?' The tone of Inspector Thomas' voice told Pippa that this was the second time the question had been delivered. She blinked, wondering how long her mind had wandered for. Her restless nights were catching up with her, hours spent staring into darkness returning to haunt her during the day.

'I . . .' She tightened her fingers against the back of her hands. 'I've already spoken to officers about this. Given my statement.' She nodded to the digital recorder not so discreetly positioned on the far side of the table.

'We know,' Thomas nodded. 'But given the . . . development, in the case, we need to ask new questions. And perhaps you might have remembered new details?'

Development.

Such a delicate way to say *murdered.* But no one had actually been specific about how Heather died. Just that she was dead before she entered the water. That it was clear that someone had killed her.

'It was raining, we walked together, and I told her I wanted to go back, that I needed to get a decent time.'

'And then what?' Thomas asked, her tone gentle but firm. Her left hand was spread against the table, showing a dulled silver wedding band.

'Then I left.'

'You argued,' said Marlin, and Pippa turned cold when she realised it wasn't a question.

'Yes,' she nodded, fighting to raise her head when all her chin wanted to do was sink down to her chest. 'She told me not to go back.'

'Anything else?' Thomas wondered.

Pippa paused, considered what was safe to share.

'Well?' Marlin asked, moustache rippling with impatience.

'She called me a flaky bitch. I told her to fuck off and then ran back to the main trail.'

'And that was it?'

'That was it.'

178

'How would you describe your friendship with Heather?' Thomas moved to grab a nearby pen and paper. Pippa frowned; wasn't the recorder enough? And hadn't she answered all these questions before? Where was Miss Rogers? Should she have a lawyer present? That's what happened on television, right? A lawyer would be called in to oversee questioning. Her heart began to pound so loudly it was difficult to hear herself think.

'You're not on trial here.' Thomas tilted her head, offered a kind smile. 'We're just trying to gather all the evidence we can to find out who did this to your friend.'

'What did they do to her?' Pippa frantically looked between them, searching their expressions for more details.

'We're not at liberty to say.' Thomas gazed down sadly at the pen in her hand.

'It may hinder the investigation if it were made public knowledge,' Marlin added. 'Right now, the best thing you can do for Heather is tell us everything you know.'

'Do you know anyone who would have wanted to hurt her?' asked Thomas. *Hurt her?* Abbie considered the question. Every other girl at Waterbridge Prep had an axe to grind with Heather. An unsettled grudge. She had trampled on feelings as though they were ants. If you were too fat, too skinny, too spotty, hair too greasy – Heather would tell you. Many, many people would have wanted to hurt her. But to actually kill her, that was different.

'Hurt her?' Pippa breathed in, tried to make herself as still as possible even though her legs jittered nervously. What was she supposed to say? That *everyone* wanted to hurt Heather because Heather hurt everyone else? The inspectors were staring at her, smart in their suits. 'No one would want to hurt her,' she told them. 'Everybody loved her.'

Pippa trembled as Thomas scratched a note against the notepad, the light on the recorder shining brightly. It was a lie but a necessary one. Because what they needed to ask Pippa was who would want to *kill* Heather. And that would have been a much smaller list.

P Dog,

I understand why you don't want to believe me. I was the same when my parents were splitting up. And your parents are going to split up, trust me. The signs are most definitely there, you just don't want to see them. I know you think they're happy. But they're hardly going to come to you with all their marital issues, are they?

First sign between my parents was them both working late. Like all the time. They never wanted to come home. Then Dad got that new haircut along with the sports car and started staying away for entire weekends. My mum reckons he fucked his way through half of London. I think that's giving him too much credit. Obviously he's handsome, he made me after all. But he can be such a dick. And he's rich for Waterbridge, but not London. In London people are millionaires.

I'm thinking when I'm twenty I'm going to go to London and find a millionaire. Let him buy me all the stuff I want and in return I just look pretty for him.

I had a fight with Tristan after school. He invited me to some party this weekend and I asked if we were going together and he like, FLIPPED OUT. Went mental at me. Started going on about how we're not a couple and why the hell would I think that. As if the blow job and the fingering he gave me on Tuesday night was nothing.

It HURT but I still let him do it. Not that I want us to be together. I don't. I was asking if we were going together like travelling together, in the car. Or getting the bus. But of course he got confused. Because he's an idiot and I hate him. All men are idiots. Your mum will be better off when your dad leaves.

And he's defo leaving so stop denying it.

Love you,

H

xoxo

P.S. Just to add that when I said ALL men are idiots, I don't mean Mr Hall. He's different. Did you know his first name is Iain? He told me that. I like how he spells it differently to regular old Ian. Like he was just born special, you know?

29

'Does it bother you that he's barely here for dinner?'

The question caught Abbie off guard. It made a change from discussing Heather, but not a welcome one. She'd been leaning across the dining room table, placing the cutlery and was about to reach for the box of matches in her dress pocket to light the candle in the centre.

'Sorry?' She felt her eyebrows knit together as she turned towards the open doorway and her daughter's inquisitive face.

'You go to all this effort.' Pippa nodded at the neatly set table. At the place mats and matching coasters. The folded napkins. The long stem glasses. The polished silverware. 'And he's almost always working late.'

'Well,' Abbie dusted a rogue strand of mousy hair out of her eyes, 'on the nights when your father is home for dinner, I like to make sure everything is ready for him.'

'But on the nights he doesn't show,' Pippa cocked her head to the left, 'doesn't it like, piss you off?'

'Language,' Abbie warned lightly. 'And, well, no,' she continued, giving what she hoped was a light-hearted shrug, 'because you and I still get to enjoy our dinner together.'

'But we'd be happy eating off our laps in front of the TV,' Pippa noted. 'Like we do sometimes when Dad is away at a conference or something.'

'True,' said Abbie, wandering over to join her daughter and planting a hand on her slim shoulders, 'we do enjoy our TV dinners. But I like to be ready for when your father is here. To show him how appreciated he is.'

'Does he make you feel appreciated?'

Abbie's hand fell but her smile held. 'Of course.'

'Because Dad is working *a lot* lately. He normally comes home after I've gone to bed.'

Abbie cleared her throat. 'The hospital has certainly been busy lately, yes. You must remember how important your father is there. How much they depend on him.'

Pippa was watching the table, not her mother. 'You think he's always working?'

Abbie's face went hot. She wanted to ask, *what else could he be doing?* but didn't want to hear the answer. It was a question which plagued her on a nightly basis, when she was alone in their marital bed, listening to the creaks and groans of their grand house, waiting to hear the rumble of an engine in the driveway.

'I know he's taken on too much lately.' She leaned to kiss her daughter's temple. 'So it's up to us to take care of each other, and the house.'

'But he should be here,' Pippa pressed, 'especially with everything going on.'

Heather. Even unsaid, her name lingered between them.

'Do you miss him?' Pippa wondered, gazing at her, eyes wide and earnest. Abbie bit against the inside of her cheek, blaming those American teenagers Pip was so fond of watching on TV, the ones climbing into each other's windows. Romance. Love. To a young girl these were reasonable ideals. Life hadn't chipped away at that hope, decayed it with the rot of monotony and abandoned dreams.

'I did initially,' Abbie admitted. 'But I got used to him working long hours.'

The wine helped.

'So you *don't* mind?'

'Nope.' Abbie pulled Pippa in for an embrace, inhaling the sweetness of her hair, relishing the warmth of her long limbs wrapped against her own. 'I don't mind your father working late.' Her grip on her daughter was tight, protective. 'I'm just happy to do what I can to help, to keep our house a home.'

'He's lucky you're so nice.'

Abbie smiled wide. 'Yes, he truly is.'

30

John was late for dinner but home by ten. Pippa was already in her bedroom, sleeping, and Abbie had just emerged from the bath. She'd lingered among the bubbles until the tips of her fingers puckered, pawing over details in her memory.

A girl is missing.

A girl is murdered.

Blonde, beautiful Heather. As stunning as she was contrary. When was the last time Abbie had seen her? On the school run? When she'd given the girls a lift back from watching the remake of *The Texas Chainsaw Massacre* at the cinema? Abbie had been certain the girls were too young to watch it but Heather had confidently informed her that it was fine, that she knew a guy who worked at the UCI who would let her in. That was one of Heather's superpowers – the ability to disarm. Always smiling sweetly, doe eyes glistening. When they'd asked to see the film, Abbie felt the desperation coming off Pippa in waves, the silent, imploring stare that said: *Don't make me a pariah, Mum. Say yes.* So Abbie did what she always did, ignored the gnawing in her gut and said yes to make someone else happy. It was a skill she was learning to perfect.

Abbie collected the girls after dark, waiting in the car park. They both dove into the backseats, hoods of their jumpers pulled up over their heads. Heather was all giggles and excitement, chatting the entire way home about the plot of the film, labouring over the details of the more gruesome bits. Pippa was silent. It was only after Abbie had watched Heather walk through the gates to her house that she held her daughter's gaze in the rear-view mirror.

'Did you not enjoy the film, sweetheart?'

Pippa turned to look out her window at the glassy blackness of the night. 'No. It was too much.'

Abbie smiled smugly as she pulled away from the curb, thinking about how gentle her daughter was, how kind. Of course she hadn't enjoyed some macabre horror film. Abbie recalled being Pippa's age when she saw the original. Fresh-faced and sixteen. How she'd clung onto her date, Peter McCarthy, buried herself in the flannel fabric of her shirt, unable to look up at the screen. John didn't even exist to her then. Nursing was just a fragile dream she'd been harbouring since her early teens.

Abbie stayed in the bath until the water ran cold. Then, shivering, skin pink, she wrapped herself in a large towel and slipped into her pyjamas. She was still in the bathroom when she heard footsteps coming up the stairs.

'John?' She stepped onto the landing, cheeks flushed, the smell of Imperial Leather still clinging to her.

'I know, I know,' he said as he strode past her, steps heavy. 'I'm late again.' He continued towards the bedroom and closed the door behind him.

It was a signal he adopted many times. More subtle than a Do Not Disturb sign. And Abbie usually honoured a closed door. Be it to his office or their bedroom. Her husband spent his working life in a vice, always under pressure. The last thing she wanted was for him to feel the same way at home.

'A man's home should be his castle,' her mother used to tell her, 'and he should be king.'

But the questions Abbie had been navigating in her head all evening were too many in number to be ignored. They took on a power of their own, controlling her feet, propelling her forward. Even as a part of her wanted to resist, to be a dutiful wife, her curious self – the self which she spent so much effort suppressing – refused to be denied.

'John?'

He was already in his pyjamas when she walked in, drawing back the duvet, his book clutched under his arm. 'It's been a long day,' he sighed as he climbed into bed, pressing his back against his pillow and the headboard, opening up his book.

'For all of us but—'

'Abigail, I'm tired.'

'Then I'll make this quick.' Abbie strode to him and whipped the book out of his possession. John looked up at her, nostrils flaring. 'John, I need to know why you thought Heather was pushed.'

'Seriously?' With a deep-set scowl he lurched forward and snatched back his hardback. 'I don't have time for this.'

'Then make time,' Abbie demanded.

'Fine.' With a sigh he closed the book, ran his fingers across the bridge of his nose. 'But this is ridiculous, you must know that.'

'How is it?'

'Abigail, come on.' The way he rolled his eyes at her reminded Abbie of how he'd reprimanded young doctors and nurses who made a mistake in his theatre. Almost with a superior sneer. The other nurses thought him arrogant. And an arsehole. But not Abbie. If anything his disdain made him even more desirable. 'Any logical person could have deduced that Heather didn't drown.'

'Any . . . logical person.' She sucked in a breath, reminded herself that this wasn't about her, this was about seeking answers. Just because she was no longer working, no longer earning, didn't mean she wasn't *logical*. If anything, it was logic which had led her to this moment. Logic and fear.

'Heather was the picture of health. A happy, popular teenager.'

'From a broken home,' Abbie added coldly.

'The chances of her suddenly suffering a seizure, especially a completely incapacitating or life-threatening one, are similar to being struck by lightning. It makes more sense that there was an assailant. That she was pushed. The police have always been of the same train of thought, hence why they never left the school premises.'

'Because they're searching for someone?'

'Exactly.'

'But . . .' Abbie shook her head, the fragments of information she was being given failing to slot together and make a complete picture. 'If that's what you truly think, John, aren't you afraid for our daughter? That whoever hurt Heather may well hurt her too? Christ, she was with the girl just before she was killed.'

'Of course I'm afraid for her.' The anger left him so suddenly that it was disorientating. John got up from the bed, crossed the space between them and wrapped his arms around his wife. 'I'm terrified for her,' he whispered into her ear, holding her close. It was too much. His arms. His heart inches from her own. Their daughter sleeping just a few feet away, their daughter who so easily could have been taken from them. Abbie began to weep.

189

'Hey, come on now.' John rubbed her back, kissed her damp cheeks. 'We'll protect Pippa. Don't worry.'

'It could be anyone.' Abbie pulled at her husband's pyjamas, bunched the fabric into the fists her hands made as she clung to him. 'Anyone.'

'We'll keep her off school until after the funeral, give the police time to catch the bastard.'

'And if they don't?' Abbie sniffed, finally empty of tears.

John eased away from her but kept his hands on her shoulders. 'They just need some DNA evidence to link him to the crime, that's all.'

'Some . . .' She looked into her husband's eyes, searching for more answers.

'That teacher.' He squeezed her shoulders and then let go, returning to the bed and his book. 'I've heard they've as good as pinned it on him.'

'The . . .' Abbie too had heard the rumours. How could she not? It was all anyone talked about. 'The history teacher?'

'That's the one.'

'You don't think Heather was . . . involved with him? Do you?' She clung to her elbows, feeling cold now she was standing by herself.

'What? No.' John waved a dismissive hand at her. 'She was only sixteen for Christ's sake.'

'Yes, but . . .' Abbie stepped closer to the bed. 'Heather was . . . well, experienced for her age.'

'You shouldn't listen to idle gossip, Abigail.'

'I'm not, I'm listening to—'

'Heather was a decent girl. You got that?'

Anger flared within Abbie, wild and terrible. 'And what makes you so bloody sure what she was like, eh? How are you suddenly an expert on fucking *Heather Oxon*?' Her

190

pulse was a drumbeat in her ears. 'You've said yourself that she was wayward, spirited. *Trouble.*'

He looked at her so calmly, as though they weren't standing in the midst of a storm but on a beach somewhere, enjoying a distant sunset. 'I know she was no saint, but she was our daughter's friend, Abigail. Her best friend. So there had to be something redeemable about her, something good. Pippa wouldn't have hung around with her otherwise.'

'Maybe it was just habit that kept them together,' Abbie challenged. 'So used to be with one another they couldn't even imagine life apart.'

John failed to meet her heated stare, already withdrawing from the conversation.

'I'll keep Pippa home tomorrow,' she told him, her smooth demeanour now mirroring his.

'Good. It's for the best.'

'But she'll need to attend the funeral on Wednesday.' Abbie looked at him, watched as he turned the page in his book, failing to meet her gaze. 'As will you,' she added as a deliberate prompt.

'I'll see what I can do.'

'As you say, she was our daughter's *best friend*. We both need to be there.'

'Abigail, I'm done talking about this now.'

'Fine.' Abbie swept across the room, across the landing and downstairs to the kitchen and the bottle of wine waiting for her. Sometimes she wondered if she'd ever truly left the operating theatre – if John still looked on her as someone only there to assist him, to clean up the mess without question.

While Abbie drank her wine and the late night turned into the early morning, she drifted through the house and kept pausing beside the door to John's office, kept considering going in. But a creak from above or a bang of pipes within the walls always sent her scuttling away like a terrified mouse.

A girl is missing.

A girl is murdered.

Abbie kept drinking until her thoughts blurred into one intangible mass and she fell asleep curled up on the sofa, head resting in the crook of her arms. She dreamt of chainsaws and hammers and blood.

31

'We think you should stay home today,' came her mum's words just after seven in the morning as she cracked open the door, letting a sliver of light into the gloom. 'Just until things settle down a bit.'

Pippa rolled over and willed herself to fall back to sleep. She drew the duvet up over her head, squeezed her eyes shut but it did no good. She was awake. Not bothering to shower she pulled on an oversized Linkin Park hoodie and some jeans then dragged herself downstairs.

'Are you doing all right, sweetheart?' her mum asked as she slid a bowl of cornflakes drenched in milk across the island to her. 'Are you sleeping OK?'

'I'm sleeping fine,' Pippa mumbled as she plunged a silver spoon into her china bowl. She knew the lie was obvious. There were shadows beneath her eyes, a paleness to her skin which told of the hours she spent staring at nothing, willing her brain to release her from the purgatory it held her in.

'Well, I just want to make sure you're all right.' Her mum positioned herself on the stool across from her, fingers gathered around a slim mug of coffee.

'Are *you* sleeping OK?' Pippa cocked her head at her, noticing how her mum looked just as exhausted as she felt.

'I think we're all troubled by recent events,' she replied before taking a delicate sip from her mug.

'Why are the police still at school? Still asking us questions?'

'They're asking you questions?' Her mum peered at her over the rim of her mug, tired eyes narrowing.

'They're asking everyone questions,' Pippa told her, chewing on cornflakes which felt dry in her mouth, even covered in milk.

'What sort of questions?'

'You know.' Pippa swallowed. 'If Heather had any enemies. That sort of thing.'

'Did she?'

'What do you think?'

'She wasn't the most likeable girl, for certain.' Her mum drank again from her mug. 'But she didn't deserve what happened to her.'

Pippa pushed her bowl away, unable to finish its contents. 'What *did* happen to her?'

A prolonged sigh from across the island. 'I don't think anyone knows for sure.'

'The police know.'

'Well . . . yes,' her mum said, nodding as she weighed this up. 'The police know.'

'And they're all over the school,' Pippa noted bluntly. 'So do they think someone at the school killed her?'

'Pip, I—'

'What do you think they're looking for? Olivia and Hannah were saying they heard that the police might search our lockers, our houses.'

Her mum looked pained.

'Will they?' Pippa demanded, suddenly tearful.

'I don't. . .' Her mum offered her a pained smile. 'I don't know, sweetheart. Before, I'd have said of course not. But that was before people knew Heather had been . . .' To save herself from finishing the sentence she drank more coffee.

'What do you think they're looking for?' Pippa sniffed, dragged the sleeve of her jumper across the base of her nose, tried to calm herself.

'It's hard to say.' Her mum pursed her lips. 'But I suppose they're looking for who did it. Wherever that person may be.'

'And you think they'll find them?'

'Yes.' There was no hesitation from her mum. 'Waterbridge is a small place. There's not many places for someone to hide here.'

Pippa looked down at her neglected cornflakes, now wilting within what remained of the milk.

Her mum sprang up. 'Look, I'm popping out to Sainsbury's in a bit. Anything you want to cheer you up? Copy of *Empire* or something?'

'Yeah . . . sure.'

'You'll be all right? I can stay home if you want?' Her mum was beside her now, cradling Pippa's cheeks between her palms and peering down at her.

'I'll be fine.'

A kiss on the forehead. 'Keep the front door locked the entire time I'm gone. OK?'

'OK.'

'And I'll bring back doughnuts, the kind with sprinkles on that you like.'

'Thanks, Mum.' Pippa forced a smile even though her stomach clenched at the thought of something so sweet.

Certain that her mum was gone, that the driveway was clear of both parents' cars, Pippa stole out into the garden. In her Hunter wellingtons she stomped the full length of it, to the low fence at the far end where she huddled beneath the cover of a grand oak. The air was damp, the sky grey. Even though it was ten in the morning the day was so gloomy it still felt close to dawn.

Crouching down, Pippa smoothed away curled, damp leaves to reveal a patch of grass. Then she rounded the tree, found the old metal bin usually used for compost at its base and came back with its lid pressed to her chest like a shield. She placed it handle down on the ground where it shone like a silver moon. Straightening, Pippa pressed herself against the bark of the tree, glanced beyond the small fence. The hills that rolled away from her home were empty. Once she was sure she wasn't being watched, Pippa pulled a bundle of paper from the front pocket of her jumper. Paper that had once been folded over and over, shared and savoured.

Clutching all her old notes and letters, Pippa suddenly felt unbearably heavy. There was so much history in her hands. Atop the pile she saw the looping scrawl of Heather's overly elaborate handwriting:

If I tell you a secret, do you promise to keep it?

Pippa eyed the pile. Remembered unfurling little notes during quiet moments in class. Finding them in the bottom of her backpack, shoved there as a surprise when her back had been turned. But she held only half a history. Heather had the rest. The replies. Pippa considered this as she began to place the notes within the lid of the bin. It didn't matter if Heather's half was found. Because half a story was half a story. Besides, it was within Heather's words that all the secrets lay. Would she have even kept Pippa's responses? It wasn't like Heather to be sentimental. Pippa imagined her reading a letter then scrunching it up and tossing it into the bin. There would be no sentimental keepsake box. Would there?

With the notes in the lid, Pippa shoved a hand into the back pocket of her jeans and retrieved the purple plastic lighter that even her mum didn't know she had. A souvenir from a cider run to the Spar shop with Heather.

'You *need* one,' she'd insisted, shoving it in Pippa's pocket when the man at the till wasn't looking their way.

'No, I don't! And I'm not going to steal it.'

'He's hardly going to sell it to you.' Heather flicked her mascara-drenched stare towards the front of the shop. Beneath the strip lights her hair glowed like a halo. 'Just take it.'

'Heather—'

'One day, a fit guy is going to ask you for a light,' Heather said, coming close, lips glossy and pink, 'and you're going to be able to offer him one. And trust me, you'll be so fucking thankful that I made you do this.'

'I don't even smoke.'

'Because you're square,' Heather frowned, 'but I forgive you for that.'

The guy at the till looked their way and Heather flashed him her brightest smile, raised a hand and wiggled her fingers at him. He blushed and waved back.

'Heather—'

'Take it,' Heather said, pressing her hands against Pippa's shoulders. 'I won't tell you again.'

Always the General. Pippa always the soldier. She looked at the lighter now in the dim morning light, still full of clear lighter fluid which tilted as she moved it about. In the notes Heather was still alive, her voice reaching out from the time-softened pages.

Secrets.

Enemies.

The police were looking for it all.

Pippa flicked the top of the lighter. Nothing happened. She flicked again and again until finally a tiny golden flame poked out. Lowering herself to the ground she crouched against leaves and wet grass, held the flame to the corner of a note wedged at the base of her stack. It caught quickly. Hungrily.

The flame became a fire which curled the paper, darkened the edges and then turned words to smoke. And finally ash.

Head bowed, Pippa watched the notes burn, inhaled the smell of their incineration. And as the smoke cleared, she peered at what remained. Merely ashes. With a kick of the lid they were scattered to the ground, soon to be carried away by the wind. Gone. Pippa returned to the base of the oak, and crouched among its gnarled roots until her legs went numb and an icy rain set in, drenching everything within the garden.

Inside, cold and shivering, Pippa positioned herself by the fire having retrieved her phone from upstairs. Several new messages from Hannah:

You're off sick, booo! H x

OK so school are saying we all now need to travel in pairs at all times and we have a curfew of 7pm. Fuck! H x

This is all feeling real now. We have a killer on
the loose. Shit. Text me back so I know they
haven't got you too!
H x

Pippa was on the floor, knees drawn up to her chest as she
rested on the thick wool rug her mum had bought in the
Next sale the previous year. Hannah was right, everything
was feeling far too real. She tapped out a response for fear
of inciting further worry from her friend. The last thing
she needed was anyone coming over to check in on her.

Hey, I'm fine. Just a cold. See you tomorrow x

Tomorrow. Heather's funeral. A chance to say goodbye.
Even though she was beginning to dry out, the warmth of
the fire pressing against her, Pippa couldn't stop shivering.

32

The church was packed. Every pew was full, people wedged together so close that knees and elbows were touching. Those who hadn't arrived in time to grab a seat were standing at the back, a throng of them, positioned like they were attending a concert, not a funeral.

Abbie was midway up the aisle, beneath a stained-glass window depicting a white dove ascending towards a sunset. The glow from the glass spilled red across Abbie's lap. Pippa was beside her, wedged against the wall. She was in her regular school uniform save for the black ribbon holding her ponytail together. All the girls from Waterbridge Prep had adopted the same look. Dotted among the congregation, their presence was a painful reminder of how youthful the occupant of the coffin was.

'Are you sure you don't want to sit with your friends?' Abbie had asked when they walked in, instantly dropping her voice to a whisper.

'I'm fine,' Pippa had replied, leaning into her mum, 'I'd rather sit with you.'

So now they were side by side, Abbie clutching Pippa's hands which she kept balled in her lap, fingers cold.

Even as the vicar began to speak, the great wooden doors at the back of the church kept wheezing open and closed, like an old man struggling to catch his breath.

'We are here today to commemorate the life of Heather Louise Oxon,' he began, fighting to be heard over the noise of the door, the scuffle of feet, the sniffles of sorrow, 'who was taken from us far too soon.'

Abbie had clocked Michelle Oxon before she sat down, the back of her head at least. Golden hair drawn back into a bulldog clip. Back straight. She was in the first row, her ex-husband beside her, an inch of space between them.

'Heather was beloved by all who knew her,' the vicar continued.

Abbie focused on Pippa's hands, rubbed her thumb against her daughter's clenched knuckles. She wanted each stroke to convey that she was there. That it was all going to be all right. But the awful surrealness of it all was making her heavy, pressing her into the pew, trapping the air in her lungs. Heather was sixteen. A child.

'Are you all right?' Abbie leaned close to Pippa and forced out her hushed words. Her daughter shook her head. No. Of course she wasn't. How could she be?

Abbie just kept holding onto her hands, not knowing what else to do. She wished John was there to support her.

'You're in a blue tie,' Abbie had noticed with fury when her husband had entered the kitchen that morning.

'What?' John frowned and then looked down at the offending tie, smooth against his crisp white shirt. 'Oh, yes.' It was the colour of blue skies. Bright and cheerful.

'Today is Heather's funeral,' Abbie stated, hands working more briskly to butter the toast on her plate. 'Your tie needs to be black.'

'I can't make it.'

'You . . .' Abbie kept working the knife, stroke after speedy stroke against the toast. 'You *can't make it*? John, this is a funeral. For Pippa's friend. You're going.'

'It's a Wednesday and I have surgeries I can't get out of.'

'John—'

He raised a hand at her. 'I told you I'd try and make it. And I did, I tried.'

'Clearly not very hard.'

'I'm sorry, Abigail,' he said, his eyes crinkling at the corners as he watched her, 'but I know Pippa will be fine as long as she has you there.'

'People will think you don't care,' Abbie thundered at him.

'And I don't care what people think.' He adjusted his tie and then stalked across the kitchen in the direction of his office. The knife in Abbie's hand kept shifting back and forth. Back and forth.

Her husband reappeared moments later carrying his precious briefcase. 'I'll try not to be back too late.' He drew up beside his wife, paused to place a cold kiss on her cheek and then carried on. 'Hope it all goes well,' he added at the door, as though she were attending a PTA meeting, and then he was gone.

Knife hit china. 'Fuck.' Abbie glanced down, saw that the toast had been shredded to pieces upon the plate. All that remained were butter-coated scraps.

33

Pippa just wanted to go home. She didn't want to be in the church. On the pew. Listening to some geriatric vicar talk about someone he didn't even know.

'Heather was a keen student.'

No, Pippa thought. She was just good at cheating.

'She had many, many friends.'

No, again. She had those who admired her from afar. Anyone who got too close quickly turned from friend to enemy. There was a barbed cruelty to Heather. She was like a rose, so beautiful to look at from a safe distance, but once you touched her there were thorns. Thorns which pricked. Thorns which drew blood.

Pippa dared to raise her head a fraction, let her gaze travel along the pew ahead of her. She recognised the back of her mum's friend Ashley's head. Neat in a dark bob. Beside her the chestnut curtains of sons Tristan and Jasper. Tristan who'd received a blow job from Heather at a house party just three months ago. Afterwards she'd remarked to Pippa that he 'tasted like a hangover'. Pippa had no idea what that meant. She wondered if Tristan was thinking about that moment now, about how his dick had been in the softness of Heather's mouth, pink lips slick with him. Pippa shifted awkwardly against the hard wood of the pew. Her mind was taking her to places she didn't want to go. Every story she had about Heather was sour.

Ahead of Ashley and her sons were Olivia, her younger sisters and her parents. At a sleepover Olivia's youngest sister – Pippa couldn't remember her name – wet the bed and Heather had been so cruel about it. Taunting the girl. Laughing at her. Calling her 'Miss Pissy-pants'.

But Heather *could* be nice. With effort, Pippa freed her hands from her mum's vicelike grip so that she could push her fingers deep into the pockets of her blazer. There they settled around the plastic of her purple lighter. Given in Heather's own version of kindness. Because beneath it all, she had been looking out for Pippa, hadn't she?

Pippa blinked, felt her eyelashes grow heavy with tears.

'One day, one day you'll leave this shitty town,' Heather announced, a hiccup escaping from her lips. For a moment the metal groan of the swing was the only sound in the playground.

'What?' Pippa withdrew the bottle of cider from her mouth, certain she must have misheard her friend. Above them the sky was clear and speckled with stars. Stars which Heather now craned her beck to look at, leaning back in the swing, hands on the chains, golden hair sweeping across the tarmac beneath her.

'You'll leave,' Heather repeated, a slight slur to her words.

'You will too.' Pippa drank again from the bottle Heather had got from the Spar, ten swigs in and no longer caring if her parents smelt the booze on her when she wandered home.

'You'll go to some fancy-pants uni. Meet some fancy-pants guy and forget all about Shitbridge. All about me.'

'What? No.' Pippa drank again, feeling warm all over. 'You'll be at uni too. We all will.'

'Not me.' Heather shook her head, almost horizontal on the swing as she glided to and fro.

'Of course you will,' Pippa objected, almost choking on the apple-flavoured bubbles which fizzed down her throat. 'You cheat enough to have the best grades in our year.'

'Ha.'

Pippa watched a soft smile draw across Heather's pretty face, blue eyes sparkling from the cider and the starlight. 'But I won't leave.' The smile quickly faded.

'Course you will.'

'No, I'll die here.'

Pippa screwed the top back on the bottle, wedged it between her knees as she clung to the chains of her own swing and swivelled to look directly at her friend. 'That's ridiculous.'

'Live fast, die young,' Heather whispered to the stars in a sing-song voice.

'You're insane.'

'Maybe it's what I want,' Heather continued, chains creaking above her. 'Maybe I don't want to get old, to look tired, to have a baby and get fat. Maybe I want to be forever sixteen.'

'Nobody wants that.'

Heather sat up so suddenly the swing rattled in shock. Her eyes were wide, wild. 'Maybe I do, what's wrong with that?'

'You're drunk.' Pippa turned away from her, focused on swinging herself back and forth. 'We're both drunk. We should head home.'

'Promise me that when you do leave . . .' Heather was plateauing again, base of her spine pressed to the swing, legs extended, head swung back. 'That you'll always remember me.'

'Stop being so bloody maudlin. Cider always makes you like this.'

'Promise!'

Pippa ceased swinging her legs, felt the nauseating pull in her stomach as gravity began to claim her. 'Fine, OK, fuck. I promise. Now can we go home?'

Heather looked up at the heavens for a few moments longer. 'Yeah, OK. Now we can go home.'

Pippa didn't realise she was crying until her mum pressed a tissue into her hands. 'It's OK,' she whispered soothingly as Tristan glanced back to peer at her. He was paler than usual, with an outbreak of acne across his forehead. But he was still annoyingly handsome. Pippa glared at him, then pressed the tissue against her eyes.

'It's all right, sweetheart, it's all right.' Her mum drew in close and rubbed her back. At the front of the church the vicar was charting Heather's involvement in various school activities.

Badminton. Netball. Cross-country running. Chess.

Then he moved on to her brief love affair with ballet. Pippa tuned him out, focused on slowing her breath, calming her tide of tears.

'It's OK,' her mum whispered again. 'I'm here.'

'I want to go home,' Pippa muttered, lips sore. 'I just want to go home.'

34

The house was still, with the kind of calm that followed a storm. Abbie was in the kitchen, at the island, tips of her nails tapping against the pale china of the mug she was holding. Upstairs Pippa was sleeping. She'd wept all the drive home after the funeral the previous day. Cried herself to sleep that night. Whimpering and gasping, choking on her own grief. Abbie wished she had the words. But all she could say over and over, like a record with a stuck needle, was '*It's OK,*' and '*You'll be fine.*' Which was ridiculous, as her sixteen-year-old daughter had just lost one of her closest friends. She'd be neither of those things.

In the churchyard as people had stood shivering, heads bowed as they waited for the coffin to be lowered into the ground, there were whispers. And loaded looks. They moved back and forth among those who had gathered, like a macabre Mexican wave. Behind every stare was the same question: *Was it you?*

Because someone had killed Heather. Had followed her out along the path that day. Walked in the rain. Watched Pippa turn back. Chosen their moment. Then they'd pounced. And that person could well be at the fresh graveside with them, cheeks wet with rain instead of tears.

Or not. Maybe they were elsewhere.

Abbie had thought, then. About her husband. About his absence. It was completely reasonable that he was working. And yet . . .

Abbie didn't like the road her mind was taking her down. She knew her husband. He could be judgemental, yes. Unfeeling, certainly. But a murderer? It was out of the question. John Parks dedicated his life to saving lives, not taking them.

But there was something off about him of late. Abbie tried and failed to place it. He was quicker to temper, more exhausted when he came to bed.

'It's just work,' he'd insist whenever she asked what was wrong. 'You know how it is at the hospital.'

And she did. It was draining, emotional. Yet also invigorating, affirming.

'I wonder if she knows?' Carol had eased in close as they all commenced the cold walk back through the cemetery.

'Knows?' Abbie had one arm protectively wrapped around Pippa's shoulders. Her daughter watched her feet as she walked, cheeks red and sore from all her crying.

'I bet she does.' Carol laced an arm through Abbie's free one, but not before doing an exaggerated lean behind her, back towards the open grave, back towards the two figures who lingered beside it – Michelle, and her ex-husband.

'Knows what?'

'Who did it,' Carol said,' dropping her voice so low that Abbie had to strain to catch her words even though they were inches from one another. 'They say it's always someone you know.'

'They?' Abbie questioned dubiously.

'Someone you trust,' Carol continued. 'We're so busy telling the girls to avoid strangers, to move in pairs, to be home before dark, we're forgetting to tell them to search a little closer for the danger.'

'Carol.' Abbie tightened her grip on Pippa as she raised her eyebrows at her friend. 'I don't think Heather's funeral is perhaps the right place for this kind of talk.'

'They've yet to bring him in for questioning, you know.' Carol spoke with more urgency now.

'Who?'

'The history teacher,' Carol hissed. 'They'll be waiting on physical evidence but it's all been washed away by now. I've petitioned the school to fire him with immediate effect.'

'But he's surely innocent,' Abbie objected, 'at least until proven guilty.'

'Not when it comes to our girls,' Carol countered savagely. 'He's a potential risk to them and I won't have it. I've sent you the email to be signed. I suggest you do.'

Abbie inwardly groaned, uncomfortable with tying a noose around Mr Hall's neck, at least until they knew more. She was about to say as much when Carol swept over to someone else, probably to spread the word about her petition.

Abbie drained the last of her tea and listened. The house remained still, Pippa tucked up in bed, sleeping off the sorrow of the funeral. Abbie's nails continued to tap against her mug. She studied the distant shape of the door to John's office.

Click clack.

He called it his sanctuary. Dark walls lined his framed certifications. A vast bookshelf full of heavy medical journals and some carefully chosen biographies. Behind his desk there was a window which overlooked the garden, and it often bathed him in late afternoon light when he worked in there on weekends. And adjacent to the bookshelf was a print of Rembrandt's only seascape. The original was stolen in an infamous art heist in Boston. Abbie and John had visited the city on a holiday early on in their courtship. Together they'd browsed the museum and become intrigued by the story, the robbery. Whenever Abbie looked at the painting of men desperately clinging to a boat in a stormy sea, she found comfort as it was the only sign of her within John's stuffy study. A reminder of brighter days. Of greater love.

Click clack. Click clack.

A girl is missing.

A girl is murdered.

There is something off about her husband.

The thoughts ran in a loop in her mind. If there was a connection she felt loathe to find it. And yet . . .

Leaving her mug on the island she marched to the door, moving quickly, knowing that if her steps were sluggish she might yet turn back. John was out at work; there was next to no chance of him returning home so early in the day. But this didn't stop Abbie's heart rate from lifting from trot to canter as she pushed open the door to the study. The smell of dust and wax filled her nose. Carefully she entered, leaving the door ajar behind her.

The office was impeccably neat. Not surprising for a surgeon. All the books lined up neatly, the stack of papers on the desk completely straight. Abbie approached them, turning to glance at the framed picture of the seascape. A part of her wished she were still twenty-one and in awe of all the beauty around her, holding hands with a man ten years her senior who she didn't just love but adored.

But now she had Pippa. And John . . .

Abbie scanned the contents of the study, knowing that the slightest movement, the smallest thing left out of place, would be noticed. John was such a stickler for details, with a memory that was flint sharp.

Hardly daring to breathe, Abbie made for the stack of papers and carefully leafed through them. Print-outs of work-related emails. A timetable. An invitation to a conference. Another invitation. A photocopy from a journal with an article on fistulas. All very standard. Expected.

Next Abbie opened the top desk drawer. It groaned at her as it slid forward to reveal its contents. A small black book which she knew to contain the names of all the patients John had lost. And beside it a diary. Now *this* was unexpected. Abbie delicately lifted the slim Moleskin diary from the drawer. It was dated 2003. She frowned, turned it over in her hands, studying the exterior. She knew that John had a work diary. A huge tome of a thing he kept back at the hospital, full of surgery rotas. At home he had no need for such a thing; Abbie monitored all their social engagements.

Unless . . .

Abbie pulled it open, nervously firing a glance towards the gap in the doorway. She wondered if maybe her husband did need a diary to keep track of his golf dates with friends. Not that he'd had many lately; John was most definitely a fair-weather golfer. Instinctively Abbie leafed through to the current week. There was no writing on the weekly page. Only three black stars had been marked out, on the Wednesday, Friday and Saturday. Abbie looked at them, then flipped back to previous weeks. Previous months. Those same stars were speckled throughout the book like a strange constellation.

'What the?' Abbie looked at them, struggling to draw any meaning. She searched for significant dates.

Her birthday – no star.

Pippa's birthday – no star.

John's birthday – a star.

'What the hell are you up to, John?' Abbie wondered aloud as above a floorboard creaked. 'Shit.'

Pippa was awake. Abbie placed the diary back in the drawer, shoved it closed and hurried from the room. It was time to be a mother. Her investigation into John's strange diary would have to wait.

Peep-po,

I've stopped replying to Tristan. He's being a complete asshole and there's NO WAY I'm going to that party with him this weekend. We'll go to the park instead. I'll bring some vodka if I can get some.

And I can't stop thinking about Mr Hall. I loved the grey waistcoat and shirt he wore today. Made him look SO sophisticated. And did you notice how he laughed when I made that comment about Henry VIII? Like, proper laughed, eyes crinkling, the works. Because he gets me. Him and me, we've got this secret code. An understanding.

I know where he lives. I saw him in Sainsbury's Tuesday night when my mum dropped me off to grab a fresh pizza for tea. He'd walked in so I followed him. He's in a little terrace on Albert Street. Number . . . 35. Red door. Nice little place. We need to walk by it a couple of times this weekend, try and catch a glimpse of his wife. What do you think she's like? She must be pretty. Do you think she's blonde too? Or not, and maybe that's why he likes me, because I'm different to her?

If he and I had sex do you think he'd lose his job? Or only if we got found out? I really can't stop thinking about him. His eyes have this . . . energy. They like, fizzle. Don't you think? Or maybe that's just how they are when he looks at me and no one else can see it. I'm not sure.

But yeah, his house. This weekend. I'll wear my short shorts and do my make-up. Wear my hair up in a bun.

Love you,

H

xoxo

35

Friday morning and Pippa stirred within her bed, roughly pulled from a dream like a fish from the sea at the sound of her mum's voice.

'I said Hannah's on the phone for you.' The same words again, disturbing the murky darkness of the bedroom Pippa had enveloped herself in for the previous forty-eight hours.

'Urgh.' Pippa drew herself into the foetal position, pressing her chin against her knees.

'Want me to tell her to call back later?'

Yes.

'No.' Pippa knew that Hannah would just keep calling, refusing to be ignored.

Just as Heather would have.

'It's fine, I'm coming.' She left the warmth of her bed, grabbed a soft dressing gown from the back of her door and wrapped herself in it before following her mum downstairs. As she padded through the hallway, making for the lounge, she spotted the time marked in roman numerals on the antique clock her parents had found in a flea market in Boston, a story they used to love to tell. It was almost midday.

The sofa was her destination. En route she grabbed the cordless phone from its cradle on a side table and dropped against the plumpest cushion, pulling her legs up underneath her. She pressed the green button and then croaked out, 'Hello?' Immediately she wished she'd taken the time to drink something before answering. Her throat felt like it had been coated with stale fur during the night which she now struggled not to choke on.

'Pippa, hey.' It was reassuring to hear Hannah so close. But the brightness in her voice was dimmed from its usual wattage.

Pippa wondered how her friend had spent the days since the funeral. Waterbridge Preparatory had remained closed so that 'students and staff can mourn their loss'. That was the official line which went out in emails and letters. But the pain held by those within the red-brick walls had seeped into the community. Pippa heard her parents discussing how still everywhere was. How quiet. Shock and fear were keeping people indoors.

'Hey.' She adjusted the pillow behind her back, could tell it had been furiously plumped by her mum earlier that day.

'How are you holding up?'

A click on the line as Pippa's mum hung up the phone in the kitchen.

'OK . . . I guess.' It was hard to know how to answer Hannah's question.

'Well I feel like shit,' Hannah told her. 'I keep wondering about what happened to her, you know, before she went in the river.'

'Mmm.' Pippa began to pull on a loose thread in her dressing gown, tugging on it, extending it. 'Same.'

'Like did someone *stab* her, hit her? What?'

Pippa imagined Hannah replaying her VHS of *Scream*, eyes widening as she considered what horrific fate might have befallen their friend in her final moments.

'I don't know.'

'Well, we *deserve* to know,' Hannah insisted. 'At least so we can know what we're up against, how to protect ourselves.'

'I suppose.'

'Was it a French thing? You know, like a crime of passion? Or something more calculated? Something that could happen again?'

'Who knows?'

'Are we in danger?' Hannah demanded, sounding almost panicked. 'I mean, is it safe for us to be out in Waterbridge? How can it be?'

'Do you miss her?' Pippa interjected. She heard the intake of breath on the other end. This wasn't safe territory. Speculating over how Heather left this mortal coil was exciting in a sadistic way, like obsessing over a celebrity death. But feelings . . . those were different. Those cut deeper, left a wider mark.

'Miss her?'

'I know she was . . .' Pippa yanked on her thread and it snapped.

'A bitch?' Hannah finished for her.

'Yeah, sometimes she was a bitch.'

'Heather could be really bloody cruel. Do you know she used to call me a dyke behind my back? Just because I don't have a boyfriend.'

'Yeah,' Pippa admitted, face heating with shame, 'I knew. But that was Heather. She said shit about everybody.'

'You heard what she was saying about your parents?'

At this Pippa froze, a breath caught in her throat.

'She was telling everyone how they had a sham marriage,' Hannah continued. 'Which is complete bullshit.'

'Complete bullshit,' Pippa muttered, eyes growing heavy with tears. She'd thought Heather's remarks about her family had been for her ears only, that she wouldn't stoop low enough to spread her incorrect speculation around the school. Pippa's chin began to quiver. She should have known better. This was Heather after all. And with Heather no one was safe. Had the police caught wind of those rumours? But then the amount of lies Heather told in the name of gossip were so vast, enough to form a gale, it would be difficult to decide what mattered and what didn't. And yet still Pippa felt her stomach swirl uneasily.

'But yeah, I do miss her,' Hannah announced breathily.

'Mmm.' Pippa coughed, blinking back tears. 'Me too.' Though she was growing less and less certain of that. Her feelings towards Heather were like the tide, ebbing and flowing in volume.

'As awful as she was, she was our friend.' Hannah was starting to sound like the eulogising vicar from a few days earlier.

'Uh-huh.'

'But we'll know the full truth soon enough.'

'Meaning?' Pippa leaned forward, head low, feet now resting on the carpeted floor, spread apart. The brace position.

'I overheard my mum talking to Ashley last night. The police are going to reveal what exactly happened to Heather before she went into the water. I think they're hoping it might help provide a lead to the killer or something.'

'When?'

'Soon,' Hannah confirmed vaguely. 'But I'm not sure I want to know. Not really.'

'You're not?'

'Think about it . . .' For a moment both girls were silent. 'If she *suffered*,' Hannah continued quietly, 'like, really suffered. Doesn't that make it all worse?'

'I mean, she's gone either way.'

Hannah snorted. 'Christ, that's cold. You sound just like her.'

The comment landed like a punch in Pippa's gut. Was she like Heather? Somehow slipping into the void her death had created? She blinked, cleared her throat, steadied herself.

'Sorry.'

'Don't be,' Hannah said gently, 'that was one of the things I liked about Heather. How direct she was. How she refused to take any bullshit.'

'Yeah,' Pippa replied honestly, 'me too.'

After Pippa ended the call she doubled back to the kitchen, found a fresh bacon sandwich and cup of tea waiting for her on the island. But she couldn't eat the sandwich, could barely sip down the sweet tea. She kept thinking about what Hannah had said. How soon everyone would know what happened to Heather in her final moments, how she really died.

36

Saturday mornings just after eight were always blissfully quiet at Abbie's local Sainsbury's. Most people were still sleeping off the night before, enjoying their first lie-in of the weekend. But Abbie was always up and dressed by seven no matter what the day, her internal body clock hardwired to her routine, unable to break it. And so she adopted the weekly habit of visiting in the morning to do the big food shop. She'd push her trolley along almost empty aisles, revelling in the peacefulness, savouring the solitude. There was no risk of bumping into anyone, of having to make small talk beside the cereals. It was about the task at hand and nothing more. And Abbie craved efficiency. In her nursing days, she strived for the most well-run ward, took joy in a surgery completed under its allotted time. Now she had to settle for a swift supermarket run.

The wheels of her trolley squeaked as she rounded the corner of the dairy aisle. She needed both green and red milk, because John refused to drink skimmed, even though it was Abbie and Pippa's preference. So she stacked the large plastic containers in the end space of the trolley, beside a litre of Coke and a bottle of white wine. She was almost at the yoghurts, about to reach for a multi-pack of Muller Fruit Corners when she felt eyes on her. Frowning she looked down the aisle ahead, immediately regretting it.

Michelle Oxon was clutching a basket which contained two bottles of wine and a French stick. And she was staring.

Abbie abandoned her yoghurts and turned her trolley around, wheels shrieking with disobedience.

But she wasn't quick enough to get away. 'Abigail.' Michelle was soon by her shoulder, face thunderous. 'I thought I'd find you here.'

'I'm just here to shop, Michelle, so if you'll let me—'

'I just need to talk.' Michelle's hand grabbed her shoulder, a gesture meant to anchor her in place. Abbie gritted her teeth.

'Like I said, I'm just here to shop. I don't think this is the place to discuss anything or—'

'The police told me how Heather died.' The fingers against Abbie's shoulder felt bony and sharp. She glanced the length of the aisle, wishing the supermarket were bustling, that other shoppers were careening towards them, preventing them from lingering.

'I know what happened to her before she went into the river,' Michelle continued, blinking rapidly. Even without make-up, and lacking sleep, she had a glow, a beauty which just couldn't be turned off. In contrast Abbie had on a full face – mascara, concealer, foundation, lipstick, eyeshadow. All carefully applied at her vanity that morning. Even though she didn't expect to see anyone. But *just in case*, she had to look her best. And now, facing Michelle Oxon, she was grateful for those fifteen minutes she'd spent applying her products.

'What happened to her?' Abbie couldn't contain her curiosity. It slipped out of its own bidding.

'Ask Pippa.' Michelle started darkly.

Abbie shook off Michelle's hand, eased several inches away from her. 'Don't bring my daughter into this,' she threatened, fingers twisting around the handle of her trolley like pythons, tightening their grip.

'She knows what happened.' Michelle positioned herself at the end of the trolley, preventing Abbie from escaping.

'No,' Abbie replied sharply, 'she doesn't. She exchanged words with Heather, then she returned to the run. You know all this already.'

'She *knows*.' Michelle tightened her hand against the trolley. Her golden hair was swept back in a tight bun, revealing razor-sharp cheekbones.

Abbie scanned the food littered between them. A box of cornflakes, some dried pasta, several tins of spaghetti sauce, a tub of vanilla ice cream. She wondered which item she could hurl at Michelle's face. A cucumber perhaps? A loaf of bread wouldn't do. Too soft.

'The police are going to question her again.' Michelle shoved the end of the trolley slightly, forcing the wheels to edge closer to Abbie, the handle to press into her chest. 'They think she's lying too.'

'Let them ask all they want.' Abbie felt her chest tightening, palms growing slick against the trolley. She was no longer aware of the hum of the strip light above or the pop music gently playing in the background. All she saw was Michelle Oxon. Michelle in her blue mac, fresh-faced and vengeful. 'My daughter had nothing to do with how yours died.' She shoved the trolley. Hard. It surged forward, slamming into Michelle who staggered back, cheeks flushing red.

For a moment Michelle looked like she was about to either scream or cry. Abbie glanced around, fearful she'd perhaps gone too far, pushed a woman already on the edge over into the abyss. Lips puckered, cheeks burning, Michelle glared at Abbie. Then one hand lifted, a long finger pointing towards Abbie, shaking.

'She knows who killed my Heather,' she declared as a single tear marked a path down her porcelain cheek. 'And she's protecting them.'

'That's not true.'

'They're going to find out who killed her, who took her from me. And then Pippa is going to pay for her silence.'

Abbie bristled. She knew a threat when she heard one. 'Maybe if you'd kept a closer eye on your daughter, on who she associated with, on what she got up to, she'd still be here now.' Her voice rose as she spoke.

Michelle didn't move except to swipe the tear from her cheek. 'Are you calling me a bad mother?' she asked icily.

'I'm calling you a terrible mother,' Abbie confirmed, feeling like her entire body was on fire. 'Everyone thinks it. And everyone knows what kind of girl Heather was.'

Michelle's eyes narrowed. She studied Abbie for a moment and then shifted to the far side of the aisle, granting her space to move on. 'You think you have this perfect life,' she told her as Abbie squared her shoulders, raised her chin and pushed her trolley. 'But you live in a house of cards, Abigail. And I for one can't wait until it all comes crashing down around you. Which it will, very soon. Trust me.'

Abbie should have kept walking. She should have followed the dairy aisle to the end, to the fresh bread and doughnuts on the back wall. But instead she released her trolley and marched right up to Michelle, so close that the other woman could feel her breath against her cheeks. Abbie was taller, leaner. And if it came to it, she knew she was stronger, too. Michelle was all bones, built too slim, too slender.

'Intimidate me and my family again,' Abbie told her, fighting to remain calm, 'and you'll regret it.'

'Is that a threat?' Michelle's blue gaze bore into Abbie's.

'No,' Abbie said softly as she withdrew back to her trolley. 'It's a promise.'

Back in her car Abbie couldn't stop shaking. The trolley that still held her shopping was sat in the empty space beside her as she couldn't yet face loading the boot. It had been a battle just to reach the checkout and help bag everything up. Half of her list she'd failed to even get. But she needed to get out of there, needed to breathe fresh air. And it was only as she pressed her forehead against the wheel, waited for her lungs to stop working like frantic accordions, that she considered Michelle's initial comment.

I thought I'd find you here.

Was Michelle watching her? Stalking her? Did Abbie truly need to fear for her family? The thoughts plagued her the entire drive home. It was only as she pulled into the drive that Abbie realised that she'd left without her shopping, left with it all still in the car park neatly bagged in the trolley and paid for. She permitted herself to cry for five whole minutes before she smoothed her cheeks, dragged her fingers through her hair and entered the house.

37

Have you heard? H xx

They know how Heather died! xx

Can you even believe it? I can't! It's mad! How did it even get in her?! Xxx

Why aren't you answering your texts? You'd better be in school today! Xxx

Hannah's bombardment of text messages began at 8 a.m. on Monday morning. Each time Pippa heard her phone buzz against her vanity table her stomach lurched. Four messages in ten minutes. And it was nearly time to leave for school. She glanced at herself in the full-length mirror wedged in the corner by her wardrobe. Her blazer was starched to perfection, skirt stopping at the regulation length of just below her knees. With her dark hair scraped back in a high ponytail she looked paler than usual, shadows lingering like craters in her cheeks, shadows which she didn't recall having seen before.

'Pip, we need to go,' her mum called up the stairs.

Pippa looked at herself. At her tired, dark eyes. The mystery was no more. Everyone knew how Heather had died. What had occurred beside the riverbank in her final moments. And it was awful.

'Pip!' Her mum was now in the doorway, dusting hair out of her eyes, already in her Burberry Mac, ready to leave. 'Sweetheart, I've been calling you. We're going to be late.'

'Hannah says everyone knows how Heather died,' Pippa whispered, feeling oddly detached from her words, her body, as though this were all now happening within a dream.

She heard the awkward grumble that caught in her mum's throat. 'It . . . She . . . Yes. I heard from Carol first thing. The police have released the results from the autopsy.'

Pippa bowed her head, studied the fabric of her grey tights with intense curiosity.

'Do you want to stay home today?'

Yes.

'No,' Pippa managed, sniffing hard. 'I should be around friends, I suppose.'

'If that's what you want.'

'Nuts.' Pippa blinked, raised her head so quickly to stare at her mum she made herself dizzy.

'Nuts,' her mum repeated. 'She had some out by the river, like a snack or something, didn't realise what was in it and had an anaphylactic reaction.'

Pippa was silent.

'There was no way you could have known.' Her mum approached her, held her close. 'When you left her, you thought she was safe. That she was OK.'

'So do they still think someone murdered her?' Pippa asked, words muffled against the Chanel-scented fabric of her mum's coat.

'I don't know how they can.' Her mum eased away, cupping Pippa's cheeks between her warm hands. 'From where I'm standing it all points to being a very tragic accident.'

226

Pippa scratched at her lower arms, nails digging into the stiff fabric of her blazer, trying to get some traction against her skin. The officers she'd spoken to during her second interview were across from her. Just as stony-faced.

'As we mentioned last time, I'm Inspector Thomas and this is Inspector Marlin. Given this latest evidence, we have some additional questions about Heather.'

Pippa nodded. Wished she hadn't been pulled out of class, was still back at her desk, hiding in text books. Everyone had whispered as she left the room. Pippa hadn't dared to glance back at them.

'Were you aware that Heather had a severe nut allergy?' Marlin asked.

'I am. I mean . . . I was.' Pippa felt confused as to which tense she should be adopting.

'Were other people aware?' Thomas asked, pen poised in her left hand.

'Well, everyone knew,' Pippa confirmed. Like everything with Heather, if it had the potential for drama it was always exaggerated.

At birthday parties when the cake came out, she'd exclaim, 'Keep it away from me, it could be lethal to me,' running from the birthday girl and candles. Anxious parents would go to great lengths to keep their entire party a completely nut-free zone. And the school was just as cautious, preventing snacks such as Snickers bars and bags of peanuts being sold in the canteen. Heather *loved* it.

But her revelry in her allergy always surprised Pippa. Like a Greek god revealing their Achilles heel, she wondered why Heather gave the information so freely, so gladly. Perhaps she was just that delusional.

'And her EpiPen,' Marlin asked. 'Do you know where she kept that?'

'I assume in her bag,' Pippa ceased scratching to look up at him, 'since it was supposed to be on her person at all times. And on the cross-country run we are permitted to wear our sports backpacks.'

'We recovered Heather's backpack several days ago,' Thomas stated, beginning to make notes. 'It is currently being tested.'

'Where was it?'

Thomas ceased writing.

'Further down the river than where the body was located,' Marlin stated. 'Since it was lighter, it was able to go farther. We're lucky to have found it at all.'

'No EpiPen though.' Thomas tipped her head at Pippa.

'Maybe it fell out,' Pippa suggested, trying to be helpful, knowing full well that wasn't the case. Heather never, ever took her EpiPen out with her. Not to the cinema, not on shopping trips, not on cross-country runs.

'Ugly thing,' she'd explain to whoever asked, 'so bloody cumbersome. If I take that I can't have a nice little shoulder bag. I have to have some big, bulky thing. And like I explained to my mum, I'm sixteen, not some dumb baby who might actually eat a nut.'

Usually her EpiPen was buried at the bottom of her school bag under a pile of overdue library books. Pippa wondered if it was there now. If the police had thought to check. She looked between the inspectors, tried to read their hard faces. Then she realised – of course they'd found it. It was why they were here with yet more questions – they still suspected foul play.

'Sometimes she forgot to take it with her.' Her words ran together, delivered too quickly. It was almost a betrayal, the lingering fibres of loyalty drawing tight against Pippa's mouth, trying to seal it shut. To admit that Heather failed to take her essential medication with her made her seem reckless, foolish. Not worth saving. And still Pippa kept playing her part, as though she didn't know any other role, kept doing her best to shine the best light on her friend, even in death.

'OK.' Thomas nodded, checked her notes. 'Did you see the contents of Heather's sports backpack at all?'

'No,' Pippa said, shaking her head. 'But we all have the, um, regulation sports bottles, so I guess that would have been in it.'

And lip gloss.

And a mobile phone.

But if the backpack had turned up then those had too. Though the phone would surely be no longer functional after its prolonged swim in the Severn.

'What do you have in the bottles?' Thomas raised her pen to tap it against her chin.

Pippa swallowed.

'I mean . . . water, usually.'

'Usually?' the woman queried sharply.

Sometimes vodka.

Or gin.

Heather loved to lace her drink with any clear liquor she could find. She'd sip on it innocently as she ran a cross-country race or attended a netball game, eyes crinkling with menace.

'We're allowed to have squash in them.'

'Squash?' Marlin's nostrils grew wide with disapproval.

'Like blackcurrant or orange,' Pippa explained.

'Did anyone have access to Heather's water bottle that day?' Thomas was writing again, her gaze flitting between her notebook and Pippa.

229

'Access to . . .' Pippa frowned, tapped her fingers against her knees. 'I mean, anyone on the bus could have had access to it.'

'So, a friend?' Thomas raised her eyebrows.

'I don't . . . I guess.' Pippa shifted awkwardly. 'Did you . . . find her water bottle?'

Her mind raced along with her pulse, wondering how long it would take fingerprints or peanut oil residue to leave a plastic surface? Would the river wash it all away? The officers shared a look before Thomas spoke.

'No, we have not. We're still searching for both the bottle and Heather's sports bag.' Pippa nodded tensely.

'And are you quite certain you didn't see anyone else before you ran back to join the others? That Heather was completely alone?' Marlin stared at her, pale eyes expectant.

Pippa drew in a breath, remembering her departure. Trainers sinking into mud, feet almost slipping out from under her. It had been raining so hard that day. And she was desperate to get back to the others.

I suppose we do need to kill a bit of time.

Those had been some of the last words Heather had said to her.

Pippa hugged her arms against her chest, a tear slowly tracing a line down her cheek before falling and dying upon her tie, which was tight against the nape of her neck.

'I'm quite certain,' Pippa told the inspectors, 'that the last time I saw Heather she was alone. Completely alone.'

They nodded in unison.

'Then we have no further questions for you,' Thomas announced flatly.

38

Since the news broke the day before, it was all anyone seemed capable of talking about. From the reports on the radio to the messages in her phone, Abbie was being bombarded by it.

Allergic reaction.

Nuts.

Innocent mistake or foul play?

Waterbridge was once again thrust into a panicked frenzy over Heather Oxon. And what Abbie wanted more than anything was to ask her husband about it, to study his expression as he answered her.

On Monday night she lay in bed, awaiting his return, staring at the ceiling until her body went numb and she was unable to fight against the sleep which claimed her. On the drive to school the following morning, Pippa fired questions at her with the rapidity of a machine gun:

'What does it mean?'

'How can they know it was an allergic reaction?'

'Can they figure out what she ate?'

'She must have done it to herself, right?'

Abbie tried to muster up the right response but failed every time. *I don't know* just felt so inadequate. But there was so much she didn't know. Like how Heather came to ingest nuts. What that truly meant. Where her husband had spent the previous night. She wanted to believe he'd slept in one of the stiff cot beds in the On Call room but her gut clenched in rejection of the idea.

'Did she suffer?' This was the question Pippa ended on as Abbie pulled up against the curb, the gates of the school in the distance. She tapped her fingers against the steering wheel.

The nurse in her wanted to give the logical, honest answer.

Yes, she would have suffered. In her final moments, her body was fighting against an internal assailant. There would have been vomit, an outbreak of hives, and fatally, her throat would have swollen to such an extent it would seal off her airwaves, strangling her. Abbie had witnessed severe allergic reactions first-hand. But usually she was able to administer life-saving adrenaline in time.

The mother in her wanted to shield her daughter from the horror of Heather's death.

'It would have been quick,' she stated, glancing in her rear-view mirror at the cars parking behind her, considering how busy the traffic was, how long it would take her to reach the hospital.

'OK.' With a pained expression, Pippa ducked out the car.

Abbie watched her daughter walk away, hating how slumped her shoulders were. But Pippa could hardly hold her head up high; she was weighed down by grief, they all were.

As Abbie waited for the road to clear enough to pull away, she considered the agony of Heather's last moments. How she'd have gasped for air, clawed at the space around her, at her own throat. And whilst it would have taken minutes for the nuts to work their lethal magic, to Heather it must have felt like an eternity.

Tired of waiting, Abbie pulled out in front of a black BMW causing the driver to slam hard on their horn. She didn't care. She had somewhere to be, and precious little time to waste.

The hospital was always busy during the day. A mixture of outpatient appointments, visiting hours, scheduled and emergency procedures kept the place packed. After finally claiming a parking space, Abbie hurried towards the main entrance, handbag tucked up tight beneath her arm, hair blowing in the wind.

Her high heels clicked along the linoleum corridors. In her past life she'd raced down them in worn-out trainers. Now she strutted, her echo bouncing off the walls. It was Tuesday morning, which meant John should be in his office, preparing to attend some outpatient appointments. Abbie checked the time on her Rolex: 9.05 a.m. She was cutting it close. She rounded a corner, almost collided with an orderly pushing an old man in a hospital bed who was so still he appeared to have already passed, his head lolling to the side of his pillow, eyes closed. Just two more wards and then she reached it. The Gastroenterology department. Abbie pushed open the double doors and strode in. Several patients were already gathered in the waiting area, all various shades of grey. They glanced up when she entered but Abbie didn't even offer them a sideways look. She made straight for the reception desk, manned by a plump blonde with a name badge that read 'Linda'. When Abbie had worked for the department she knew every nurse, every receptionist, ever doctor. Now most of them were strangers to her.

'I'm here to see Mr Parks,' she told Linda. Linda who tapped angrily at the keyboard in front of her and smelt like cheap coffee. 'Do you have an appointment?'

'No. I'm his wife.'

'Oh?' Linda's face was almost perfectly round, like the rest of her body. Her thin blonde hair struggled to reach across her scalp. 'Well . . .' The woman began to turn a shade of beetroot. 'I'm afraid he's not in.'

'Not in?'

'He's on leave today.'

Abbie felt as though she were at the point on a rollercoaster right before the big fall, when you're tipped, able to look down and see what fate awaits you. Stomach coming up to meet her throat, she forced a smile at Linda. 'Of course,' she said briskly, 'silly me. I'm all over the place at the moment.'

'We all are,' Linda nodded, treble chins melting into one another. 'Such terrible, tragic news. I think the whole of Waterbridge has felt it.'

Abbie didn't answer. She turned on her heel and marched back along the corridor, steps echoing as she went.

John hardly ever had leave. And when he did, it was for family holidays or golf tournaments. Neither of which were happening on a cold Tuesday in late November. The part of Abbie which had fallen so hard for him all those years ago wanted to believe he was off in a shopping centre somewhere, carefully selecting her Christmas gifts. Eyeing up diamonds and designer handbags. There was a time when John lavished her with expensive treats.

'Diamonds for my diamond,' he'd say.

But Abbie was older now, too cynical to daydream. On her journey back to the car she considered where her husband might be. And her internal compass kept pulling in the same direction.

It took twenty minutes to reach the street Michelle Oxon lived on. The same amount of time it would have taken

Abbie to drive to her own home. And for every one of those minutes she willed herself to be wrong. Mistaken. Paranoid. But as she rounded the corner, felt the shadows cast from ancient oak trees sweep over her, she slowed to a crawl and looked up ahead.

Mercedes. Black. With a private licence plate, black on yellow like a wasp. Parked in plain fucking sight. Like he was goading her. Mocking her. Like he didn't even care if she saw it there.

J PARK 40

A gift for John's fortieth. From Abbie. She pulled her car to the side of the road, turned off the engine.

So he wasn't at the hospital, at work. He was at Michelle Oxon's home. *With* Michelle Oxon.

Abbie began to pant, her breathing too shallow, too rapid. Details from the previous months clicked through her brain like the pages of a flip book. Alone they were just images, but played out together they made a neat little film for her.

John working late.

John always championing Michelle.

The diary with the marked stars.

John refusing to see the worst in Heather.

John failing to attend the funeral.

It all pointed to the awful, inevitable truth – he was sleeping with Michelle.

Abbie ceased panting to howl. Dropping her head against the steering wheel, causing the horn to blare dully. Shoulders shaking, she thought of what Michelle had said in Sainsbury's.

I knew you'd be here.

So John had talked about her. Betrayed her. And he'd done this after committing the ultimate betrayal. And Michelle's questions about Pippa, her insistence that she knew more – so he'd betrayed her too.

Slowly Abbie raised her head, didn't lift a hand to wipe away the mascara-streaked tears falling darkly down her cheeks. She peered through the windscreen at the distant shape of her husband's car, wondering if her hatred was powerful enough to make it combust. She wanted to see flames, fire, destruction. But the street remained calm, bathed in gentle autumnal sunlight. The only sound in the car was the hollow wheeze of Abbie's breath.

She had been a *good* wife. No, a *great* wife. John had been a king in his castle. But still that wasn't enough. Abbie looked at his licence plate until the letters and numbers began to blur together.

Was he fucking Michelle at that very moment? Did he push her onto all fours, demand she arch her back and stay quiet like he did with his wife? Abbie ground her teeth together.

When John wanted to fuck, they fucked.

When he wanted roast lamb for tea, she cooked.

She'd given him a daughter. A life. *Her* life.

A girl is missing.

A girl is murdered.

When Abbie pulled away from the curb, body drenched in sweat, she began formulating a plan. She didn't know how, or when, but she was going to make him pay for wronging her. She'd take everything from him, just like he'd taken everything from her.

39

Her mum had been quiet both to and from school. Which wasn't like her. Pippa's mum always talked – about the weather, the girls at school, what was on the radio. It was one of the things Pippa liked most about their daily car journeys together, the free flow of conversation. But today had been different. The clouds in the sky were thick and grey when Pippa left for school. She tried to fill in all the empty spaces as they drove. Needed to. The silence was too much. In the silence she could hear her own thoughts.

But it was like asking questions in a letter, forever one-sided.

It was at dinner that evening when Pippa finally attempted to chip through the wall her mum had suddenly put up around herself. The table was set, as always, for three. Her dad's seat empty but his plate and cutlery laid out anyway, like a shrine.

'Mum.' Pippa gripped her knife and fork as she tried to savagely cut her way through an overdone pork chop. 'Is everything all right?'

Across the table her mum cradled her chin in the heel of her hand, gazed out towards the garden, which had slipped over from dusk to darkness whilst the meat roasting in the oven had burnt.

'Mum?'

With a start her mum dropped her hand, looked across at her. Her dark eyes didn't sparkle with interest in the way they usually did. They seemed waxy, vacant.

'I said, is everything all right?' Pippa asked, knife finally connecting with china as she successfully broke off a chunk of her chop.

'It's . . .' Her mum looked down at her plate as though she were surprised to find it there, laden with mashed potato, meat, gravy and broccoli florets. 'I'm fine, sweet-heart. Just a lot on my mind.'

Pippa placed a forkful of meat, mash and gravy into her mouth and commenced chewing, knowing how her mum felt.

'How was school today?'

The meat was impossibly tough. Pippa worked it until her jaw began to ache, frowning at her mum. They usually had the discussion about her day when they drove home, freeing up the rest of the day to talk about anything else. There was a new series of *Friends* coming up; she'd heard Hannah talking about it during IT that afternoon. Rumours suggested it might be the final season. And Pippa was keen to watch it with her mum. Keen to talk, keen to keep the voices in her head muted.

'Did you have a good day?'

It was too much. The pork refused to submit. Pippa leaned forward and spat out the contents of her mouth into the centre of her plate. An act which would usually illicit banishment from the table. But her mum's expression was distant, mouth pulled in a tight line.

It's what Heather said.

The voices found a slice of silence and slid into it. Loud and demanding. Pippa winced, scooping a forkful of mash into her mouth, swallowing hard.

Heather said there were troubles at home.

'Is it to do with Dad?' Pippa asked, daring to position her elbows on the table as she gave her mum a hard stare.

'Your dad?' The waxy brown eyes glanced over to the empty space, the plate neatly waiting. 'He's working late.'

'He's always working late.' Pippa loudly placed down her cutlery. 'Is that what's going on with you two?'

Now a light returned to her mum's eyes, burning and brilliant. But also pained. She pinned Pippa with the intensity of her gaze, her entire face twisting, cheeks flooding red. 'Pippa . . .'

Pippa didn't dare to breathe. To move. Her mum blinked, clasped her hands against the solid oak of the table, held onto it tightly. 'Your dad and I are working through some issues. But his working late . . .' She looked down at her lap, cleared her throat, then stared anew at her daughter. 'I've never had a problem with his workload. Your dad saves lives. I respect that, I always have.'

'Then what's wrong?' Pippa peered at her dad's place at the table. When he was there everything in the house felt tighter, more constricted; especially her. His piercing gaze seemed to find every fault. He wanted the world to be perfect, in order.

'He can't switch off his surgeon's brain,' her mum had explained back when Pippa was seven and it was all too much to bear. 'He needs the house to be neat and tidy, or else he feels like he's losing control.'

The tea towel straight against the oven handle.

Toilet paper stacked in a single, seamless pile.

Duvet pulled tight against the bed, no creases.

Cushions always plumped on the sofa, always set at just the right angle, evenly spaced from one another.

Pippa knew the way the house was supposed to be presented, how *she* was supposed to be presented. Uniform – ironed. Hair – clean and pulled back. No make-up. No earrings. It was as though her dad had swallowed the school's handbook on proper etiquette.

'It's nothing for you to worry about,' her mum stated as a tremor appeared in her lower lip.

'But I am worried,' Pippa announced desperately, pushing back her chair and moving round the table to kneel at her mum's side. 'You're not yourself. And we tell each other everything, right?'

'That's the problem.' Her mum glanced down at her, tremor easing, mouth pulling into a sad smile. Releasing a hand from the edge of the table she stroked Pippa's forehead.

'What do you mean?'

'Your dad, he . . .' She kept looking at Pippa as she frowned deeply, a crease appearing in her layer of foundation. 'He kept something from me,' she concluded vaguely. 'Something he should have told me. And now . . .' She shook her head.

Pippa usually hated vague answers. Loathed them. She dealt in certainties and absolutes. A trait her parents with their dual medical histories had taught her. But her mum's words began to sway and dance in her mind, moving in a loop over and over.

Something he should have told me.

'We don't keep secrets, do we, Mum?' she asked, voice suddenly small.

'No, sweetheart.' Her mum's smile reached her eyes. 'We don't. We tell each other everything.'

'Then there's something I need you to do for me.' Pippa placed her head in her mum's lap.

'What's that?' Her mum's fingers swept across her head, back and forth, gentle and loving.

'Tomorrow, instead of taking me to school, we need to go to Sefton Park.'

'Sefton Park?' The hand withdrew. Her mum pushed her chair out, pulled Pippa onto her feet so that they were both standing. If a mirror were placed between them, it was like looking between the past and the future. So equal in standing, in beauty, they were. 'Why on earth do you want to go there?'

'I've been putting it off.' Pippa began to fidget with the cuff of her shirt, blazer long discarded and tossed on her bedroom floor. 'But I need to go.' Her tone became insistent. 'I need to say goodbye, properly. Where it happened.'

'Well, if that's the case we can go over the weekend and—'

'Please. It needs to be tomorrow.'

'Why?'

'Because I've already left it too long,' Pippa started to cry. At first the tears were light like summer rain, but they quickly thickened.

'Oh, sweetheart, OK, OK. I'll take you. Tomorrow, I promise.' Her mum drew her in close, held her tightly. Let the tears soak into the soft fibres of her pale blue jumper.

Pippa kept crying as the voices in her head taunted her.

Something he should have told me.

Something he should have told me.

Something he should have told me.

Pip Parks,

I am not infatuated with Mr Hall. And my feelings are NOT one-sided. If you weren't some square virgin you'd understand but you don't know what it's like to be in love, to have actual feelings for someone.

Pip, you've never even kissed a boy. So don't start judging me! It sucks you won't walk by his house with me but I'm still going. He's bound to see me. And if his wife isn't there I bet he invites me in. It'll be all innocent at first but then we'll get down to it. I bet he's a good kisser. He's got those kind of soft, inviting lips. Not like Tristan with his outbreak of acne.

Did I tell you he showed up at my house? Your dad had to tell him to sod off. Because your dad was there. Again. And no I'm not lying. Tristan came and started hammering on the doorbell, shouting up to my window that I'm a bitch and why aren't I replying to him. I keep telling my mum that the whole point of having a gate on the drive is to CLOSE IT. But she never does. She can be so dippy it winds me up. Forgetting keys, bank cards, all the time. How she actually looks after people at work I don't know.

Tristan will lose his mind when I start going with Mr Hall. Like straight up IMPLODE. I can't wait to see it. Will teach him a lesson for being such a dick to me.

But yeah, stop being so negative about it all, Pip.
I get that you're jealous but enough already.
  Write back,
  H
  xoxo

40

Her father was in his study. Already it was dark outside. She heard the rustling of his papers, the clearing of his throat. It was strange to have him home; usually the house was compensating for his absence. But now he was here. Pippa lingered by the doorway, chewing on the ends of her nails. She knew that her mum was upstairs, on the phone, her voice rising and falling like an endless tide.

Probably talking about Heather.

Because that's all anyone wanted to do. To talk about. At school. On the TV. The radio. Heather. Heather. Heather. Even in death she was dominating everything.

'Hey.' The door opened and Pippa bit down on her thumb too hard in surprise, drawing blood. Lowering her hand she blushed with embarrassment at her father who was now in the doorway to his study, tie loose about his neck, watching her, forehead creased. 'Everything OK?' He stretched to look beyond her, towards the empty kitchen. 'I thought I heard someone out here.'

'I . . .' Pippa looked to her pink slippers. Fluffy and soft. They seemed so grotesquely girlish against the sombre backdrop of her father's study. The one place in the house her mum's feminine touch couldn't reach. It was all dark wood. Plaid. Framed accomplishments. No frivolity. No flowers. Air thick with the dust held by the vast tomes he lined his bookcases with. 'Dad, I need to talk to you.'

Heather. A record on repeat, even in Pippa's mind. 'OK.' He returned to his desk, casually placed himself in his leather chair. Across the ocean of wood Pippa shrank into herself. Shoulders raised, chin dipped. 'What is it, sweetheart?' he prompted.

Pippa raised her gaze to meet his. She wondered where the man who had once made monkey faces at her and blown raspberries against her belly had gone. Lately he was always so . . . so serious. As though he never really left the operating theatre. Over time, his ability to separate his life had diminished. And Pippa wanted to believe so badly that it wasn't her fault. That if she'd stayed young and fun and playful, he would have too. 'The thing is. . .' She reached for a strand of hair, twisted it between her fingers. She knew what she had to ask. What she should have asked months ago. But to ask was to admit it might be true, right? Twining her hair around her index finger, Pippa peered at the edges of the room from the corner of her eye. Such a solid space. Grand. Secure. Her home, her life, could it all fall? Even when it was made so sturdy? 'Heather said something about you.' She said it quickly, ripping off the plaster of her hesitation.

'Oh?' Leather squeaked beneath her father as he straightened.

'Yeah . . . before she . . .' *Died.* But Pippa didn't want to say it aloud. Didn't want to feel it on her tongue. 'She said something about you and her mum.'

There it was.

Pippa flicked her gaze to the open doorway, the glow of the kitchen beyond, burning with betrayal. Should she really be doing this? Asking this, when her mum wasn't around?

But if it's not true it doesn't matter.

'What did she say about me and her mum?' Her father neatly clasped his hands together atop the desk.

'That you . . .' Pippa rolled her eyes, feeling foolish with her enquiry. 'That you guys were, like, sleeping together, having an affair.' She couldn't look at him, instead stared at the flamingo fuzz on her feet.

'I see.'

She dared to glance up and noticed how tightly her father was holding his hands together, knuckles draining of colour. 'And who else did she say this to?'

'I don't . . .' Pippa shook her head. 'I'm not sure. I thought just me but . . .' She chewed her lip. 'Knowing her, she told more people.'

'I see.'

Was that all he was going to say? *I see. I see. I see.* Of course he fucking *saw*. But what Pippa wanted was the truth. Why wasn't he insisting it was just an ugly rumour, created to inflict pain, standard Heather?

'Well is it true?' Pippa asked in a squeak.

'Sweetheart, relationships are complicated and—'

'*Is it?*' Pippa felt her pulse pounding in her temple, face growing hot. 'When did Mum stop being good enough? Does she not keep the house nice, cook decent dinners? Everything she does is for you and you go and fucking—'

'Pippa.' He said her name sharply. Suddenly. Like a cowed animal, she froze, corners of her mouth dipping low. 'I know that Heather was your friend, that you were close, but she was at times a troubled young woman. Wayward. She wasn't *good* for you.'

Pippa was silent, chin trembling.

246

'You know that I love you, don't you, sweetheart?'

'Do you love Mum?' Pippa whispered.

'Of course.'

'Because if you've hurt her . . .' A single tear sliced down her cheek. 'I won't let you hurt her. Hurt . . . me.'

Her father and pretty Michelle Oxon. Their bodies pressed close, his lips on hers. Just thinking of it was like pouring acid on her brain.

'Oh, there you two are.' Behind them, her mum's sweet voice instantly diffused the tension. 'Dinner is ready.'

Without another word Pippa followed her father out of his study, noticing that outside it was now dark. He hadn't confirmed what Heather had said, he'd denounced her credibility. Pippa knew what he'd said about Heather was true.

And yet he hadn't denied the accusation either.

The thought plagued her like an errant fly, refusing to leave as she sat down for dinner and did her best to force down the food her mum had worked so hard on.

41

Abbie was at John's desk. She'd heard him leave just under an hour ago, his dinner barely settled in his stomach, muttering something about an urgent alert on his beeper. A small lamp offered a rectangle of light within which she'd piled numerous documents. Beyond, the house was plunged into darkness. Abbie needed the shadows to keep her company. With all the lights on, everything felt too bright, too open.

Upstairs Pippa was sleeping. Abbie knew this as she'd checked in on her daughter several times before coming downstairs. She'd crack the bedroom door ajar, peer in, watch the shape beneath the duvet shift and move. But just after eleven the moving ceased and Abbie crept away.

Now she was in the study, at the desk, she did her best to be methodical. Like an investigator surveying a crime scene. She needed to gather facts. But her emotions were a rope around her neck, squeezing and lethal. Her thoughts kept trying to lead her away from her home, through Waterbridge, to the oak-lined street, past the iron gates, through the door and upstairs, to what was happening in Michelle Oxon's bed.

'Abigail, come on,' she chided herself through clenched teeth. Now was not the time to fall apart. She could do that later. Her hands sifted through old letters, utility bills, her mind like Chernobyl. Ideas were slamming together like atoms with such force that she feared her skull might explode and paint the walls of John's beloved study with her brains.

'Focus. You can do this.'

Water bills. Gas. Electric.

'Ah.'

Finally, the stack of old credit card bills. Abbie hauled them out from a drawer of the desk and reached for a highlighter pen. Doubling over the pages, only her face illuminated by the lamp, she trawled the numbers. The dates. The payments. Her memory had always been sharp. It helped her succeed in school, pulled herself up out of the drudgery which claimed so many of her peers. She had taken that memory, that skill, to university and ensured she did something useful with it. She wanted to help people. But she also wanted to help herself. She'd watched her mother rot away in a council house, drinking shots of cheap whiskey and cackling at daytime television. That wouldn't be her fate.

Faced with the bills, Abbie quickly found the anomalies she was searching for. Streaked them neon yellow.

A night in a Hilton in Bath.

Sixty pounds spent at Ann Summers.

A night in a Marriott in Bristol.

Eighty pounds in La Perla.

Three hundred pounds in Tiffany's.

Gifts Abbie had never received. Dates taking her back one year, then two. And then, after highlighting over eighty entries she found nothing untoward. She leaned back in John's chair.

Two years.

He had definitely been cheating on her for two years. Seven hundred and thirty days. Each one of them had been a lie.

Abbie folded against the table, pressed her forehead to the scattered results of her search and cried. Her back spasmed as she soaked the paper but couldn't stop. She kept thinking of her wedding day, of the white lace dress she'd worn, her hair tied up in a bun held together in a crisp blue ribbon.

'You're just who I've been searching for,' John had told her, pressing his lips against hers. 'I'll love you forever.'

Serious, stoic John Parks. Renowned at the hospital for being cruel, for being cold. But with Abbie he opened up, he let her in.

'Smart girl,' her mother had commented when informed of the engagement, 'attaching yourself to a rocket who is only going up. But what is *he* getting?' she'd asked coldly, cheap port on her breath.

'He gets a wife who he loves,' Abbie had declared with certainty so absolute she'd have staked her very soul on it.

'He gets a wife he *needs*,' her mother had corrected her. 'You'll push out a kid, keep the house tidy. He won't let you work.'

'You don't know that!'

'I do,' her mother had smiled sadly at her. 'Powerful men like him, they don't marry powerful women. Be careful, Abigail. Because in your marriage, the odds will be stacked against you.'

Abbie had put it down to the drunken lament of a jealous woman. Her own dad had walked out when she was three, only to move to a different county and father three more children in the space of two years.

But her mother had been right about John not letting her work. He had thrown out so many excuses.

You're needed at home.

Pippa needs you.

Your job now is to be a mother.

And most crushing of all: *What you'd earn as a nurse doesn't warrant you going out to work. I make six times what a nurse does.*

When Abbie had worked with him, John was distant from the nurses. The porters. Disinterested. She never stopped to consider that he held them in contempt. Her wage, so pitiful against his, even though she assisted on surgeries, helped his patients through post-op. She'd remove sutures, dressing, drains, help them out and into bed. She was there when they *healed*. John just cut them open.

'People become nurses because they care about the patient,' an old tutor had told her during her time as a student. 'Other people become surgeons because they care about the science.'

With John this was most certainly true. People didn't interest him. Their anatomy did.

Straightening herself, Abbie wiped her cheeks, did her best to tidy the credit bills haphazardly spread across the desk like neon-streaked confetti. She wondered if that was what John saw in Michelle Oxon, someone as interested in medicine as he was. Or was there more to it? Was he now just merely done with Abbie? No longer in need of her?

Two years.

Abbie considered the timeline in her mind. So when Michelle's husband had moved out, it hadn't taken long for John to move in.

Last summer they had gone to Disneyworld in Florida. Pippa had loved it, shrieking with pure excitement and joy when she saw the castle, met characters and went on rides. John had been morose, blaming his cynicism for all this on Disney.

'It's all so corporate,' he'd complain over and over, shuffling away from his wife and daughter to check his phone.

'You just can't see the magic,' Abbie told him. And glancing at his messy desk, Abbie realised that had always been the problem, not just when an Orlando sun was beating down on them. John failed to see the magic in his marriage. In his daughter.

Abbie massaged her temple which throbbed with an aching pain. She needed to concentrate, to present her thoughts with a clear path they could neatly walk down.

A girl is missing.

A girl is murdered.

Her husband – a liar. A cheater. Sleeping with the dead girl's mother. Who knew what else he could be concealing from her? Abbie tasted the bile of her own rage, knew she needed to wash it away with something fermented.

So after tidying the study she went into the lounge, glass of wine in hand, and curled up on an armchair, turning on the fire, letting the flames be the only source of light. And as she drank, she plotted.

The fire spat and she watched the flames curl, dance and twist. And as she did she mentally ran through dozens of scenarios, playing them all out in meticulous detail. This was how she used to prepare for an exam, a surgery – by imagining it all play out second by second. From the first incision to the final loop of a closing stitch. At each stage her objective changed.

Suction.

Pressure.

Sutures.

And if something went wrong she had to know how to react. So once she settled on a scenario she played out all possible missteps. And how to navigate them. When the light outside softened from black to grey her glass was empty but her plan was complete. Now all she had to do was execute it.

42

The car radio played an eighties medley, which Pippa tried to ignore. Head pressed against the window she watched the landscape slipping by. The neat streets of Waterbridge quickly being replaced by barren farmer's fields. Winter had nearly arrived. Next week it would be December. A ten-foot pine tree would go up in the centre of the high street. Lights would glow in windows. A sense of magic would creep in with the turn of the calendar page. But not for Pippa.

Cyndi Lauper's 'Time After Time' filled the space between her and her mum as they veered off the main road and passed through the gates which marked the entrance to Sefton Park. Pippa looked across the cultivated fields, her left eye beginning to twitch as the grand house came into view.

'Are you all right?' her mum asked as they entered the car park.

'I'm fine.'

Sefton Park had only recently reopened following Heather's disappearance. The grounds had been closed off entirely for the police to conduct a thorough investigation. But now it was welcoming guests again. Pippa saw dog walkers clad in Joules coats and Hunter wellingtons jogging towards the entrance. Elderly walkers with binoculars hanging from their necks.

'Are you sure you want to do this?' her mum turned and asked, engine still running.

'I'm sure,' Pippa told her, opening the car door and stepping out onto the gravel. It was cold. The damp kind which clung to your clothes and sunk into your bones. Pippa reached for her parka from the back seat, eagerly pulled it on along with a turquoise bobble hat and some fingerless gloves in a matching shade. She was decidedly warmer than she had been during her last visit to Sefton. Lingering close to the car while her mum put on her own additional layers, Pippa scanned the scattering of people approaching the entrance. Searching for ghosts.

Within the grounds nothing had changed. From the main courtyard, which had previously been the stables and now housed a charming café and gift shop, they followed the curve of the path towards Sefton Hall. Pippa always liked to take in a moment to appreciate its grandeur, to marvel at all the great house had seen. While time would erode her in just a few decades, it would take much longer to steal away the beauty of the stone mansion. Nestled on the edge of Waterbridge it was a monument to what had been before. To history. But today Pippa kept her eyes trained on her feet, guiding her boots to take her beyond the house, to not follow the path down towards the dual bridges that crossed the river, but to continue along the side of the house. The side of the river.

'Urgh, I'm freezing.'

Pippa turned, blinked in surprise when she saw her mum at her side, cheeks pink. For a moment she'd expected to see the golden glow of Heather's hair, see her turn and frown.

I said I'm fucking freezing.

'Pip?' Her mum had ceased walking, was studying her.

'I'm . . . fine.' Pippa shook her head, kept moving, aware that she was beginning to sound less and less convincing when she said that. Because she was beginning to think she was the furthest from fine that someone could actually be.

She rounded a corner and the drab slate of an English November morning was gone. Replaced by an explosion of colour.

Flowers. So many flowers. Tulips. Carnations. Roses. Lilies. Peonies. All spread along the riverbank in bouquets ranging in size and colour.

'Oh my,' her mum said beside her. They both stopped just shy of the first blooms. There had to be hundreds of bouquets there. Maybe more. Nestled among them were stuffed teddy bears, some clutching big hearts. A pinwheel had been erected beside some red roses and it turned swiftly in the breeze. Its playful appearance, all the colour, the beauty, it was all so misplaced that Pippa wanted to vomit. She huddled close to her mum, shielding herself from the sight and the wind.

'We should just go back,' her mum was saying, rubbing her back and holding her close. 'I was worried this would be too much for you. It's all just too soon, too raw.'

'Mum.' Pippa edged back from her, cheeks slick with tears.

'It's all right.' Her mum used her gloved hands to wipe away the worst of them. 'Don't worry, darling. Heather will know you wanted to say goodbye. And you came. So now we can—'

'Mum!' Pippa stepped back, knocked her mum's hands away. They were alone. The dog walkers, the bird watchers, they'd opted to do the longer route. The one Pippa should have done that day. 'I need to tell you something.' She began to shake.

Something he should have told me.

'OK, what is it? Sweetheart, are you cold? You're shaking, let me—'

'And you're not going to love me anymore once I've told you.' She shrunk back from her mum's outstretched hand.

'What? No.' Her mum let her hand fall, face hardening. 'There is *nothing* you could ever tell me which would make me stop loving you. Do you understand? Nothing.'

Chin trembling, Pippa looked between her mum and the offerings of flowers. A sea of petals, some already browning at the edges.

'Let's just go,' her mum insisted sternly. 'You're clearly upset and—'

'I lied.'

Her mum said nothing.

'To you, to the police. I lied.'

'About what?' Her mum took a cautious step towards her, glancing over her shoulder.

'All of it.' Pippa blinked back more tears.

'What do you mean?'

'I wanted to tell you, Mum, I did, but . . . I was scared and I know I should have just *told* you. Because we don't keep secrets and—' Pippa's rambling ceased when her mum grabbed her arm, drew her away from the flowers, back along the path, back towards the mansion.

'Sweetheart, you can tell me anything,' she whispered against her head, 'absolutely anything. But not here, not when anyone could be listening.'

Pippa nodded numbly, tasting salt on her lips.

Back in the car, still shivering even though she'd kept on her hat, gloves and coat, Pippa took a deep, steadying breath.

'The beginning,' her mum had urged, 'just start at the beginning.'

'You know what Heather was like.' Pippa picked at the tips of her nails. 'She was a complete bitch. Not just to me, but to everyone. And no one ever stood up to her, ever. It was like . . . because she was beautiful she was untouchable.'

Her mum nodded, mouth hardening into a tight line.

'And I mean, whilst she could be nice, in her own way, when she was mean she was just . . . the worst. And she'd started saying shit about you and Dad.'

'Like what?' her mum asked tightly.

'That you weren't happy. That your marriage was a lie.'

'Pippa—'

'That he was sleeping with her mum.' Pippa looked at her lap, unable to glance over at her mother. Outside a dog yelped excitedly as it was released from the boot of a nearby car.

'And . . .' Pippa continued, mouth growing dry, 'I hoped she wouldn't spread it around the school. But . . . I could never trust her. I was scared she might . . . might try and shame me with it. So I wanted to . . . I don't know. I guess I wanted to shame her first. Take away the beauty, take a hammer to her ivory tower.'

'So what did you do?' her mum asked evenly.

Pippa cleared her throat, wishing she had something to drink. Hating the irony of that desire. 'The morning of the run, I got up, got my sports bag ready. Including my water bottle. Only I added something to the water.'

Her mum watched her patiently.

'Peanut oil,' Pippa whispered, waiting for the car to suddenly implode. Only nothing happened. The world was as it had been seconds earlier; she hadn't burst into flames or been struck down by lightning. 'It was a *joke*,' she quickly insisted. 'A prank. I wanted her to break out in some ugly hives, be forced to get back on the minibus like that. I didn't think she'd . . . she'd . . . die.'

'How did you give her your water?'

'I swapped the bottles on the bus,' Pippa explained, face aflame. 'It was so stupid, anyone could have seen me do it.'

'But did they?'

'I don't know.'

'And did you see Heather drink the water?'

Pippa closed her eyes, felt her intake of breath rattle all the way down her throat and settle in the empty vacuum of her stomach. She had watched Heather's throat as she swallowed from her own bottle. Only that hadn't been their final moment together. Pippa had watched the golden girl, waiting for the grenade she'd just thrown to explode. And she didn't have to wait long. The bottle had barely left Heather's glossed lips when she began to cough.

'Fuck.' She pressed a hand against her mouth. More coughing. Her face turned pink and Pippa noticed a blemish upon the skin. The angry red of a hive. 'W-what?' Heather kept clearing her throat, struggling to speak. 'The . . . the . . .' She suddenly threw the bottle to the ground. Her eyes were wide with panic when she looked over at Pippa. 'Get . . .' She doubled over to vomit. 'Help,' she panted as she managed to right herself. Her lips had now doubled in size. Bulbous and crimson they opened as Heather tried to catch a much-needed breath of air. She was now covered in hives. Hand extended she reached for Pippa, gripping her arm.

'H-help,' she wheezed, beginning to shake. Pippa wasn't sure what she was seeing. It was all happening so fast. So much faster than she'd ever anticipated. Heather was still clutching her arm when she dropped to her knees, withdrawing her hand to claw at her own throat making strange, strangled sounds. She was so red, so swollen. Almost unrecognisable. Snots and tears washed down her no-longer-perfect face. 'Mum,' she panted on her knees beside Pippa. 'Mummy.'

Pippa turned to her own mum, whose face was drained of all colour. 'That was the last thing she said. "Mummy." And then she just dropped into the mud. For a while she kept wheezing and trembling. But then she was still. So awfully still.'

'Then what happened?' her mum asked calmly, as though she were asking about Pippa's day at school.

'Mum, why aren't you freaking out?' Pippa whispered fretfully.

'Because,' Abbie told her stoically, 'it's my job to look out for you. So tell me what happened next and let me do that, OK?'

'I panicked,' Pippa said, choking at the memory. Crying, she recalled to her mum how she rolled a lifeless Heather down the embankment, shoved her into the river. Then kicked in her bag and discarded bottle of water, its incriminating contents mixing with the murky flow of the Severn. 'I *knew*,' she sobbed as her mum leaned across the handbrake and gearstick to embrace her, to hold her while she shook. 'I knew that if I came forward, if people knew what I'd done, my life would be over. And I didn't *mean* to do it. Mum, you have to believe me.'

'I believe you,' her mum promised, holding her.

'I just wanted to bring her down a peg or two. I didn't mean to—'

'Shh.' Her mum leaned back several inches, caressed Pippa's cheek with her thumb to wipe away tears, her brown eyes wide. 'I need you to listen to me. You are never again to speak of this. Do you understand? Never.'

'But I—' Her mum pressed her hand against Pippa's mouth. 'Never. If anyone saw us today, you were crying and publicly mourning the death of your friend. Understood?'

Pippa nodded. Confused and afraid.

'I'm going to fix this,' her mum promised.

'But,' Pippa sniffed, needing to be sick, 'the police know it was an allergic reaction, it won't be long until—'

'I'm going to fix this,' her mum repeated more firmly. 'Pippa, I'm going to sort this out.'

'But Mum—'

'Like I said, it is my job to protect you.' She kissed Pippa on the forehead. 'Please, darling, let me do my job.'

43

Abbie cleaned. She hoovered the lounge, hallway, dining room and John's study; she mopped the floor of the kitchen, utility and conservatory. Then she cleaned the windows, scrubbed the toilets. Her house sparkled, air thick with bleach. Upstairs, Pippa slept.

Over and over on the drive home, Abbie assured her that everything would be all right. That she loved her. She wasn't quite sure how they made it back to their driveway, couldn't quite remember turning the key in the ignition, leaving Sefton Park. On autopilot she'd found her way back home, her mind a scrambled mess.

A girl is missing.

A girl is murdered.

Peanut oil in the water bottle. An innocent prank. Pippa had said as much. But then Pippa had kept it all from her for so long. Abbie grunted as she dragged her scouring pad back and forth across the stainless steel of the draining board beside the sink. She pushed hard against the metal until the bleach in her cleaning solution began to burn both her nostrils and fingertips.

Fear had kept her daughter silent. That was all. The truth was out now. So easy for someone to misjudge the intensity of an allergic reaction. Anaphylaxis was quick. She'd seen cases before, airways blocked, paramedics too late on the scene. Even if Pippa had called for help, it was unlikely Heather would have lived. Just a prank that had gone wrong.

Only it had gone horrifically wrong. It had been fatal. Heather was dead and her blood . . . it was on Pippa's hands.

Abbie tried to force a way through her maze of questions.

Did anyone else know?

If so − who?

And how likely were the police to piece everything together? They knew about the allergic reaction being the cause of death. The autopsy had shown that. Had it also revealed the contents of Heather's waterlogged stomach? Was the peanut oil still detectable, or had it been washed away by the river, or reduced by an overwhelmed immune system to mere bile? Did it even matter? They knew that someone needed to have given Heather something laced with peanuts. The water bottle was an easy guess. Then all they needed to do was consider who had access to said water. Girls on the bus. Pippa.

Panting, Abbie ceased scrubbing. She was going to protect her daughter. She just had no idea how. Exhausted, she carried herself to the island and draped against it, letting her cheek rest against the cool marble. Everything was unravelling. Her perfect marriage. Her perfect daughter. Her perfect life. Just as Michelle had threatened. Abbie seethed at the thought.

That morning she'd woken with the intention of finding a decent divorce lawyer, of severing herself from John. She'd taken joy in how much he'd hate that. He cared about appearances more than she did, though he'd never admit it. He presented himself as the virtuous high-ranking surgeon. A family man. He liked his home neat and in order. His wife tidy and reliable. A divorce would be messy, would allow whispers to follow him along the corridors at work. And he loathed any sort of mess. John and his never-ending desire to have everything just so.

Leaning against the island, Abbie considered her kitchen from this new angle. Everything on its side. She felt like Alice when she tumbled into Wonderland and discovered a world of oddities where nothing made sense. Only there was no waking up from this. This was real. And Abbie needed to think. To find a way out for both her and Pippa.

Her thoughts were disturbed by the shrill bleat of the doorbell. When it rang a second time, echoing through the house, Abbie righted herself.

'Fuck,' she muttered as spots danced in her line of vision. Then she hurried to the hallway, forgetting that her sleeves were shoved up her arms, hands damp and pink from all the cleaning. She just needed to get there before the sound of the bell woke Pippa. Pippa, who needed to rest, who had cried and shook the entire way back from Sefton. Back home she'd collapsed into bed, completely exhausted. And Abbie thought also, relieved. Because the secret was no longer hers. It was theirs.

The doorbell chimed a third time.

'I'm coming,' Abbie called loudly to the blurred outline beyond the paned glass. Opening the door she drank in a lungful of crisp air and nearly choked on it. Michelle Oxon was on her porch. Immaculate in a grey wool coat, hair drawn back in a sleek bun.

'Abigail.' Her mouth twitched with distaste as she greeted her.

'Michelle.' Abbie filled the doorway, fighting the urge to slam the door right in the other woman's face. 'What can I do for you?' Civility was an effort Abbie barely had the energy for.

'I came here as a courtesy.' Clutched to Michelle's chest were a pile of white A4 sheets, edges fluttering gently in a stiff breeze. By way of explanation she passed the stack over to Abbie.

'What is this?'

'Letters,' Michelle explained flatly. Abbie glanced down at them, immediately recognising the neat cursive of her daughter's own hand. And sure enough, at the bottom of the top page, the letter was signed off by her:

Pip xoxo

'I'll save you the effort of reading through them since I've already done that,' Michelle announced icily. 'Today I went through the contents of my shed, to keep myself busy, and I happened upon something Heather had tried to hide away from me. A tin box containing these letters. And some weed.'

Abbie scanned the top letter. There didn't seem to be anything untoward in it.

'I'm guessing your daughter has the corresponding letters,' Michelle continued. 'In them she threatens Heather.' Her icy blue eyes pinned Abbie in place. 'Heather informs her about John and I, and Pippa lashes out. Calls her a liar. Says she needs to be careful what she says.'

Abbie neatly cleared her throat, tightened her grip against the letters. 'I don't see what is so threatening about that.'

John and I.
John and I.
John and I.

Michelle was the one making threats. Driving over to her home to take a shit on her doorstep. Abbie felt her jaw tighten, felt her heart rate begin to climb.

'You're probably right,' Michelle agreed, though her tone remained sharp, words clipped. 'But put that together with the fact that Heather died from consuming nuts. Nuts which needed to have been slipped to her without her knowing. Perhaps in her water bottle. Then I think we all draw the same conclusion that it was Pippa.'

'They never found the water bottle, did they?' Abbie asked coldly. 'Your theory is nothing more than the hysteria of a desperate woman grasping at straws.'

'Do you think the police will think as much?' Michelle taunted.

Abbie turned to stone. She said nothing. Did nothing.

'Because that's the line of enquiry I'm going to insist the police follow. I'm taking a set of the letters over to them now.' She nodded at the stack Abbie was clutching. 'Don't worry, those are merely copies. And I have many, many copies.'

'Try and drag my daughter down into the muck you live in and you will live to regret it,' Abbie seethed, her hands beginning to shake.

'Wow, so you're threatening me, again,' Michelle laughed falsely at her. 'Like mother like daughter, eh?'

Abbie's nails dug into the paper, leaving crescent moon indentations in the sheets.

'Like I said,' she continued, 'this a courtesy for John. He asked me to leave this alone. Pleaded –' her eyes shone with this '– but I kept waiting for him to speak to Pippa and he never did. So now the police will.'

Abbie kept sinking her nails into the letters. Thinking of her husband who never, ever pleaded for anything.

'Your daughter has motive,' Michelle continued coolly, 'these letters prove that. And she's sixteen. She'll be tried as an adult.'

'My daughter has done nothing wrong.'

'Neither did mine,' Michelle glowered at her. 'Yet here we are.'

'Get off my property.'

'Gladly.' Michelle turned and began striding back down the driveway to her sleek, silver car parked beyond on the street. 'Oh,' she said, glancing back when at the edge of the driveway, 'tell John I said "hi" and that I'll see him tonight.' She waggled her fingers at Abbie.

Abbie breathed in through her nose. Fast and heavy. She watched Michelle leave, watched the shape of her car pull away. Then she slammed her front door, pressed her back against it and ripped the letters in her possession to shreds, all the while screaming.

44

Pippa was frozen on the landing. Incapacitated by the fear which now consumed her. It gnawed on every nerve, every bone; it all she could feel.

The doorbell had pulled her from a dead sleep. Groggily she'd turned over, tried to fall into darkness once more. But then the doorbell came again. Shrill and piercing.

'Urgh.' With a groan Pippa had left the warmth of her bed, shuffled towards her bedroom door, cracked it open and slumped against the doorframe, wearily rubbing her eyes. She was about to shout down towards the hallway, call for her mum to come and answer. But then she heard footsteps, the twist of the lock, the creak of the door hinges. Pippa was prepared to slink back to bed, if not to sleep then just to hide beneath her duvet in the warm haze. But she knew the voice at the door. Had heard it countless times before.

Oh, Heather, you look so pretty.

Pippa, why don't you try wearing more mascara?

Pippa, don't you ever straighten your hair?

You shouldn't ever wear red lipstick, Pippa, it will wash you out. It suits a stronger skin palette, like Heather's.

Michelle Oxon with her comments. Her ongoing quest for beauty. Perfection.

'My mum says a woman needs to have brains *and* be beautiful,' Heather used to state with pride. 'She says that's called being a double threat and only those women succeed.'

Pippa had considered her own mum at that moment. How statuesque she was, slim and slender but with the same severe, dark eyes she'd passed to her daughter.

'That's why your mum wouldn't succeed alone like mine,' Heather had crowed, climbing aboard Pippa's train of thought. 'She has neither.'

Previously, Pippa might have fought such a remark. But Heather had worn her down over the years, made her so accustomed to her cruelty that it just washed over her.

Creeping from her doorway, Pippa ventured onto the landing, moving on the tips of her toes, wincing at the creak of every floorboard. When she reached the banister she gripped it tight, curled up against it.

Her mum was talking to Michelle. But it was easy to deduce that the conversation had quickly turned unpleasant.

'That's the line of enquiry I'm going to insist the police follow,' Michelle was saying below her. 'I'm taking a set of the letters over to them now.'

Pippa had to move. Had to clasp her hands against her mouth to stifle the mournful whimper which seeped out of her.

The letters. The fucking letters.

Heather's mum had found them. Pippa cried into her hands. She'd burnt hers, watched them turn to ash, but that wasn't enough. All the things she'd said. How she'd finally stood up to Heather, told her enough was enough, to watch her back.

And for a prank. A little prank! Just a chance to show Heather she meant business, that she refused to be her punching bag anymore. That her parents were off limits.

Only . . . Pippa gulped and slowly lowered her hands. Yesterday, in the car, her mum hadn't denied the affair. And now, face to face with Michelle Oxon, she still didn't refute it. So was it true? When all along Pippa assumed it was just a lie that Heather had concocted to toy with her, hurt her. And if it was true . . . Pippa leaned forward to peer into the hallway. Her mum was now demanding that Michelle leave.

Pippa scurried to her feet. She knew she'd made a mistake. Far too many of them. And she'd hurt the wrong person. If Heather was right, if the affair was real, then it was her father who was the enemy, who was trying to blow up her entire life. He'd not only brought the wolves to their door, but left it wide open so they could just force their way inside. Her chest ached with it. The pain. The sting of humiliation. Her father hadn't just cheated on her mum, he'd slept with her *friend's* mother. No boundaries. No care. And Heather *knew*. He let Heather see him, be privy to it all, but kept this information from his own daughter. Pippa clasped her hands to her mouth to catch the whimper that left her. The truth was there, unbearable to see – her father didn't love her mum, and he didn't trust his daughter. Her suitcase was open on the unmade bed. The one she'd dragged through both Heathrow and then JFK airports on their last family holiday. Pippa thrust open drawers and threw handfuls of clothes towards the suitcase. Pants. Bras. Socks. T-shirts. Her Sony Walkman. A couple of books. Her purse. Her piggy bank. Pyjamas.

Downstairs she heard screaming. But she didn't stop. Hoodies. Joggers. Trainers. Slippers. She threw anything and everything into the suitcase, desperately trying to pack up her entire life as swiftly as possible. Passport. She'd need

270

that. But wasn't it kept in her mum's bedroom? Or was it her father's study?

'Pip?' The door squeaked open and Pippa stopped, several T-shirts bunched in her fists, about to be flung across to the overfilled suitcase. 'Sweetheart, what are you doing?'

Her mum entered the fray, scraping her cheeks with her fingertips. Her skin was red and blotchy, mascara smeared beneath her eyes.

'Mum . . . just . . .' Pippa threw the T-shirts, turned to root around in her wardrobe for more clothes. Her warmest coat, she'd need that. Pulling it off the hanger, she tried to bunch it into a ball.

'Hey, hey.' Her mum was at her side, prying the garment out of her hands. 'Pip, come on, calm down. What are you doing?'

'I'm leaving!' Pippa explained, on the edge of hysteria. Voice so brittle it could break at any moment. 'I *heard* Michelle. She knows! She knows what I did! Soon everyone will know and I'll . . . I'll . . .' She was shaking so much her teeth clattered over her words.

'Hush, hush now.' Her mum folded against her like a vanilla-scented wave. 'Stop, stop panicking.'

'But I . . . I heard . . . her,' Pippa hiccupped uneasily. Michelle Oxon knew everything – her part in Heather's death, how she'd done it, *why* she'd done it. 'I'll go to prison,' she whispered, wondering what that would be like. No college. No university. No job. No life. No family. Just prison. Four small walls and a locked door. Her sobs bubbled out of her thick and fast, making her entire body convulse.

A prank. A joke. Nothing more. A simple accident. Her life for a prank. A mistake.

'Shhh, shhhh.' Her mum was stroking her head sooth-ingly, swaying on her feet. 'Don't worry, darling. You're not going to prison. I won't that let happen.'

'How? I did it, Mum. I'm a murderer, I'm a—'

'It was a simple mistake,' her mum stated fiercely, sealing her certainty with a kiss against Pippa's temple. 'One which you have already paid for with your grief. I won't let anyone take you from me.'

'But Heather's mum *knows*.'

'I'll stop her.' Her mum's arms tightened around her. 'How?'

'I don't know yet. But I will.'

'The police they'll find out and—'

'You have to trust me, Pip,' her mum whispered against her head. 'I'm going to keep you safe, sweetheart. Whatever it takes.'

'Then why did you scream?' Pippa wondered despond-ently. Her mum's screams had filled not just the hallway but the entire house. 'If you think you can fix this, why did you scream?'

'Because I'm angry, sweetheart. I'm so, so angry. At your father. At Michelle. I'm full of all this anger and I needed to let some of it go. Like a kettle boiling. I didn't mean to scare you; you don't need to worry about my screaming.'

'I get angry too.'

'I know.' Her mum kissed her cheek. 'I know, baby, I know.'

'What do you do?' Pippa asked earnestly. 'When you're so angry you feel like you can't breathe?'

Her mum clasped her chin with her cool hands. 'I told you. I find a way to fix things.'

'You can't fix this,' Pippa's face crumpled. 'I b-b-burnt my letters,' she admitted woefully. Within those pages she'd gotten so extremely angry at Heather, risen to all her taunts. 'And I'll burn the letters Michelle has too,' her mum instantly replied. 'And if I don't get to, I'll just change the narrative, that's all.'

'How?'

'I don't know yet, sweetheart. I need to think.'

Calming, Pippa leaned back, wiped her cheeks with the heel of her hand. 'Is it true,' she said, looking into her mum's eyes, 'about Dad?'

Her mum's lips set in a tight line, eyes crinkling at the corners. 'It's true.'

Pippa whimpered and crashed back into her. Her father. Heather's mother. It was too much to handle. And worst of all, Heather had known all along. Whilst Pippa and her mother had been kept in the dark, oblivious to it all.

'He was meant to love us,' Pippa said, holding her mum tight.

'He loves you, sweetheart.'

'How can he when he tried to destroy our family?'

'Oh, Pip.' Her mum stroked her head.

'He needs to pay,' Pippa whispered tearfully. 'For hurting us. For ruining *us*.'

Her perfect family. Their perfect life. The portrait above the fireplace taken a year ago, all three of them smiling, sat beside one another like they belonged on a Christmas card. Her dad might have well taken it off the wall, smashed the frame in front of them and then ripped the picture to pieces. He didn't care about them. Pippa wondered if he ever truly had as she hugged her mum, crying until her eyes felt raw.

'Don't worry,' her mum said as she rubbed her back, continuing to sway back and forth, 'I'm going to make him pay. Him and her both.'

45

Whatever Abbie was going to do, she needed to do it fast. She had the fragments of an idea, a blueprint, but nothing concrete. As she drove to the hospital, windscreen wipers flitting back and forth against the rain, her temple throbbed from the pressure of thinking, plotting, desperately trying to dig a way out of the grave Pippa had placed herself in.

Because that's what it was – a grave. A death sentence. If the police figured out what truly happened to Heather, guided by Michelle's delivery of the letters and what evidence they had, Pippa could be convicted. Found guilty. And what then? Abbie merged onto the motorway, hungrily picking up speed. Even if Pippa wasn't found guilty, the accusation would stick, be burned upon her like an unsightly brand. Waterbridge was small. But it had links to every prestigious university, all the high offices in London. It was a breeding ground for achievers. No place for someone labelled as a murderer.

Abbie swerved awkwardly into the fast lane, inviting an onslaught of car horns to blast at her. She didn't care. She was going to the hospital, cradling the delicate shoot of an idea in her hands. Once there she would water it, nurture it, and she hoped against hope that come the dawn it would be large enough and grand enough to save her daughter. Because that's what mothers did.

She thought of Michelle. Finding those letters too late. Too busy sharing her bed with other people's husbands. With *Abbie's* husband. It was only natural that Pippa had been angry at Heather, had wanted to punish her for what she believed to be lies. Abbie understood the desire for revenge. It boiled in her blood. Throbbed behind her eyes like a third party to her thoughts.

A girl is missing.

A girl is murdered.

It was all Pippa. But Abbie's hand had been forced. Not by Heather, but by Michelle.

She clocked her exit a fraction too late, had to zigzag through the traffic, tyres skidding on the rain-slicked tarmac. More honking from fellow drivers, lights flashing at her in disapproval. She noticed a raised middle finger from the car behind. It didn't matter. She was nearly there, at the hospital. At the source of all her troubles.

John was on call for the weekend shift. Which meant that he wasn't in his office or doing his rounds on the ward. He'd be helicoptering around the A&E department. Which on a wet Friday evening in late November would be heaving with drunken accidents.

Abbie checked her watch: 10 p.m. She raised her chin, pushed back her shoulders and strutted along the corridor like she belonged there. Like this was a regular visit. Heels clicking against tiles, she fretted over whether to check in with Pippa. When she'd left, Pippa had again drifted off to sleep after spending the better part of the evening crying and shaking. Abbie considered texting her but didn't want to risk waking her. Better she sleep through the next part.

Gliding along the corridors was easy. Abbie could pass for a consultant in her Burberry coat. Or worst case, a visitor to some infirm patient who wasn't expected to last the night. It was quiet – a couple of porters, a heavily pregnant woman shuffling about in fluffy slippers. They barely gave Abbie a cursory glance. This was the great thing about hospitals – everyone there was too swept up in their own problems to care about hers. Abbie reached the clusters of offices which belonged to the Gastro consultants. The main doors were open but the reception desk was shuttered closed. And following a quick inspection, Abbie found that John's office was locked tight. But she had been expecting this. Reaching into her handbag she rooted around for the spare key to the office John insisted on her having. Even though she no longer worked for him, he was regularly sending her off on errands.

I've forgotten a file, can you get it? There's some photocopying I need doing.

Though he had called on her less frequently in recent years, Abbie kept her key close. She liked feeling that John trusted her more than his secretary. That even though she no longer worked at the hospital she could be useful to him. She stepped into the darkened office, not bothering to turn on a light. Better to not attract unwanted attention. Abbie moved quickly, knowing what she was after.

This office was stark and bare compared to the one in their home. The regulation NHS walls were white. The desk housed a computer monitor, keyboard, pen pot and note tray. A noticeboard was adorned with various notifications about the department but they were swathed in shadow. Abbie approached the desk, pulled on the handle for the top drawer. It was locked.

'Urgh.' She pulled out the door key again, collected the small silver key beside it on its loop, slid it into the waiting keyhole and turned it. The drawer opened easily. Abbie spied her prize. A prescription notepad. Slowly, carefully, she peeled away the top sheet, which wasn't easy in the thin cashmere gloves she was wearing. She fumbled towards the edge, yanked hard and managed to cleanly pull the paper away. Grabbing a fountain pen from the pen pot, straining to see in the darkness, Abbie leant against the desk and scratched the pen tip against the paper. She filled out the prescription, then with a flourish signed it off with her husband's signature, something she'd been forging for years. Clicking the cap back onto the pen, she returned it to the pot, folded the signed paper and placed it within her handbag.

John knew she'd sign his name when needed. For cheques for the school mostly. He'd just wave a dismissive hand at her when Abbie pressed him about it, concerned.

'I don't have time for admin,' he'd tell her. 'That's your job.'

Abbie smiled smugly to herself when she considered what a good job she was doing. Because whilst she'd taken something from the drawer, she'd also added something. A change in a diary entry to help form the nail to hammer into the cross. Left there for someone to find. She was being so very diligent. So very careful. She was being the good wife and mother John had always expected her to be. Leaving no stone unturned.

It was midnight when Abbie was back in her kitchen, still clothed beneath the dressing gown she now wore. With each tick of the clock above the oven she felt her nerves fray a little more. John needed to be home soon. Had to be home soon. He wouldn't have gone to Michelle's, would he? Not after what she'd done to their daughter. But if he had then her efforts were all for naught. And it was time to run.

If he hadn't returned home by 3 a.m. then that's what she'd do. She'd clear out the safe in his study, take their passports and run as far and as fast as she could. Pippa was still sleeping, Abbie had checked on her at least ten times since she'd come home. How quickly could they pack, leave the house? Should she start preparing now, should she— Tyres on gravel. Showtime.

John came in, hair and shoulders damp from the rain.

'Welcome home, stranger,' Abbie said from the kitchen doorway, a glass of wine in her hand.

'Sorry I'm late.' He looked towards her but failed to meet her gaze. So Michelle had spoken to him, told her about her distasteful little doorstep visit.

'It's OK,' Abbie drawled out her words, 'I thought I'd wait up for you.'

'It's been a long evening.' He placed down his briefcase and began loosening his tie. 'I'd just like to—'

'Have a drink with me.' Abbie cocked her head at him, pouted playfully.

'I think you've already had enough.' He made for the staircase.

'One drink,' she said, her tone hardening. 'You owe me that at least.'

She watched her husband's posture sink in defeat. 'Fine.' He turned back to her. 'One drink, Abigail.'

He followed her into the kitchen. 'I made you your favourite.' She pointed to the leaded glass tumbler of neat Irish whiskey.

'So you did.' He approached the drink, placed his fingers around it, nails short and neat. He perched on one of the stools whilst Abbie remained standing. He went to take a sip and then lowered the glass, studying his wife. 'Abigail, look, I know we need to talk and that I've—'

'I've only ever been good to you, John.' Abbie carefully raised her wine to her lips. 'I take my vows seriously. For better or worse. And I appreciate that right now, things are worse.'

'Abbie, I . . .' He shook his head, looked down at the marble, cheeks flushing red. She approached him quietly, placed down her glass and began massaging his shoulders. After a few seconds of needling with her fingertips, he leaned appreciatively into her touch.

'It's been a long day for you, darling,' she whispered, stooping to lean in his ear, 'have a drink, relax a little.'

'Abbie, what is all this?' he asked but didn't turn around, enjoying the massage too much to break the connection. 'I was certain I'd come home and you'd be aiming my old hunting rifle at me.'

'No, no, no.' She worked his shoulders harder, pushing deeper into the tissue. 'You've made me realise, John.' Her voice was low, seductive. She watched her husband lift his glass, tilt it as it reached his mouth, amber liquid sliding in. Heard him gulp it down. 'You've made me realise that I need to stop being the wife you want,' she planted a kiss upon his cheek, 'and start being the wife you deserve.'

Ten seconds later he was passed out against the island, head pressed to the marble as a pool of drool gathered beneath his open mouth.

Pee-Pee,

I'm so over going round in circles with you. YOUR DAD IS SLEEPING WITH MY MUM. I've literally heard them doing it. It sounds very gross. Old people sex is nasty. But they're doing it, I'm not lying to mess with you and you need to get it in your head that it is happening. That soon everyone will know. They'll know because he'll leave your mum and if he doesn't I'm telling everyone. I'm sick of the lies. The secrecy. My mum is a hypocrite as she left my dad for the same shit she's now doing. You might not agree but I'm not keeping her sordid secrets anymore. I'm going to tell everyone what she's doing. And with whom.

Look on the bright side – when it all comes out, if your dad moves in with my mum we'll basically be sisters. And I'd love that – wouldn't you?

Love you,

H

xoxo

PS: WEAR. THE. BRA. With that red lipstick I got you. To the party this weekend. Maybe we'll finally find someone to get off with you.

46

Pippa crawled out of the clutches of exhaustion. Bleary-eyed, she pulled her duvet around her shoulders like a cloak and stared into the musky darkness of her bedroom. Somehow she had slept. No dreams. Just a void she kept falling through. And as she slept she wondered how far her truth had travelled. Did all of Waterbridge now know what she'd done?

Clutching her duvet tighter, she shuddered. She yearned for more sleep but she didn't dare close her eyes now her thoughts were tiptoeing towards what she'd done. Now her mind's eye would only show her Heather. Those awful final moments. The gasping. The reaching. And then finally the emptiness in her eyes as they glazed over, losing their sapphire sparkle for good. How heavy her body had been, how listless, as Pippa pushed it towards the mud-streaked water, trainers sinking into the soft ground. The rain had beat down upon her, washing away the signs of her sin almost has soon as it had been committed. And then Heather had landed in the Severn, awkwardly, like a bag of falling potatoes. She hadn't sunk as Pippa had hoped she would. She just drifted. Away she went, carried by the current. And Pippa watched, rain stinging her eyes, too afraid to look away. Waiting for the shouts of someone who had seen what she'd done, someone who was coming for her. But no one came. It just kept on raining. And so she turned from the scene and ran.

Pippa listened to the distant sounds of her house. There was the hum of the immersion heater in the nearby airing cupboard, the bang of old pipes compressing. No pounding on the door. No ringing of the bell. Cautiously she left her bed, moved towards the window which overlooked the front drive and peeled back the curtain, keeping herself fully wedged in the surrounding shadows as she chanced a glance outside.

She was expecting lights. Blue and flashing, with streaks of neon. Instead all was dark. All was quiet. Only . . . Pippa placed her hands on the window sill, peered down at the driveway where only one car was parked. Her mum's 4x4. Her dad's longer, smoother saloon was absent. He must still be working. Or else— Her stomach churned uncomfortably at the thought. Was he currently intertwined with Michelle Oxon? Comforting her? Consoling her?

'He's fucking my mum,' Heather had declared two months ago in the golden September twilight as they sat side by side on their swings.

Pippa shook her head, feeling instantly dizzy from all the cider she'd consumed. The start of a new school year was merely days away. Their final year at Waterbridge Preparatory as senior students; the next phase was sixth form. A Levels. Another chapter in their young lives. They were supposed to be feeling euphoric, infinite, on the cusp of such change. But Heather was pouting and morose. Pippa sensed she'd rather be at the party Tristan Jenkins was throwing that night instead of stuck at the park with her. But Tom refused entry to girls he deemed 'lower than a seven' and he'd once kindly informed Pippa that she was 'a six and a half on her best day'. God, she hated him.

'You're lying,' Pippa scowled. Heather had been lacing toxic breadcrumbs for weeks. Hinting at how unhappy Pippa's parents were, that it was all for show. But what did she know? She was just jealous because her dad had left.

'Am not.' Heather swung high, kicking her legs out. 'He's there most nights. Truly smitten.'

'Liar.'

'No.' Heather dropped her feet to the ground, bringing the swing to a sudden halt, blue eyes bright, sky pink threaded with gold behind her. 'He's fucking my mum. It's been going on for ages. Your mum is just too dumb to notice.'

That was it. Pippa left her swing, stood up, crossed her arms against her chest, wishing she hadn't drunk so much. If only Heather wasn't forever taunting her for being boring, for being square. 'My mum isn't dumb and my dad isn't cheating on her.'

'Fine, don't believe me,' Heather gave a flippant shrug, 'but I'm doing you a favour, telling you, being a friend.'

'No, you're being a bitch.' Pippa began to walk away. She was just past the slide when she turned back, hands clenching at her sides. 'You're never being a *friend*, Heather. You're always just being a bitch. To me. To everyone.'

Heather said nothing but resumed swinging. Up and down. Up and down. Blonde hair fanning out behind her as she swooped towards the ground.

Muttering with annoyance, Pippa marched away, wishing she had the courage to say more. To do more. Because this was classic Heather. She was jealous of Pippa's stable home life. Inventing cruel lies to ruin everything. But Pippa wouldn't stand for it. She'd stop Heather, teach her a lesson.

'You'll regret this,' she shouted over her shoulder. 'You'll regret lying to me.'

When school started they didn't speak again of what was said at the park. At least not out loud. Pippa channelled her anger into her letters, which seemed to humour Heather. But she was becoming increasingly distracted by a fresh batch of victims now they were around the other girls in their year again. And each week there was a new boy Heather was gushing about, usually one who drove a car. She seemed to move on from what she'd said.

But Pippa didn't. She kept thinking about it and wondering when Heather would use it against her. As the weeks wore on she became determined to be the one to strike first. She had to protect her name, her family. It's what her mum would have done.

Pippa drew back from the window, heart beating hard in her chest. Just because the police hadn't come to her house yet didn't mean that they wouldn't soon be there. She glanced at her bed, wanting to hide in it for all eternity. But her mum had been so certain when she held her just hours ago, when she'd kissed her cheeks and promised over and over that she'd fix things. The smell of her perfume still lingered in the air.

'I'll protect you,' she had told her daughter, eyes wide and sincere. 'I'll fix this.'

Listening to the house around her, to the throb of her heartbeat in her ears, Pippa knew she had no choice but to trust her mother. But she wanted to hear it again, the promise that all would be well, the strength in her mum's delivery. So she left her room and headed across the landing, thinking of how alone Heather had looked that night on the swings. A solitary figure, atop the hill the park was placed on, gliding back and forth through the air, silhouetted against a darkening sky.

47

Abbie had never liked driving John's car. It was too long, too low. He jokingly called it 'the barge'. Now as she steered it through the darkened streets of Waterbridge it felt impossibly large around her. Like she was behind the wheel of a hearse. It didn't help that she was wearing John's golf gloves. The soft leather was too loose against her fingers, making her grip slippery and unpredictable.

As she approached some red lights she flicked her gaze to the rear-view mirror, seeing an empty street behind her. It was late. Whilst she waited, rain peppering her windscreen, a taxi drew up behind her. People younger than her but older than Pippa would be in the midst of their Friday night out, dancing drunkenly beneath strobe lights on the sticky floor at Passions. Pippa had told her how Heather had snuck into the club a few times. Had gyrated with strangers, knocked back shots.

'I don't want to go clubbing with her when I'm older,' Pippa had admitted fearfully, hair wet from her bath, cheeks rosy as she perched on her bed, bundled in her favourite pink dressing gown. 'She's too intense.'

'Then don't go,' Abbie had replied simply. 'Only go out clubbing with people you like when you're old enough to go.'

'It's not that simple.'

Abbie had stroked her daughter's cheek, smiled gently at her. She understood. Some people were like a drug. And even though they were bad for you, you couldn't stop being around them. Sometimes she wondered if that was what happened with John. That he shifted from object of infatuation to obsession. She built her world around him so tightly, so desperately, that there was no escape for either of them.

The lights turned green and Abbie accelerated, the car awkwardly shifting forwards, her touch on the clutch not quite hard enough. She missed her own car, and knowing intuitively how much pressure to apply.

As a nurse, she knew the only way to successfully come off any drug was to go cold turkey, to completely cut it out. No chance of relapse, only redemption. She turned onto a quiet road bordered with oak trees. Her heart began to work overtime in her chest. Checking her rear-view mirror, she saw the taxi was no longer behind her. She was alone.

Back home John should still be slumped against the kitchen island, a slave to the sedatives in his system. Abbie had been exacting with the dose, refusing to take any chances. By the time he woke up she'd be back there, beside him, and everything would be done. She pulled up against the curb, killed the engine. Leaning back into the headrest, she considered all that she knew.

Heather was dead.

Pippa had killed her.

Only it wasn't murder, it was an accident. But no one would see it that way, would they? Not with Michelle's fucking letters and Heather's general reputation.

And not with John's affair.

John. The man she'd built her life around. The man who was now set to implode it all. He provided their daughter with motive. And worse, he *knew* Michelle's intentions and had done nothing to stop her.

He asked me to leave it alone. Pleaded. Behind the wheel, in the dark, Abbie chewed on her inner cheek. No, that wasn't John. He'd never lower himself to begging, not even for his daughter's life. Michelle was merely goading her. Wasn't it enough that she had John in her bed?

Abbie glanced at the street beyond, the grand trees breaking out of the tarmac, their bare branches reaching up to street lights which highlighted the falling rain.

That was her saviour. Michelle's jealousy. John's failure to leave his wife and daughter. For two years he'd shared another woman's bed. And for two years he'd kept coming home to Abbie. She knew why. Appearance, stability, cleanliness, these were paramount to John Parker. He loathed mess in all its forms. Abbie imagined it was Michelle who kept pleading, asking over and over for John to come and be with her, let their relationship be out in the open. Abbie tightened her fingers against the wheel, wished John's hands were closer in size to her own. She had the motive she needed. Cracking the door to the car she stepped out, taking care to pull up the hood of the sole hooded jumper John possessed. One he'd bought at Disneyland several years ago. Black with a picture of Mickey Mouse on the front.

Abbie locked the car, thrust the keys into her pocket, tucked the hood over her head and approached the gates of Michelle Oxon's home. Just as they had been during her last visit, they were ajar. Abbie pushed them open a fraction more, squeezed through and began walking up the driveway, keeping her head low. There was just one more job left to do.

48

'Mum?' Pippa crept down the stairs. The light was on in the hallway, making the darkness visible through the glass of the front door seem impenetrable. 'Mum?'

Though the house was big, it was old. And in the dark hours the walls like to rattle and shake, floorboards wheezed. Pippa reached the final step and listened. The sounds which had terrified her as a child now comforted her.

'Mum?' She followed the light from the hallway and headed into the kitchen. Darkness greeted her. 'Mum?' Pippa reached for the switch on the wall beside her. Flicked it, instantly banishing the shadows in a blaze of burning white. Then she screamed.

The sound flew from her like a poorly struck chord, jarring against the surrounding silence. Clasping a hand to her own mouth Pippa stared at the figure slumped against the island, head upon the marble and turned away from her. As she recognised the salt-and-pepper curls, the initial feeling of dread began to seep out of her.

'Dad? Dad, are you all right?' She rushed to him, placed one hand against his back as she moved to his side, peered up at his comatose face. 'Dad!' His eyes were tightly shut, mouth slaw, skin warm. 'Dad!' She shook him at the shoulders. Why wasn't he waking up? Was he drunk? But that didn't make sense. Her dad was never, ever drunk. At least not in front of her.

'Dad?' Hot tears slid down her cheeks. Maybe he was just drunk. Maybe she didn't usually venture downstairs at such a late hour. Maybe she didn't know her dad at all, just the illusion he presented to her. 'Dad, what the fuck?' she sobbed, scrubbing the back of her hand against her eyes. She looked at the draped man in her kitchen, felt a sinking sensation in her stomach when she realised the man she thought she'd known wasn't there anymore. She was looking at a complete stranger.

He'd been sleeping with Heather's mum. Behind all their backs.

An image of his bare body against Michelle's flashed in Pippa's mind and she balked. How many times had he come home late and lied, said he'd been at the hospital? How many times had he been at the Oxon house when Heather woke up in the morning? Did he hang around to fix her breakfast? Wish her a good day at school?

Pippa began to tremble as her tears dried up. 'Wake up.' She punched his shoulder. 'Fucking wake up, Dad! You don't get to keep abandoning me!' Had he been downstairs knocking back whiskey while she slept in bed? Did he know everything, know what she'd done, and was this his response to it all? Rather than attempting to fix things, he was drowning in his preferred malt? 'Dammit!' Pippa edged away from him. Blinking hard, she threw a glance at the clock on the wall. Half past one in the morning. She frowned, her gaze drifting to the door and the illuminated hallway beyond. There was only one car in the driveway – her mum's. And yet it was her dad who was passed out in the kitchen. Pippa need her phone, needed answers. She was about to race upstairs to retrieve it when she spotted a note tucked in beneath one of her father's elbows. Pippa closed her fingers around its edge and plucked it free.

The stiff white paper belonged to the notepad attached to the fridge, usually used for shopping lists. She recognised the neat penmanship of her mum's hand.

Pip,
   Don't worry about your father, he will wake up soon with nothing more than a mild headache. And don't worry about anything else, either. I've gone to fix it and will be back soon.
   Love,
   Mum xxx
PS: BURN THIS AFTER READING

Pippa stared at the last line, the final instruction. The paper fluttered in her grasp. Where had her mum gone? What was she doing? And what had she done to Pippa's father? The questions pressed against her temple but Pippa did her best to blink them away. Her mum was going to fix things, she'd said as much in her letter. Pippa turned the slim piece of paper over in her hand. She looked towards the door which led from the kitchen to the conservatory.

Minutes later she was walking the length of the garden, still in her pyjamas but she'd pulled on her warmest boots, snuggled into her parka coat and put on a bobble hat. Still the cold snapped at her like an angry dog. Pippa ignored it, kept walking, hands thrust deep in her coat pockets. She moved from memory. There was no moon to guide her way, just an endless pit of darkness which had swallowed her whole. Pippa descended the trio of stone steps, manoeuvred around terracotta plant pots, sidestepped large roots which broke through the ground like fingers scratching against the surface.

Once she was certain she was far enough from the house, she pulled the note from her pocket along with her plastic purple lighter. There, at the edge of the garden, she produced a tiny flame which flickered and then grew as it tore through her mum's tidy handwriting. Just as the flame was about to singe her fingers Pippa let it fall, watched the bright arc of amber and gold descend towards the abyss beneath her.

49

As a student nurse Abbie had spent time with cadavers. Upon them she'd learnt how to insert a central line, perform intubation. Conduct CPR. All the ways to keep someone alive. And in learning how to preserve life, you also learn all the ways it can be taken away – where all the key arteries are. Arteries which once severed could render someone dead within minutes. Like John, like Michelle, Abbie had dedicated her professional life to aiding others. But she was no longer a practising nurse, her commitment to the Hippocratic oath long since lapsed. Hands encased in her husband's beloved leather golf gloves, she raised a finger to the doorbell, pressed down and waited.

'Abigail?' Michelle was swathed in a thick dressing gown when she came to the door, cheeks tinged rose. She looked beyond her unexpected guest at the driveway in which only John's car stood. 'What the hell are you doing here at this hour?' She laughed lightly, mockingly, as she delivered her question.

'May I come in?'

'Look.' Michelle leant against the door frame, crossing her arms against her chest. She smelt like an orange orchard. 'You're wasting your time coming here. I'm going to the police *first thing* with those letters.'

Abbie quickly assessed the other woman – the fragrance of her skin, dewy and freshly bathed, her hair bundled atop her head but with several ringlets having slipped loose, framing her face. Lashes dark with mascara, the nails which dug into her upper arms freshly painted. Michelle had been hoping for John to appear on her doorstep that night. Had the letters just been a taunt to lure him? Is that what she had to do now – find reasons to attract him to her bed? Was her honey no longer sweet enough? This should have been victory enough for Abbie. But it wasn't. Of course it wasn't. Michelle still had the letters, the potential to damage her daughter with them. And if John wasn't lying in a pool of his own drool, what's to say he wouldn't have come here, and inhaled her sweet perfume up close?

'John asked me to come and speak with you,' Abbie said, raising her chin.

Michelle's eyes instantly narrowed, shoulders dropping a fraction of an inch. 'He did?'

'He thought it better for you to speak to me.'

Chewing on her lip, Michelle again looked behind Abbie, at the shadows upon the driveway, perhaps hoping that John was lurking somewhere, that this was all just a game. 'Fine,' she eventually declared, stepping aside to permit Abbie to enter. 'What the fuck are you wearing, anyway?' she remarked, mouth drawn in a snarl of disapproval.

'It's laundry day,' Abbie muttered as she slipped by her and headed for the kitchen, footsteps awkward in her boots. Or rather *John's* boots – the winter walking boots he rarely wore as he deemed them too tight. For Abbie they were too loose but she could just about get away with wearing them.

'So what is it you want to talk about?' Michelle demanded tensely, hands on hips where she stood several feet behind

Abbie, lingering on the edge of the kitchen. 'Because I'm pretty sure we've said everything we need to.'

Abbie had always had a great memory. It had always served her well. Through school then onto university, she felt it was the gift which kept on giving. Then, as a mother, she never forgot a playdate or a doctor's appointment. Every birthday was remembered. And now, as she looked about Michelle Oxon's kitchen, sleek with its silver fridge and polished granite surfaces, she was thankful that she could recall every detail. The positioning of every item. Like the knife block upon the island, now just inches from her hand which she gently placed on the granite, fighting to keep her breathing level, to appear composed.

'I get that you want to protect, Pippa, I do.' Michelle was pursing her lips, throwing backward glances to the hallway.

She still thinks he might come.

Abbie nearly choked on the bubble of laughter which suddenly caught in her throat. John wasn't coming. He never would visit her again. And he certainly wasn't about to save her. Not that the foolish woman even considered herself to be in danger. Perhaps it was her arrogance, her complete hubris. A lifetime of being golden and glorious made you think you were beyond hurting. She was as dumb as her deceased daughter.

'But I'm showing the police the letters. They need to know the whole picture.'

'Do you know the difference between you and I?' Abbie asked, gently stretching her hand closer to the block, studying it out of the corner of her eye, assessing which blade would be strongest, sharpest. She'd thought it'd be more difficult to distract Michelle but the willowy GP was completely preoccupied with glancing back at the door, fingers nervously clicking together.

'That I can actually make your husband come?' Michelle snapped her blue eyes to briefly land upon Abbie, smirking cruelly.

'No.' Abbie's voice was smooth. As smooth as the surface she was guiding her gloved hand across. She wondered if grief had made Michelle even crueller or if the woman had always been a total cunt. She expected it was the latter. 'The difference between you and I is that I would do anything for my daughter.'

'And I wouldn't?' Michelle demanded, hands wedging firmly against her hips.

'The day Heather died you were busy fucking my husband.'

Michelle sucked in her cheeks, revealing razor-sharp bones.

'I bet you didn't even realise she was missing until someone else told you.'

'Look, Abigail, don't think you can—'

'I *always* know where my daughter is. When she should be home. I look out for her, protect her.'

A quick roll of her eyes in dismissal of Abbie's comments, and then a final, foolish glance over her shoulder at the hallway and the front door.

Abbie moved quickly. She withdrew the largest blade, sprinted the short distance between her and Michelle and thrust it straight into the other woman's side. When the blue eyes turned back to her they were wide with shock and fear.

In someone else's hands the knife might have struggled to pierce several organs successfully. Might have come against bone. Or even failed to be delivered with the right amount of speed and pressure. But Abbie knew. How to preserve life and how to take it. The knife still deep in Michelle's side, her dressing gown began to darken with blood.

'What? What is—'

Abbie clutched at the lapel of the dressing gown with one gloved hand whilst the other withdrew the knife, only to push it in again. And again. Michelle reached towards the island, a dark trickle leaking from the corner of her mouth. Abbie let her fall against it. Then she worked quickly. Several stabs to the back. All in exacting positions. Everything had to be calculated. Neat.

Even though there was nothing neat about it now. Michelle sputtered against the island, her blood forming a river beneath her. And the blood was dark like an oil slick. Abbie eased back, careful not to stand in it. Then she dropped the knife to floor where it clattered against the tiles.

'Like I said,' Abbie whispered to the dying woman, 'I would do anything to protect my daughter. *Anything.*'

50

Pippa wasn't sure of the time. She was aware of the cold which scratched against her cheeks and eventually numbed them. She was aware of the silence which spread through the darkness. Nestled at the base of the oak tree she squatted there, pressed her chin to her knees and waited. Though she had no idea what for.

A part of her wanted to go back inside, to the warmth. She could creep up the stairs, go back to bed and pretend that everything was fine. That things were normal. But in order to do that she'd have to pass by her unconscious father. And to look at him, to even *think* of him, felt like slamming into a brick wall. The reality of her situation smacking against her. There was nowhere to go. No place to hide. Not even beneath her duvet. The truth, *her* truth, was out there. In the world. In other people's mouths.

'She'll fix it,' Pippa whispered to the stiff grass, her words held in a foggy breath. Because her mum had to fix it. She had to. In the distance her house glowed, windows yellow and welcoming. But still Pippa didn't move. Preferring the cold. The silence.

'I hate these cross-country runs,' Heather had declared during Science, the day before the run at Sefton Park. 'But my mum has been so on about them lately. About the importance of extra-curricular bullshit.' With polished nails, she twisted the opening on her Bunsen burner, flicking her flame from orange to blue and back again. 'Must be your dad's influence.' She smirked at Pippa who was on the stool beside her, peering through goggles as she carefully emptied a vial into a glass beaker.

'Will you stop with that,' Pippa hissed, glancing over her shoulder in case anyone else had heard the vile lies her friend kept spouting.

'I'm just saying.' The flame whispered to her as she kept changing its supply of oxygen. 'Maybe you could tell your dad to tell my mum to stop being such a bitch about cross-country.'

'Heather!' Pippa ceased combining the two chemicals in her possession and stared at her friend, lips puckered.

'You need to stop being such a princess about it all.'

'And you need to stop lying,' Pippa stated.

'Or what?' Heather arched an eyebrow at her. Pippa looked down at her beaker. 'That's what I thought. You're all Miss Big Balls in your letters but in person you're same old meek Pip. You want me to stop talking about it, you're going to have to shut me up.' The flame turned orange. Blue. Orange. Blue. 'I dare you,' she taunted, pink lips lifting into a grin.

'Stop talking about my dad.' Pippa tipped the liquid from the vial into the waiting beaker. The reaction was quick. Bubbles and then smoke.

'Then tell him to stop fucking my mum.'

In Pippa's grasp the beaker moved quickly. She smarted briefly at the heat the glass held, then threw it to the ground where it exploded leaving only shards and a smouldering stain on the classroom tiles.

'What was that?' Mr Collins thundered from the front of the room, bushy eyebrows high and alert.

Turning red, Pippa began to mutter her apologies. How the beaker must have slipped. She crouched down and began to pick up the pieces which she could reach.

'Well, well.' Heather abandoned her burner to kneel beside her and help. 'Seems my kitten might have some claws,' she laughed to herself.

'It just slipped,' Pippa said simply. Because that was what had happened. Wasn't it? But her hands still shook with the fury with which they'd possessed when they slung the beaker to the ground.

'Yeah.' Heather was studying her with an amused expression. 'Sure it did.'

The low growl of a car engine. It pulled Pippa away from her thoughts, back to the frost of the garden. She awkwardly stood up, knees sore. How long had she waited out there in the dark? One hour? More? Numbly she shuffled back towards the house, uncertain what would await her once she was inside.

Pippa,

Threaten me all you want but I'm talking. My mum. Your dad. The truth will out. I'm exhausted from keeping their secrets. I don't care that I'm 'in dangerous territory' as you put it. Or that you'll 'shut me up if you have to'. You're just being a bitch. And I get it. It hurt when my parents split. But it was for the best.

I told Mr Hall about it, after detention yesterday. And he's not the only one I've spoken to. Can't believe I got detention for forgetting my fucking PE kit. Fucking Miss Charnley. Old bitch. I'm not going to do the full cross-country run tomorrow at Sefton. NO WAY. You and me, we'll ditch. The old crone will be too dumb to notice. She can't give me a detention and then think I'll run myself ragged when it's this bloody cold out. Although, had I known Mr Hall was the one doing detention maybe I'd have felt differently. Scratch that — of course I would have. You should have seen how he looked at me. All caring. He touched my hand at one point too and I WAS ON FIRE. He and I — we're destined. Like star-crossed lovers or something. And I told him about my mum. Your dad. And he urged me to speak out, said that holding things in like that can cause ulcers.

So I'm telling everyone, Pip. And you can moan all you want but you can't actually stop me.

H

51

Abbie was home. It seemed strange that the house was as she'd left it. A light shining in the porch. Curtains drawn at every window. It looked as it did on any other night. With a shudder, Abbie released her hands from the steering wheel. Cracked the door, stepped onto the gravel. As though in a dream she fumbled for her keys, struggled to push them into the lock of the front door. With a grunt she was inside. Beneath the hall light she could study her clothes. Could notice the dark red smears on the golf gloves. Her eyes crinkled as she teetered on the edge of something she couldn't quite comprehend, fighting to hold herself upright.

Blood. There had been so much of it. This Abbie had been expecting. Even the moment when Michelle's eyes became waxy and unseeing. She had been expecting that too. In her past life as a nurse, Abbie had become accustomed to death. To guilt. But now in her hallway she realised that something strange had followed her home. Not remorse. Not regret. Something more—

'Mum?' A figure in the doorway which led to the kitchen, pale and shivering. 'Mum, you're back.' Pippa's voice, strained and fragile, cracked as she spoke.

'Sweetheart.' Instinct guided her closer but she stopped inches away, catching herself. 'I need to go and change.'

'Is that . . .' Pippa pointed a finger towards the leather gloves Abbie was still wearing, 'Mum, is that blood? Are you all right?'

Her daughter rushed to her and Abbie had to ease back, knocking against the telephone stand, almost sending a vase of fresh lilies atop it toppling to the floor. The flowers wavered but didn't fall.

'It's not mine,' she said quickly. Urgently. Aware that she was running out of time. 'Don't worry, Pip. I'm all right. Everything is going to be all right.'

'But . . .' Pippa blinked at her, eyes red and sore. It was there in the look she gave her, the question she couldn't dare breathe life into.

What have you done?

Abbie smiled at her, heart clenching. Because that was the change. Her soul was forever marked now. She had been close to death before but failing to save someone was different to harming them. Ending them. She had taken a life. Just as Pippa had. Once more they were the same, two sides of the same coin.

'I need to go and shower,' she told her daughter. 'Go and wait in your room, I won't be long.'

'Will Dad be OK?' Pippa fired a look over her shoulder.

Abbie inhaled slowly. 'Well, that depends which way you look at it.'

She scrubbed her skin until it burned red. She rubbed her scalp until her fingers and wrists ached. Every speck of blood, every trace of Michelle, swirled down the shower plughole along with the gel she had lathered herself in. Then, once she was freshly clean and dry, Abbie drew her still-damp hair back in a low ponytail and pulled on her pyjamas. The clothes she'd previously worn she placed in a bin bag and then carried out onto the driveway, placing the bag in the boot of John's car. All the while her mind churned, trying to thicken her plan into something concrete, something secure.

What if she'd missed something? What if she hadn't done enough?

But there wasn't time to dwell on doubt. Abbie needed to be swift. As the sky softened against the horizon she entered John's study, grabbed what she needed. Placed several notes in his drawer. Moving her husband was more difficult than she'd assumed it would be. In his state of lethargy he was heavy and uncooperative, head lolling back and forth. With some effort she managed to get him on his feet and then muscle memory helped his sluggish feet shuffle across the floor as she walked him to his study, dropped him into his beloved chair. A king on his throne.

With a groan he tilted his chin upwards, lifted heavy eyelids. He was waking up. Abbie dashed away, back upstairs.

'Sweetheart.' She opened Pippa's bedroom door, found the young girl sitting on the edge of her unmade bed gnawing on the tips of her nails. 'Put on some pyjamas and get in bed. Pretend you've been sleeping there all night, got it?'

Pippa nodded and said nothing. Eyes wide.

'It will be all right,' Abbie said as she approached her, reached out and cradled Pippa's cold face in her hands. 'I promise. I've taken care of everything. You're going to be fine, Pip. You're going to be safe.'

Her daughter felt like she was made of ice.

'I need you to trust me,' said Abbie. 'Do you trust me?'

'I trust you.'

'Good.' Abbie kissed her forehead, squeezed her cheeks. 'Because there's one final thing I need you to do for me.'

'Anything,' Pippa said with sincerity.

Back in John's study Abbie watched her husband squirm awkwardly in his chair, push his hands through his hair, blink, take in his surroundings. He was awake, and momentarily helpless. Clothes crumpled, eyes bloodshot. The immaculate surgeon was gone. Replaced by a dishevelled, confused man.

'John.' She said his name loudly. Firmly. Needing him to listen to her. To understand. 'John?'

He glanced around his study as though he'd never seen it before. Abbie began to worry that she'd used too much sedative, left his mind too sluggish for what was to come next. But when he twisted his head to peer up at her, his eyes widened, their usual sharpness returning to them. Cocking his glance to one side he studied her as an eagle might a mouse. Only Abbie was the one standing, the one on the other side of his desk, the one holding all the cards.

She remembered what it was like to love him. It was like drowning.

'What . . . what have you done?' he demanded gruffly, scratching at his throat.

'John,' she repeated, saying the name sternly, finally in the role of teacher. 'I need you to listen very carefully to what I'm about to say.'

52

THE FOLLOWING STATEMENT WAS GIVEN BY MR JOHN PARKS AT WATERBRIDGE POLICE STATION ON THE MORNING OF SATURDAY 29TH NOVEMBER 2003.

Just over three weeks ago, on the afternoon of Wednesday 5th November, I drove out to Sefton Park. I'd been in clinic all morning and told my assistant I was going home due to a headache. This was not true. I felt fine. I was actually going to Sefton to intercept the cross-country run I knew would be going ahead. A run I knew my daughter was participating in. That Heather Oxon was participating in.

Upon my arrival I did not park in the main car park. Instead I pulled into the side road, Jockey Lane, and parked my car on the edge of a farmer's field. I then walked back towards the boundary of Sefton Park and climbed the surrounding fence where it is only several feet high. I walked towards the main house. It was raining, so with my hood up and boots on, I knew I'd blend in with any other dog walkers who might be about. Except it was unusually quiet, even given the weather, because of the school run.

I'd asked my daughter to do two things for me that morning. One – to ensure that Heather was removed from the main group. She assured me this would be easy. Second – to swap her water bottle with Heather's prior to the run. Pippa had no idea why I wanted her to do these things for me. When asked I told her not to question me. I'm ashamed to admit that this does somewhat characterise the relationship we have.

So when I rounded the main house I saw in the distance Heather and my daughter. When my daughter saw me, she jogged away to rejoin the others on the run. Once Heather realised I was there she understood the intention of my visit.

'You're here to warn me about talking about you and my mum,' she said.

Here I should disclose that for the past two years I have been engaged in extra-marital activities with Heather's mother, Dr Michelle Oxon. I confirmed to Heather that this was indeed the reason for me seeking her out. She had been discussing the affair with my daughter, Pippa, even though I'd insisted to Heather on numerous occasions to keep it private. I did not wish to hurt my family. But Heather was always a girl who loved drama so she couldn't resist discussing what was going on between me and her mother.

My intention that morning was merely to scare her. To set off the allergy attack I knew she'd have, to demonstrate to her that I would hurt her, if I needed to, to ensure her silence. But I had misjudged the severity of her allergy. Or rather, had been ill-informed of it. When Heather herself spoke about it previously, she had been dismissive. She also failed to keep an EpiPen on her person, which further made me suspect it was only a mild intolerance at best. However, it was not. As soon as she consumed the water I had laced with peanut oil, she quickly succumbed to a violent anaphylactic attack, her airways became compromised and she transpired within minutes. I did not intercede. Once I was certain she had died I felt I had no other choice but to push her into the river. Hide the body. I think I had the foolish hope it would float away and everyone would believe she had just fled Waterbridge.

When the truth of her death surfaced, my daughter did not come forward to say she had seen me. Why would she? I'm her father, it is only natural she wanted to protect me. As more and more information was leaked about Heather's death, Michelle began to grow suspicious. She knew of my disdain for both her daughter and her daughter's ability to gossip so freely about us.

I wanted to protect my family. Our name. Our legacy.

Michelle was a smart woman. It didn't take her long to realise what had really happened to her daughter. On the evening of Friday 28th November 2003 I visited her home, as I regularly did on Friday nights, and she confronted me. Our ensuing altercation became violent. I stabbed her. Out of self-preservation.

[For the purpose of our records can you recall how many times you stabbed her?]

Six. I stabbed her six times. As I said, things became heated. And in the end I was lost to the anger I felt towards her.

308

[She'd have died from the first wound. Why continue?]

Things got heated. It all happened so quickly.

[And you'd been romantically involved with the victim?]

Yes. For two years. But I never wanted a life with her. A future. And she knew that. But I think she employed her daughter to try and reveal our affair, to force my hand into making it public. And I never wanted that. I love my wife. My daughter. I didn't want to ruin our family. Destroy our home. What I had with Michelle was only ever physical. Things escalated more than I could ever have expected, first with Heather and then with Michelle. I never intended to kill either of them. They were . . . mistakes. Accidents. Two awful, horrific accidents. And that is why I am here now. Confessing. Because things have gone too far. This all needs to end. So I am turning myself in, pleading my guilt. I see now that in my efforts to protect my family I have only further hurt them. And I don't want that. I want only to keep Abigail and Pippa safe. They are all that matters. They are why I am sitting here today.

STATEMENT ENDS HERE

53

May 2004

Abbie didn't like the drive to the prison. It took her out of Waterbridge, across the border into a different county. She ended up in the middle of a historic town boasting more charity shops than pubs. Once parked, she climbed a hill, signed her name, passed through a scanner and then eventually got to see her husband.

Gone were the suits. Now he wore his regulation prison uniform which was so oddly reminiscent of hospital scrubs it added an eerie hilarity to their meetings. She always visited on a Tuesday morning. Setting off right after the school run. Their time together was always brief. And awkward. John barely uttering a word from where he was sitting on the other side of a table, hands cuffed together in his lap.

But on this bright morning in early May, Abbie had news to deliver. News which might extend her visit beyond the usual ten minutes. So instead of updating him about Pippa's time at school, how her GCSE preparation was going, she opened with: 'I'm going back to work.'

Hair in a bun, skin flawless in a layer of foundation, Abbie felt confident. But her posture slumped in the seconds that followed. John's chest rose and promptly fell with an exaggerated sigh. He then stared at the table before asking, 'And how is Pippa? Ready for her exams?'

'That's it?' Abbie crossed and uncrossed her legs. 'No interest at all in my going back to work?'

'No.' He raised his head to look at her. He looked so very tired. 'None.'

'Well, I need to pay the bills somehow,' Abbie protested loudly, folding her arms against her chest. 'Aren't you even interested in which department? How my re-entry exams went?'

Her husband wearily shook his head.

'You just want to know about Pippa,' Abbie noted flatly.

A stiff nod.

'She's all that connects us,' he said. 'All that matters between us.'

Abbie blinked. He was right. She smiled thinly at him. 'I think it's been that way for quite some time.'

A resigned sigh.

'When I met you, you were everything,' she remembered wistfully, a hand lifting to girlishly tuck a strand of hair behind her ear. 'You were so admired by everybody. So *feared*. And such an accomplished surgeon.'

'And yet here I am,' John raised his bound hands half an inch, 'completely diminished because of you.'

'Because of *you*,' Abbie clarified bluntly. '*You* were the one who had the affair. *You* were the one who prompted Heather Oxon to commence gossiping about you. Pippa spiralled, because of *you*. So you have no one else to blame for being in here. You did this all to yourself. And you had the hubris to leave your car outside her house, in *plain sight*, John. Where anyone could see it. It's like you wanted to get caught.'

He considered this for a moment. 'Perhaps I did.'

'You destroyed everything,' Abbie released her venom in a whisper, 'everything we worked so hard to build. You deserve to be in here.'

'I understand why I'm here.' He cocked his head at his wife. 'I'm doing my part to protect my daughter.'

'Only because I left you no choice.'

'And I'm a prominent surgeon with a very good lawyer. I'll be here for a handful of years at most.' He shuffled in his chair, clearly uncomfortable against the cheap plastic. 'I've operated on half the guards in here,' he continued. 'People know me. Respect me. I'll regain my life, Abigail.'

'And with you locked up I'm finally able to regain mine,' she declared, nostrils flaring. 'I can finally practise nursing again. Be myself again.'

'No one stopped you being yourself.'

'No, John, *you* did. Time and time again. I had to be your wife, your maid, your cook, your cleaner, your accountant. Constantly. You left it so there was no space for me to exist.'

'You lived for Pippa,' John muttered, eyes narrowing, 'never for me.'

'I lived for you both,' Abbie corrected him. 'But you didn't see that.'

'The day you became a mother you stopped being a wife.'

Abbie blinked. Took a second to gather her thoughts, clasping her hands into a ball on the table before her, leaning towards her husband. 'Do you know how hard it is to be a woman?' she asked. 'The demands which are placed on us?'

'Don't start with the feminist bullshit.' He glanced to the door.

'I had to be everything for you. And I was. And I had to be everything to Pippa. And I was. There was nothing left for me. You think you fell into Michelle's bed because she was so alluring, so desperate to please you? You think you're diminished? I've been fading away for nearly two decades, you should try how that feels.'

'I made you.' John pushed back from the table, chair scraping on the concrete floor. 'I gave you everything. Before me, you had nothing.'

Abbie's jaw clenched.

'That's why I married you, Abigail. Because I knew you'd be forever grateful. Because before me you were living in a council terrace with your mother. I gave you a wonderful life.'

'No, John, it was a wonderful lie. We were supposed to love each other.' Her cheeks burned, knowing that she had truly loved him. Back when she was young. Idealistic. Back before her stomach had swelled and she'd had to divide that love.

'And we *did* love each other, once.' Crinkles deepened in the corners of his eyes. 'I was happy in our marriage, Abigail.'

'Then what changed?'

'The day we brought Pippa home from the hospital I saw it in your eyes. She was your world. And I just became the man who paid for it.'

'That's not fair,' Abbie snapped.

'Maybe not,' John conceded, 'but we were built on passion and hunger. I was the surgeon, you the beautiful young nurse. But after Pippa, all that heat went away. You became cold, clinical. I felt like I was forever trapped in this . . . this surgical world.'

'I became a *wife*, John. A mother. I did what I had to. What I needed to.' She blinked quickly to push back tears.

'I never wanted Pippa to end up like you, to lack . . . empathy.'

'Like *me*?' Abbie squeaked, incredulous. 'You are the one who set her on her dark path,' she said, pointing a perfectly manicured nail at him, 'not me, John. You.'

'You need to listen to what I'm saying.'

'Look, John—'

'I understand that you want to protect her. I do. But what will you do next time, when you don't have me to be your scapegoat?'

Abbie frowned. 'Next time?'

John released a chesty laugh. 'You truly are so blind to it all. Do you still think Heather's death was an accident?'

Throwing an anxious glance over her shoulder, towards the door on which two guards were positioned on the other side, she hissed her response across the table: 'Of course I do.'

'Then you're a fool.'

'Our daughter made a mistake. That's all.'

'Heather was Pippa's best friend.' Abbie opened her mouth to speak and John raised his cuffed hands to silence her. 'I don't care about the nuances of what that means between teenage girls. The bottom line is that Pippa *knew* Heather. Knew the true severity of her allergy.'

'No, Heather was always downplaying it and—'

'*Knew* that Heather didn't keep her EpiPen close.'

'She had no idea that the attack would be so violent, so swift.' Abbie was speaking quietly, urgently, needing to silence her husband. 'It was a mistake. Plain and simple.'

'Then why not alert somebody?' John stretched closer to her. 'The moment Heather began struggling to breathe, why not scream for help? Why not run back to find the teachers? Instead she waited for the girl to take her final breath. Then she pushed her into the river.'

Abbie was silent.

'That's not the response of someone acting in the moment. Someone having a panicked reaction. That's the action of someone who knew what they were doing. Who planned it. I know because it's part of what I'm being accused of. Calculated murder.'

'John, she didn't know what would happen with the oil and she—'

'Christ, Abbie, she *knew*. Open your eyes.' John was glaring at her, veins raised in his forehead. 'Protect her this time all you want. But she needs help. Real, actual psychological help. Promise me you'll at least get her that.'

'Our daughter is fine.' Abbie was getting up, pulling her handbag against her shoulder. 'What she needs is a stable home life. Love. Security.'

'For weeks she kept what she did from us. From you. That isn't normal. It's . . . it's the actions of a sociopath.'

'No,' Abbie said, clutching her handbag tightly to her side, 'it's the actions of a terrified teenage girl, that's all.'

'You gave it to her.' John studied her as she pushed in her chair. 'What she did with Heather, you did with Michelle. You're both broken.'

'Yet you're the one sitting in here,' Abbie remarked coldly.

'You think I'm blind?' John's face scrunched up in anger. 'You think I never saw what was going on in my *own home*?'

Abbie grimaced tightly at him. 'Perhaps, *dear*, you were too busy occupying yourself in other people's homes. And that was the problem.'

John clicked his fingers, the sound like a bullet, and pointed at her. 'When you had to pull her out of *The Nutcracker*. Back during your ballet phase.'

315

Abbie's face crinkled with disdain. 'The whole process was just too stressful for Pippa,' she declared breathily. 'The schedules, the strains upon on her body, the—'

'She put those razors in that poor girl's shoes. Tammy . . . Tammy something.'

'Tammy Collins,' Abbie effortlessly corrected him.

'That's it.' Another click of his lean fingers, the sound rattling in her bones. 'You told me Pippa pulled out of the show because her heart wasn't in it. But people talked. Michelle talked.'

Abbie felt her entire body steel at the sound of the dead woman's name.

'There were whispers about the incident with the ballet shoes. About how that poor girl's feet were cut to ribbons. I remember at the time, noticing in my cabinet, several of my razors were missing. I spoke to you about it and you dismissed me out of hand.'

'You merely forgot how many razors you had.'

'I don't think I did.'

'A moment ago you couldn't even remember the name of the *poor girl* who was so afflicted. So don't pretend your memory is some iron vault from which nothing ever escapes.'

'The point is you lied to me.' John's hand slapped against the table, the sound hollow. 'You lied to protect Pippa. But what she did . . . it was cruel. Malicious. She didn't even *care* about ballet, she just disliked the girl.'

Abbie arched an eyebrow and said nothing.

'She hurt that girl on purpose.'

'She didn't,' Abbie stated briskly. 'Accidents happen, girls play pranks on one another all the time.'

'Abbie, she needed help back then.' John stared at her with watery eyes. 'The ballet shoes were more than a . . . *prank* . . . it was her acting out. It was no accident.'

'How can you say that?' Abbie narrowed her eyes and sharpened her tone.

'And you kept it from me,' John lamented, still in the past.

'Pippa did nothing wrong.'

'You know that's not true,' John declared with a lump in his throat.

'She's my daughter. I know my daughter.'

'You know she placed the razors. Spiked the water. You can't protect her forever.' The statement echoed in the sparse room.

'The ballet shoe incident is hearsay. Nothing more,' Abbie told him primly.

'And Heather?'

'You're comparing a dead teenage girl to a dance slipper?' Abbie mocked.

'It'll happen again,' John warned, expression darkening. 'There's something wrong with our daughter. With you.'

Abbie squared her shoulders, inhaling sharply. 'I'm leaving.'

'You think the reason I didn't want you to return to nursing is because I wanted to keep you at home, keep you as a housewife?' The question came as her hand reached for the door. Twisting round Abbie looked back at him.

'That's what you said,' she recalled. 'You told me my role was to be a mother and homemaker.'

'I saw it in you, Abigail,' John was watching her with sad eyes. 'You could be so cruel with patients. So cold.'

'That's not true,' she uttered in a strained breath.

'The errors on charts, the denial of medication to anyone who was rude to you.'

'I was a *good nurse*, John.' The sting of his words left her breathless.

'No,' he softly corrected her. 'You were not. You were always missing that vital ingredient – compassion.'

'Are you –' she clasped a hand to her chest, breathing hard '– questioning my *compassion*? Everything I do is for my daughter. For Pippa. Because I love her.'

'You love her because you see yourself in her. The mark of a narcissist. I've always known it but kept looking the other way.'

'Well, aren't you just in a prime position to judge?' Abbie seethed, gesturing around the small room.

'Michelle was kind. Was good.' John bowed his head and she saw the sorrow wash over him. Clenching her jaw, Abbie made herself poker straight.

'You deserve to be in here, John,' she told him sincerely. 'For all you've done to our family.'

'I knew there was something broken in you. But I hoped becoming a mother would fix it. You were so beautiful, and so in love with me, it was intoxicating. We fell into the routine of marriage and I kept hoping that the house, motherhood, it'd make you kinder, gentler. But Abigail, I was wrong. You, Pippa, you both need help.'

Abbie absorbed his comment with stoicism. Staring into his eyes she asked the question that prodded at her in the dead of night, persistent as a starved mosquito. 'Do you still think about her?'

She saw her husband's jaw clench, a ripple of sorrow flutter across his tired features and her heart ached.

'Yes,' he admitted in a strained breath.

Abbie wanted to fling the table between them across the room, hear it land against the wall with a satisfying crash. Instead she rose, smoothed out the creases in her dress, her expression blank.

'I'm leaving.'

'You and Pippa need help,' he told her urgently.

'Goodbye, John.'

'I'm just telling you what you need to hear,' he called after her as she opened the door and marched into the corridor. But Abbie wasn't listening.

54

Things were different at school. Initially, in the days and weeks following her father's arrest, Pippa hadn't wanted to go back. Hadn't wanted to be confronted by her peers, endure their relentless whispers. That's if they had the grace to say their comments behind her back. She anticipated verbal onslaughts to her face. And worse.

But it never came.

For two weeks, she hid away at home, safely concealed away from all the drama thanks to a doctor's note. But she couldn't stay away forever. So just before the Christmas holidays she returned to Waterbridge Preparatory. No longer Pippa Parks, best friend to Heather Oxon. She was now Pippa Parks, daughter of a killer. Perhaps it was through fear, or maybe just confusion, not knowing what exactly to say to her, but in those first few cold weeks and months, people avoided her. They darted to the other side of the corridor rather than risk making eye contact with her. Only Hannah lingered. 'I get it,' she told Pippa early on, 'how scared you must have been, knowing it was your dad all along. I get why you lied, said you saw nothing.'

The truth of the affair was out. Along with the revelation of the double murders. First Heather, then Michelle. People were much crueller about the latter. Pippa would hear old ladies gossiping together in the aisles at Sainsbury's.

She'd huddle close to her mum, both bending their heads, moving with quick, stealthy steps. As they moved she'd catch fragments of their conversation. And no matter the day, the weather, the time, the locals of Waterbridge were always setting their words to the beat of the same song.

For two years.
Can you imagine?
No wonder the husband left her.
And to do it all behind her friend's back.
No wonder he killed her.
No wonder she's gone.
She had it coming.

Because that was it, wasn't it? Michelle, Heather, they weren't innocent. They never had been. Had Pippa not intervened, fate would have. Pippa did what she had to, just as her mum did. And now her father too was atoning for his sordid part in it all. Because after all, it was he who began the turning of the tragic wheel of death that came to claim the mother and daughter. If he'd never shared Michelle's bed, he wouldn't be left standing over her grave.

'We did what we had to,' was her mum's response when she asked her. And so Pippa followed that mantra. *What we had to.* As though there had never been a choice.

Now it was May. The days were getting longer. Warmer. And things were different at school. Most notably there was a framed picture of Heather in the main hallway, smiling proudly in her school uniform. Up there, on the wall, she looked even more perfect than she had in life. And that was how she would forever be. Perfect.

'Will you be OK today?' her mum had asked as she pulled up beyond the gates. It was the question she asked every morning, features pinched as she anxiously awaited the answer.

'I'll be OK.' And Pippa would be. Because she willed herself to be. It was tempting to want to return to the sanctuary of her bedroom, to the warm comfort of her bed. She had done something truly terrible and yet the world hadn't stopped. Everything hadn't changed in the loaded second after she slipped over from schoolgirl to killer. The world kept turning, carried on. Meaning Pippa had to do the same.

Hannah was waiting by the gates, blonde hair blowing into her eyes, and greeted her with a smile. 'Morning, Pip.'

'Morning.' They fell into an easy stride together.

'How much revision did you do last night?' Hannah was speaking quickly, on a high from the three coffees she'd downed that morning. 'I focused mainly on physics and was up until after two.'

Ah, GCSEs. The saviour of Pippa's social existence. The girls at Waterbridge cared about one thing so much more than a murdered peer – their own futures. And with the biggest exams of their young lives looming, it was all anyone could talk about. Spare time was spent cramming. The space for gossip, for speculation, had all but been entirely squeezed out as soon as spring arrived.

'I did some,' Pippa confessed, 'mainly English Lit.' The textbooks, they helped. When Pippa was studying, trying to commit a multitude of information to memory, she couldn't think about Heather. About those final, strained gasps for air. About how everyone just accepted her part in it all without further questions.

My dad told me to switch the water, didn't tell me why. I saw him in the grounds at Sefton Park and he told me to stay away.

Everyone understood why she'd been silent. Why she'd protected him.

'I'm so sick of Shakespeare,' Hannah announced with a roll of her eyes.

Pippa wasn't. She had read over and over the scene in *Othello* where he kills Desdemona. The compulsion to kill someone you love, out of jealousy, out of rage. Pippa was fascinated by it.

She had it coming.

'I hear Tristan Jenkins is having a huge party at his after final exams,' Hannah chattered on as they swept beneath Heather's beaming portrait.

'Oh yeah, I heard about that,' Pippa nodded. That was the other thing her infamy had granted her – a golden pass into all the upper circles. Everyone wanted to be around her now she was notorious. 'I've been invited, we should go.'

'Defo,' Hannah linked arms with her. 'I think Tristan is so bloody hot, don't you?'

'Sure.' Pippa kept staring ahead, willing the last few metres of the corridor to pass quickly, not daring to glance back over her shoulder because she hated the way the eyes in Heather's portrait always seemed to follow her, no matter where she went.

55

The sky was blue at Sefton Park. It stretched across the trees which were adorned with tentative green shoots. Abbie walked briskly, arms pumping by her sides.

Her feet whispered across the ground as she moved, taking short, sharp breaths. It felt good to move, to stretch her legs until they filled with a burning ache. Abbie upgraded to a jog, sailing past a dog walker with an excitable cavalier which turned to watch Abbie, tail flapping madly.

Abbie gave a polite nod and kept moving. The river came into view. A wide streak of muddy brown that curved away from her.

This is where it happened.

In the sunlight, the scent of fresh cut grass in the air, it was hard to imagine rain. And mud. And death. White daisies dotted the embankment. The embankment Heather's stilled body had rolled down. The murky waters which had claimed her. Abbie had seen enough.

She stole a glance at her watch. Just after ten. There was plenty of time to finish her run around the grounds, get home, prepare a lamb joint before she had to pick Pip up from school. And then after tea she'd be heading off for her shift at the hospital. Not on the Gastro department. She'd been assigned to Head and Neck. This suited Abbie just fine. On that ward there were fewer things to remind her of John. Not that it really mattered. His name still travelled the length of the corridors just as much as Heather and Michelle's names did.

That doctor who went mad.

Murdered his lover and her daughter.

He worked here. For years. Was well thought of.

Shows how you never really know someone.

As Abbie ran, her mind worked. Over and over she picked at the details from the night she'd visited Michelle. She picked and she picked until the memory was raw. Always she circled back to the same, agonising thought.

What if I missed something?

What if there were some trace of evidence that would exonerate John and condemn her? A thread of hair in the kitchen, a speck of DNA upon the countertop? *But you'd been there before.*

Yes, it was reasonable there'd be traces of her. John too. Abbie had been so careful in her set up of it all, so thorough. On the day Heather died he'd been with Michelle. His little black diary delivered that shred of information. So Michelle was his only alibi for that first murder. With her out of the way, it was his word against . . . Pippa's. Pippa who agreed to claim to see him at Sefton Park. Pippa who would deny that he was ever slumped over the island in the kitchen, drugged.

'Are you sure you can do this?' Abbie had been so worried about asking Pippa to lie. It seemed too great a weight to place on such young shoulders. But what was the alternative? The truth would see them both behind bars.

'I can do it,' Pippa had replied, nodding, looking so solemn, so certain, and so much older than her sixteen years.

'In saying that you saw him that day, it means he'll go to jail.'

'I know.'

'I appreciate that it is all quite—'

'He did this.' Pippa's voice had hardened. 'He slept with Heather's mum. Kept it from us. Lied to us. Heather. Michelle. They're both on him.'

Abbie could only nod, unable to argue with the logic as it was the same rationale she employed in the small hours of the night, when she questioned what both she and her daughter were truly capable of.

'Dad deserves to be in jail for what he did to us.'

And that was where he was. Locked up, awaiting sentencing. Despite his usual serving of arrogance and bravado whenever Abbie visited, she'd bet that her husband feared a severe sentence, that perhaps his professional credentials wouldn't be enough to solicit leniency from the judge.

Chest tightening, Abbie finally slowed. Hands on her lower back, she arched to look up at the clear sky, filled her lungs with air, tasting the early flavours of summer. There was birdsong, the whisper of leaves on a soft breeze. All was tranquil. All was well. She was smiling as she made her way back to her car.

56

Pippa was in the garden. The sky was a smear of dusky pink above her. Squatting at the base of the oak tree, she studied the sheet of A4 paper in her hands. Distantly she heard the cries from the stragglers still on the golf course, struggling with the eighteenth hole. Soon the sun would slip from the sky and it would be dark.

She looked to the house, standing large and empty at the other end of the garden. Her mum had departed for her shift at the hospital, leaving Pippa alone.

'You'll be all right?' her mum had asked, cradling Pippa's chin in her hands, which had grown rougher since her return to work. 'I'll be fine, I promise.'

Her first GCSE exam was on the coming Monday. History in the morning. Then Maths in the afternoon. She'd spend her entire weekend cramming.

'You are on the precipice of greatness,' the headmistress had declared as she addressed the gathered Year Elevens in the hall, her clipped voice echoing off the high ceiling. 'Do not squander this opportunity. Seize it. Seize it and claim it.'

Pippa knew that people expected her to fail. Teachers were telling her not to worry if she struggled with the exams, that the coursework she'd already turned in was good enough to warrant a decent grade. But she had no interest in *decent*. She had to do great. Or else what was it

327

all for? Her father in prison, her free? She really did have to seize the moment, make it all count.

A bird chirped in the branches above and Pippa tightened her grip on the paper, causing the edges to soften and curl. With the light fading she drank in the cooling air and read her final letter to Heather one last time.

H,
    There's a lot I want to say. And a lot I can't say.
I'm really not sure when things got so fucked up between
us. Maybe it was always that way, or maybe it happened
slowly, crept up on us both. Either way, you're gone.
And it is all my fault.
    You were telling the truth about my dad. I know that
now. I guess I'm supposed to say that I'm sorry that
I didn't believe you. But you told so many lies it was
hard to see the truth. My dad was an asshole. He did
something really shitty to me and my mum. Especially my
mum. But then he's been there for me when I needed him
to be. So I don't know. Maybe he is a good dad. Or at
least he was once. Things changed, I guess. People change.
    And I'm sorry about your mum. I don't really know
what I believe about what happens next but I hope
you're together somewhere. Wherever that may be.
I know I'd want to be with my mum.
    GCSEs start on Monday and I'm determined to do
better than Hannah. She thinks she's going to finish top
of the year. I know how much you'd hate it if she did.
    That's the thing – I think about you a lot. Every
day. I think about what you'd say, when you'd roll your
eyes, the snarky notes you'd send me during school about
something someone said. You could be such a bitch. But

I miss you. We were friends. And somewhere along the way that got messed up into something else. I wonder if we were both to blame for that.

But Heather, I'm sorry. So fucking sorry. I was SO angry at you. What you were saying about my dad, that you were telling people. I felt like you were pushing me to do what I did, goading me. My mum thinks it was an accident. I think you deserve the truth.

Remember when you said you saw the dark in me? Is that why you pushed me? I wanted you to do more than break out in hives. I wanted you to suffer. I knew that without your EpiPen you'd die. And I let it happen. So what does that make me? A monster? I regret it. I see now I went too far. But I still did it. And now everyone thinks my dad is a murderer when it was me. I wanted you gone, Heather. I was tired of living under your rule. And the fucking, Alanis-level irony is that I miss you. How lame is that?

If I could bring you back, I would. But obviously I can't. So I need to move on from what happened. Do my exams, start sixth form, try and get into Oxford or Cambridge like I always planned. Because I'm still here. You're not, but I am. And I can't waste that.

I promise to do better. And to never wear colours that clash.

We'll be friends always.

Pip

xoxo

The golf course was empty. The shadows in the garden thick. With a shaking hand, Pippa took the plastic purple lighter from her pocket, ignited the small flame and held it to the lower left corner of her letter. She watched it burn, smelt the sweetness of the fire, and let the ash gather at her feet.

Epilogue

September 2004

Pippa's bag swung at her side as she sailed through the school gates, newly flaxen hair fluttering against her neck. Everything was new, from her black Morgan tote bag to her freshly dyed and cut hair. Even her blazer, maroon. The colour the sixth formers wore.

'There you are.' Eyes lighting up when she saw her friend, Hannah released the wall she'd been slumped against to dash to Pippa, lightly planting a kiss upon her cheek. 'I feel like I've been waiting *forever* for term to start.'

'I know,' Pippa agreed with a rueful smile.

Sixth form.

A Levels.

Parties.

Boys.

Gone was their girlhood and school years. The summer had burned long and hot and they'd all emerged from it rounder, greedier. Yearning for life to give them all that it could.

Dust gathered on Heather's name. Passing girls no longer craned their necks to glance at her picture as they strode down the hallway. Arm in arm with Hannah, Pippa ascended the stone steps, her new shoes slightly too tight. But she welcomed the pain, for in time the leather would mould to her will. In time everything would fit perfectly.

'Are you going to that party at Tom's later?' Hannah was prattling on as they meandered towards their new form room. Pippa was nodding, thinking of the text message she'd yet to reply to on her phone. When it came through she originally thought there must be some mistake, that she was somehow in possession of Heather's phone, who was still being asked to all the best parties, even beyond the grave. But the phone, like Heather, was gone. This invite was for Pippa. Even addressing her by name.

'Always wait three days before replying to a boy,' Heather had once told her sincerely. So Pippa was waiting.

She smirked at Hannah. 'I mean, I might go. Maybe.'

Her friend erupted in giggles, loving this response. 'I mean, yeah, same. I'll go if you do. Loving the new hair by the way.'

Pippa's chin was high. Bolstered by her new life, her new beginning. Now only college was in her way before she could ascend to Cambridge. Her GCSEs had set her well on the path. All A's.

'Was there ever any doubt?' her mum had declared proudly when she'd seen the results, before kissing her hard on the cheek.

It was worth it. All of it. She was excelling. As she was always supposed to.

We did what we had to do.

Lost in chatter, neither Hannah or Pippa looked up at Heather's portrait as they passed it in the hallway. 'If we *did* go the party, what would we wear?' Hannah was asking eagerly.

'I'm thinking a dress, definitely.' Pippa's smile felt so free, so easy, her answer unbridled and honest. It was so easy to be herself now she was out of Heather's shadow. So easy to shine.

We did what we had to do.

And as Pippa arrived in her form room, as she settled in her chair, designer bag at her feet, face angled towards her tutor, she knew that she would do it all again.

If she had to.

Acknowledgements

I've really enjoyed working on *She Had It Coming*. It's a story that is special to me for a number of reasons and there are people who I need to thank, people without whose input and support it just wouldn't be the book that it is today.

My wonderful agent, Emily Glenister. You work tirelessly and always believe in me. You push me to be the best writer I can whilst being an awesome person. You're truly one of the best.

Huge thanks to my fabulous editor, Rhea. From the beginning you've been so passionate about this story and helped guide it to become my most thrilling book yet. Thank you for your continued support. And for dog pictures. Those always make my day.

To the wider team at Orion, I'm forever grateful for the sensational covers and for the opportunity to keep writing the stories that I love. You gave my dark mind a home.

My friends, you know who you are. Every WhatsApp, every TikTok, every FaceTime, they keep me sane. Especially when I'm knee-deep in the edit trenches.

My mum and dad. For never telling me no. For always telling me that nothing was beyond my reach if I worked hard enough.

Sam. You get to be my sounding board. You listen. You're patient. And most nights you let me pick what we're watching.

My little Rose. You're starting to grasp what I do when I disappear onto my laptop though we're a LONG way off you reading one of my books. You brighten my days. You keep me going. And you inspired this story of fierce maternal love. Because for you, baby girl, I'd do anything.

My fluffy man, Rollo. You can't get upstairs anymore to sit with me while I work. But you're waiting for me downstairs, cosy on the sofa, eager for cuddles.

And finally, the readers. The people who pick up my books, who journey into my stories. Thank you. A million times over. Because of you I get to do what I love. Because of you I get to keep telling stories. I hope I never stop.

Credits

Carys Jones and Orion Fiction would like to thank everyone at Orion who worked on the publication of *She Had it Coming* in the UK.

Editorial
Rhea Kurien
Sanah Ahmed

Copyeditor
Saxon Bullock

Proofreader
Clare Wallis

Audio
Paul Stark
Jake Alderson

Contracts
Anne Goddard
Humayra Ahmed
Ellie Bowker

Design
Charlotte Abrams-Simpson
Joanna Ridley
Nick May

Editorial Management
Charlie Panayiotou
Jane Hughes
Bartley Shaw
Tamara Morriss

Finance
Jasdip Nandra
Sue Baker

Marketing
Javerya Iqbal

Production
Ruth Sharvell

Sales
Jen Wilson
Esther Waters
Victoria Laws
Rachael Hum

Anna Egelstaff
Frances Doyle
Georgina Cutler

Operations
Jo Jacobs
Sharon Willis

Don't miss the other addictive and emotional psychological thrillers from Cary Jones . . .

Five names on a list. The first two are dead.
The third is yours.

Beth Belmont runs every day, hard and fast on the trail near home. She knows every turn, every bump in the road. So when she spots something out of place – a slip of white paper at the base of a tree – she's drawn to it.

On the paper are five names. The third is her own.

Beth can't shake off the unease the list brings. Why is she on it? And what ties her to the other four strangers?

Then she discovers that the first two are dead.

Is she next?

Delving into the past of the two dead strangers, the truth Beth finds will lead her headlong into her darkest, deadliest and most dangerous nightmares . . .

We're best friends.
We trust each other.
But . . .

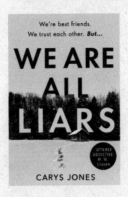

Allie, Stacie, Diana, Emily and Gail have been by each other's sides for as long as they can remember. The Fierce Five. Best friends forever. But growing up has meant growing apart. And little white lies have grown into devastating secrets.

When Gail invites the increasingly estranged friends to reunite at her Scottish cabin, it could be the opportunity to mend old wounds and heal the cracks in their friendship. But when a freak snowstorm rocks the cabin and one of the girls is found dead on the ice, their weekend away becomes a race against time – and each other – to get off the mountain alive.

And in the end, whose story can you trust, when everything was founded on lies to begin with?